MONASTERY RIDGE

MONASTERY RIDGE

A Novel of The Korean War

The Second Year

Henry West

iUniverse, Inc.

New York Bloomington Shanghai

MONASTERY RIDGE
A Novel of The Korean War

iUniverse books may be ordered through booksellers or by contacting:

iUniverse
1663 Liberty Drive
Bloomington, IN 47403
www.iuniverse.com
1-800-Authors (1-800-288-4677)

Because of the dynamic nature of the Internet, any Web addresses or links contained in this book may have changed since publication and may no longer be valid.

This is a work of fiction. All of the characters, names, incidents, organizations, and dialogue in this novel are either the products of the author's imagination or are used fictitiously.

ISBN: 978-0-595-46211-7 (pbk)
ISBN: 978-0-595-70741-6 (cloth)
ISBN: 978-0-595-90512-6 (ebk)

Printed in the United States of America

PROLOGUE

In the early summer of 1952, the Korean War had been going on nearly two years. The massive sweeps by great armies moving north and south on the peninsula were temporarily halted, but the armies were preparing to start up again. The line between the UN and Communist forces was unstable but active, which resulted in some of the most vicious small-unit, limited-objective fighting of the war, and added the names of Pork Chop Hill, Iron Triangle, Bloody Nose Ridge, Jane Russell, Snook, Old Baldy, and others to the history of the three years of the Korean War.

This is the story of how one small unit, a U.S. Army rifle company, came to be the defender of Monastery Ridge.

CHAPTER ONE

The older man turned to his younger seatmate and broke the silence maintained since the start of the journey. "Now I know I ain't got all the answers"—starting up as if renewing a lengthy conversation—"and that somewhere in the higher commands"—thrusting a thumb upward toward the top of their canvas enclosure—"there was a reason for all that. But you know I've been at this line of work a long time"—here another thumb punch, but this time into the knee cap of his companion—"and I ain't never been in such a set-to as we just got clear of. Another two or three days of that and we could have put the whole company in the back of this one truck." The younger man, deep in his own thoughts, looked up, nodded, and said nothing. The trucks were moving on a rough trail, really just a path only somewhat widened by the passage of the vehicles. They were taking them away from Iron Mountain. It was necessary because the company was completely spent.

The soldiers were the remnants of an infantry rifle company that had been at the place for nine days. For seven of those days, they had been battering on a peak unnamed on the Army maps, but known as Iron Mountain by everyone who had reason to curse it. While other units similar to theirs had been in the fight, the peculiar, persistent, *unfortunateness* of the infantry had focused on them. Because of change of higher command, change of objective, change of boundaries of lines of advance, they had for every one of the seven days found themselves at the front of the push up the mountain. It had, over the seven days, proved to be a ghastly effort. No amount of firepower and no amount of maneuver or artillery support or air strikes had enabled the attackers to gain the upper slopes of the peak. Day after day, they had continued to claw upward toward the summit, scrambling, slipping, and sliding on the slopes. They hugged the ground, squirming behind every boulder, rock, and pebble, seeking protection for a body, an arm, or a finger from the withering fire pouring down on them from above.

Men went down and continued to go down: riflemen, noncoms, officers. Sergeants, corporals, and privates took over, trying to lead. Finally, their captain, the last officer in the company, save one, was gone. He was killed attempting to rescue one of the new men, who was trying to manage a flame thrower while scrambling up the mountain as best he could. The new man—no one could remember his name—had touched off his torch, which slashed into the hillside and immediately drew all the return fire of every enemy soldier who could aim at him. The youngster jumped into a hole but couldn't find the valve to shut down his weapon. The blazing fuel continued to spew out and drew even more enemy fire power. The captain left his position to aid the flamer, but just as he reached the boy, the backpack fuel tanks exploded. Both the captain and the new man were incinerated. The young soldier became a campfire in the hole. The captain was transformed into a large lump of flaming gristle, with bits of sputtering grease rocketing off as he cart wheeled slowly down the slope. As the blazing lump bounced erratically, both sides ceased firing. The burning stopped when what had been the captain reached the bottom. The thing, now a jagged piece of charcoal, slid into a ravine.

For a moment, nothing happened on the mountain. Then, after a tension pause, the fighting resumed with escalating fury. It continued for one more day. Other units were thrown into the battle but always in support of the company, which was kept at the point of serial attacks against the mountain. After a final valiant assault by the company and attached help had driven nearly to the summit, the battle ended when the Chinese—not beaten—had simply moved off the peak and departed northward. After the Chinese left, the mountainside blossomed into a rifle woodland of stunted trees. Rifles stuck in the ground with bayonets fitted to the weapons for this purpose acted as markers for wounded or dead soldiers. Rifles sticking straight up lead the medics to their patients. Rifles with a helmet balanced on the butt end lead the burial details to their assignments. The designation code was simple: a wounded man continued to need the protection of his steel helmet. A dead one had no further use for his.

In the dark, canvas-shrouded, small caverns of the two-and-a-half ton truck beds, the men's thin shanks were pounded by the slats of the pull-down bench. Although they were not needed now, no man had taken off his steel helmet that, for most of them, was pitched slightly forward and nearly covered the eyes, which were open, fixed in a flat gaze focused on a faraway place. All of them were hunched forward, elbows resting on their knees. The hands of each, forward of the knees, were in constant motion—clenching and unclenching fingers that worked continually rubbing and kneading, scouring away the memory of the past days. And, if the hands and fingers came momentarily to rest, they twitched: a jittery tremor that sometimes crept up the arms till it reached, with a shuddering splutter, the shoulders, which caused startled glances from the other riders in the truck bed. Each man was replaying in slow motion what they had just come from; the details, forgotten as they happened, were now excruciatingly remembered. But some of the men in the truck were starting to slide into a post-battle near coma in which everything would be shut out, except the slowly subsiding clangorous din that continued to roil their heads. It would yet be sometime before they would sink into that languorous, though guilty, state of realizing that once again they were survivors.

The two most senior members of the company, First Lieutenant Horace Crayley, the only surviving officer, and First Sergeant Gleason McCoy were of a kind: both had, by different means, been fashioned by the Army. Though years apart in age, their brain waves and heart systems surged and flowed to the same pattern. They understood the pattern, and they understood each other. So, when McCoy spoke again, Horace was already ahead of his thoughts. "You know it ain't by accident that we're out of there first. The Chinks may have left, but those other companies that were up there are gonna continue to push. And here we are"—a wide sweep of both arms—"getting this limo ride back to somewhere." He paused, "To do some damn thing that ain't been yet revealed to us." He leaned back, pleased at how he had phrased the last part of his comment.

"I agree with you. We're being taken off line, because other plans for us are in somebody's head. The only thing the battalion commander said to me was, 'Go back, rest up, get fit, and be ready.' That's a helluva an operations order. But I do think we need to rest up. We took the laboring oar on the mountain, and it pretty well busted us up. However, as I see it, we've still got a good solid core that's been around the track enough times to know what's necessary. But right now, all of us are beat. We need some time off. When we get our replacements, we'll slide them in with what we already have, and after a short time, we'll be fit and we'll be ready."

The sergeant responded, "Well, you're the new boss. You've been in the company long enough. You know the men. They trust you. You got a good record, here and in the last one. The company's rightfully yours. They'll leave it that way."

Horace seemed not to hear McCoy's last words. He said, half to himself, then louder as he turned toward the sergeant, "All we need is a little recovery time. That's what I told battalion. Just a little rest. We'll be all right then. Just a little rest."

The truck convoy came to a small valley, really no more than a wide cleft in a range of hills that paralleled a broad river plain. It was separated from the plain by a thin spur that spiked up for several hundred yards along the edge of the plain. The valley was only slightly distinguished from other similar savage chops in the land by a stream churning through rocks at the tip of the valley to cascade down its center, gradually to slow and broaden as it neared the valley entrance. But the stream did not continue. It suddenly disappeared into the earth at the edge of the plain.

The stream had given life to the place, and rays of sun reflected off wood and mud huts barely recognizable as the work of man. It had been the great misfortune of the valley inhabitants to have lived so near the river plain. This broad basin had not carried a river for a thousand years, but had been carved by the forgotten river into a majestic nearly north-south highway that served the people in trade, commerce, and other ways. People came as travelers, as pilgrims, and sometimes as soldiers. The valley's most recent occupants' destiny had been to be alive when the great roadway had once again served as the route of armies. The sweeping passages up and down the broad highway had almost accidentally and quite incidentally swerved, swirled into the little valley and ended the life of the village there. The few sagging homesteads retained barely enough fragments of walls and roofs to be usable by the company's temporary presence. But it was enough to once again give life to valley. Here the company came to rest and recover from the Iron Mountain excursion. The company would be, for a short time, part of the regimental reserve. So as long as they were in reserve, the men of the company could expect relative calm. But this would not last very long.

CHAPTER TWO

On the morning of the third full day in the valley, McCoy determined to set the matter straight. It was something he'd had to do early on whenever the company got a new commander. Of late, he had had to do the exercise frequently. Although Horace was his friend, there was a different tilt to the friendship now. Crazy Horse had just become the new boss and this was bound to have some repercussions on their relationship. So it was necessary for McCoy to test the amplitude and severity of any shockwaves that might be headed his way.

Sergeant Gleason McCoy was RA all the way. He had been in the Regular Army since he was sixteen. He exited the Des Moines orphanage, where he had lived since he was seven, one night in 1917, just after America got into the Great War. A few documents were created at the recruiting office, the Army certified him as eighteen, and he was in. In short order, he was in France where he became a whiz-bang success with the medals to prove it. He had found a new home, a different sort of orphanage, where he was one of the star inmates.

Now, in 1951, McCoy was forty-nine, soon to be fifty. Thirty-four years of being mothered by, then mothering, the members of the khaki tribe, the confines of which defined his life and his family. He was not tall. He was a man in a stumpy body—a physical figure of rounds: a round torso, round hard belly, round prominent buttocks, round, that is to say bowed, legs, and a round head with sparse grey fuzz springing antennalike from above his ears. His face had a pulled-back cast to it. He seemed to be permanently standing in an operating wind tunnel. Because of this, his manner appeared to be always thrusting ahead, always pushing, always challenging. For most of his life this was his character. But in these latter years, he was mellowing—except on matters of duty. Occasionally he lapsed into a nostalgic reverie when he thought of other places, other friends. During those short periods, his men sometimes remarked that they hoped his almost genial civility was a permanent change of attitude.

Long ago when McCoy was a vigorous hell raiser, he had been dubbed "Wowser." The name fit, and it stuck. It had been his for so long it sometimes appeared on official records. Not usually as "Wowser" but often as "Worthington," as if it were some kind of middle name, and several times as "Wow," with a period after it, as if a confused clerk thought that "Wow" was an abbreviation for an unknown, more elegant name. McCoy had been for years the ranking enlisted man in all the companies in which he served. As first sergeant, he was only rarely spoken to as "Wowser" these days: by one or two senior noncoms or the company commander but never the platoon lieutenants; sometimes by old friends from other units. Mainly, it was just Sergeant McCoy.

For those who knew his record, and as it was told by others, there was no chance of McCoy fading into insignificance in their eyes. He had every medal the Army could give, except the top one from Congress. It was not just that he had them, he had most of them more than once. That was why, at a time when the emphasis was on youth able to run up and down the Korean peaks and valleys, McCoy's assignment requests were always granted. And his requests were always for a rifle company, even though he could have had a soft job far from the bright lights and big noises.

Why he made such requests he did not consciously know. He had been an infantryman since 1917. Thirty-four years at the bottom of the pile. It was here that they came after no one else would take them. After the air force, the navy, and the Army high headquarters put in their requisitions for college men, high school graduates, almost high school graduates, men with a trade, men who could type, bake, drive a truck, a boat, run a railroad, or fix any of the above—too dumb, too mean, too weird, too wild, too crazy, too sad, too much for all the other services, come to the infantry, all you misfit fuckups. This is where you belong. So had Gleason McCoy arrived long ago from a rock-pile orphanage, and he had been taken in, cared for, survived and prospered. He had become somebody in this through-the-looking-glass–world—that very small percentage of those "in the service" who actually did the pig sticking. And where would he be except with his family in times of trouble. So that's why he stayed where he was and did what he did.

McCoy knew that it was the riflemen in the few rifle companies, in the few infantry regiments, in the few infantry divisions, who decided the issue. The issue that was resolved only when the soldiers of one side walked upon the enemy ground with their guns at the foe's throat and their hands on the loot. This is how McCoy's family made its living.

Together they did it all. From the days and nights of wretched grubbiness to the few moments of exultant screaming ego gratification when yet another objective was won and held. And through and over it all, they also shared the pure distilled knife edge of ultimate fear that any second could end in a brain-shattering explosion if the other guy was smarter, faster, meaner. And so, where else could McCoy be? The infantry raised him. It had become his turn, some time ago, to raise the new children. He was still at it.

As McCoy reached the conclusion that the matter should be settled today, the sun was just starting to push into the lower reaches of the narrow valley. A strong, hard light was sliding a flood glare along the nearly smooth, almost frigid, snail-slick floor. The remnant of a night fog was swirling away in wispy plumbs to congeal into a thick pancake that would keep the valley barely warm after the early burst of warming sun.

Wowser lashed his weapon into position, strap in front and carbine on his back, with two condoms fitted tightly over the end of the barrel. The condoms weren't really needed in the present weather, but it was a habit acquired in the rain and icy sleet of the German winter of 1944–1945. It was an article of faith and McCoy's commandment of the highest order that men in his unit carry their primary weapons at all times. And he meant at all times, so he carried his own.

Just by looking at the company's activities, Wowser knew that the routine of the day was correctly underway. Such matters were largely left to the company clerk, Corporal Trent, to organize. To Trent's continuing terror, McCoy required his clerk to be in the field rather than back with others whose primary weapon was a snappish typewriter. Trent told the platoon sergeants what he needed for manpower details, and because McCoy had deputized the clerk, it all happened.

Last night there had been a small party, ostensibly to celebrate Lieutenant Crayley's confirmation by the regimental commander as commanding officer of the company. It had been carefully structured by Wowser and a few of the senior noncoms to camouflage what was actually a micro scan of Horace Crayley to determine if the company shakers and movers would validate the regimental commander's decision. Of course, Crayley knew the real purpose of the meeting, having participated in others when he had been on a lower rung of the ladder. Liquor, never officially available, had been in generous supply. It had been obtained by sending one of the company jeeps back to the nearest air field. The long distance from the front increased the value of the trading material carried by the jeeps, which was several enemy small arms, Chinese copies of Russian rifles, automatic weapons, and a few assorted handguns. This treasure had been exchanged for many bottles of smooth, energizing, lip-smacking booze.

At the modest celebration, the senior noncoms used the time between drinks to probe the new commander for his views of life, and, more importantly, their lives. Crayley had a leg up because he was well known to the party givers and to most of the company. He was one of them. He had been the company's executive officer—second in command—when the Iron Mountain ordeal had come upon them. The men knew Horace as a sensible, fair, courageous, but not foolish officer. At the party they had drawn him out, searching to see if his new job might have changed him, to try to discern if he had acquired a new drive or enlarged ego, ominous to them if he had, by virtue of pro-motion to command. Although unsaid, the messages went back and forth between them, and at the end of the party everyone was satisfied. But Wowser still needed his own understanding, and that was the focus of the day's effort.

McCoy was of an age when his participation in the field activities of the company was an exercise in tightwire walking. He knew he should be out of it. He was well past the time when he should be finished with this line of work. But it was what he knew and what he was good at. The problem was that McCoy was somewhat, actually *very*, long in the tooth to be a field first sergeant. This was a heavy duty job and was uni-versally done by energetic types, usually a couple of decades younger than Wowser. Many company commanders required their first ser-geants, particularly those with many years, many medals, and many pounds of gut billowing over their cartridge belt to stay at the company rear position with the kitchens and the supply trains. But Wowser wouldn't do it that way. He was a leader of men in battle and he would have no lesser position.

For the job Wowser wanted, he needed a commander who realized that a jewel such as McCoy needed no further cutting and polish-ing—that the McCoy brilliance was best left to shine through the stone as it was. Although he had worked with Horace before, this important matter had to be nailed down; to be clearly and cleanly resolved in his favor.

The now-dead Iron Mountain captain had been a great admirer of British military tradition. He thought *Gunga Din* was the greatest film ever made. His military attitude had a few touches from that movie that he thought were elegant. The men of the company thought they were quirky. One of the captain's Limey affectations had been to refer to the company executive officer as "Number One," meaning first among his subordinates. Now, "Number One" was the commander, but Wowser decided to see if he could carry it on. He had always thought it a bit overblown, but he recognized that, if used in a respectful way, it might put a nice spin on his relations with Horace.

McCoy steered toward the Command Post hut and pushed through the sagging opening.

"Good morning, Number One, sir."

Crayley, sitting cross-legged on his bed roll in a corner of the hut, looked up. "Good morning, Wowser. Is all well in our home-away-from-home?" Getting a nod from McCoy, Horace continued, "What can I do for you?"

"Sir, I just wanted to check in to see what you have on your schedule for me." Here, Wowser stopped. He was stumped. He didn't know how to get into the subject he had come for. He choked on asking if Crayley would allow him to continue as the company's main man.

"I've made a list of assignment changes I'm putting in." Horace handed McCoy a folded paper. "You can look at this later and give me your comments, if you have any. But for now, there are some other things I want to review."

They moved to a spotlight of sunshine hitting a grassy swale on the streambank. One of the cooks brought coffee and bread with C-Ration jam. They sat there for two hours discussing the company. Crayley did not refer to the assignment list he had given McCoy. Wowser plowed through the conversation stolidly, rejecting his itching desire to read the list.

In due course, they finished and Wowser was left to carry on with his duties. McCoy waited until Horace moved away. He unfolded the paper. If there were to be a change in his position, he would have plenty of comments for the new commander to consider. The first two lines on the list said:

First Sergeant—G. McCoy

Field First Sergeant—G. McCoy.

The assignments went on, but the first sergeant decided to look at the rest of them later. The sky was brightening, the river was buoyant, the grass was warm, the coffee was good, and Wowser felt just fine.

CHAPTER THREE

Even though the participants at Number One's evaluation party had given their best efforts, there remained several bottles of liquid cheer that had not been adequately considered. It was mandatory that such excess be disposed of, and this was done in a somewhat larger gathering of veterans of all ranks the following evening. McCoy departed the gathering somewhat the worse for wear but feeling quite good, especially when he recalled the prior night's session with the new Number One. He had left that meeting thinking that the company's prospects had been strengthened by the time spent with Crayley. There had been just enough respect, just enough polite but probing questions, just enough "old timers" genial camaraderie to make the session worthwhile, even valuable.

McCoy continued on his way home. He was only somewhat unsteady as he approached, with caution, the foot bridge leading to his sleeping quarters. The bridge was metal: a solid, somewhat curved surface. It had not been built as a bridge, and it had only been in place a little more than half a year. It crossed the narrow but turbulent stream. The late night dew settling down from the surrounding walls had made the bridge surface slippery. It was dark in the floor of the narrow valley. It wasn't quite cold enough for the thin sheen of water on the bridge surface to freeze, but it was almost too dark to try the nearly icy span. However, there was a night glow from a half moon and star-crowded sky. It was enough to make out the bulging center of the bridge. He decided to try it.

He hesitated for a moment listening to the night sounds. Only the smooth sloshing of the stream below could be heard. He looked ahead to his goal a few steps away. He raised his head to look once again at the darkening sky. He took a quick breath of cool air, held it, and started. He slid, tentatively, one booted foot onto the slick surface. A dozen and a half quick scooting little dance steps—his toes trying, through his boots, to grip the walkway—and he was safely across. He let out his breath with an explosive gasp. He squeezed through an opening he had made and proceeded to make himself as comfortable as possible in his carefully selected chamber. The rest of his companions, back on the other side of the stream, had made their own arrangements in the remnants of the village, the remaining parts of which were sticking up at odd angles against the rock wall that bounded one side of the valley.

He was in a small room of a type of glass. Clear, translucent panes bound together in a web of lightweight metal formed an enclosed dome, which was open at the bottom and a shallow part of the stream ran under it. This opening allowed cool fresh air to circulate and also admitted a soothing sound which focused inside the dome.

He'd had the foresight to devise a kind of sleeping harness so he wouldn't fall out of bed into the cold water below. He thought this would be helpful if he thrashed about when the bad dreams roiled up. He got into the harness, onto the plank bed, and lay down. Here, away from the main course of the stream, he could hear other sounds. There were several thumps—some far away, more very near. They had a heavy punch to them, even the ones in the far distance. It seemed to him like sharp thunder jolts. But he knew it wasn't thunder. The sky was too clear. As he neared sleep, the sky overhead suddenly erupted with a series of cracks into a light show. Miniature suns dotted the sky. The incandescent globes slowly drifted down, extinguishing themselves before they hit the ground. The glass of the dome sliced the glow so that slit beams bounced off every object in the dome.

McCoy remembered when he was a child of being told by a visitor of the grand Crystal Palace of the great London exhibition. She told him she had been in the Palace when the nightly fireworks display filled the interior with multicolored slashes that danced over the watchers inside the massive glass dome. He contented himself with the thought of his grandmother and the beautiful Crystal Palace show as he slipped off to sleep.

He awoke, clear headed. Bright, sharp sunlight was flashing through the glass launching miniature rainbows skittering around the chamber. But he wasn't in the London Crystal Palace. He was in the nose assembly of a B-25 bomber in a remote valley in Central Korea. He had no idea how the plane got to this place. He knew that B-25s had been used last year in the early days of the war for ground-support low-level attacks. It seemed to him that this plane had found the little valley for an emergency landing and had been pretty successful. The front part was mostly intact and in the front was the bombardier perch: a glass observatory from which to drop the bomb load. This was space of great value, and he had taken it as his sleeping quarters.

As McCoy awoke in the morning, he groaned himself to wakefulness then lay in his harness for a few moments thinking of his rifle company. Actually, not his—not even Crazy Horse could claim it. It belonged to the Army. Number One and McCoy had only temporary charge of it. A general feeling of well being was starting to simmer in him as he reflected on progress the company was making in ridding itself of the debris of Iron Mountain. He could sense a relaxing of the screw-tightened nerves that had bound the men in the first days after getting off the mountain. No longer did he see vacant eyes, recognizing and counting the faces that were no longer there. He felt so good about the way things were going that he decided to go to work. He struggled up out of his harness and got a look at what he considered to be a grand group of riflemen.

There they were, just across the stream looking like a bunch of characters in search of a clothing dump. They appeared to be outfitted as if they had been in a circle around an enormous pile of unrelated pieces of clothes when the pile exploded. Instantly, each had been dressed in whatever attached itself to them. From their feet to their waists, they looked like they were, in a manner of speaking, in similar uniform. All wore combat boots and fatigue pants. From the waist up, the sergeant regarded them as the Easter Parade of the Gargoyles. Fatigue shirts; athletic T-shirts and pullovers; sweaters, some Army issue, some letter-men from various schools, some brightly colored, suitable for the ski slopes; a few dress shirts; one frilly bridegroom number; jackets of all shapes, including a few lovely air-force flight jackets liberated when the company had been near Kimpo Airfield a few months earlier; hats to warm the heart of Dr. Seuss. There was every type of headgear imaginable; he noted that women's silk stockings pulled tight over the head and just down to the eyebrows continued to be a crowd favorite. He also noticed a lack of steel helmets.

He didn't care about the grand fashion show. The company had lost a lot of everything in their last effort. It was that excursion that had brought them to the valley to recover. They were now in reserve—expected to be out of harm's way—for at least several more days. He knew that before they moved from this place, they would be replenished with clothes, equipment, and new men. He knew when they departed they would look like what they were—a working infantry company that knew its trade.

The sergeant watched them assembling on the other side of the stream for their morning ablutions. Stretching, yawning, shivering, yawning again, the men gave notice of their existence. The place echoed to the sounds of their wake-up exertions: gasses being vented out top and bottom body openings—sharp cracks, timid hisses, languid sighs, an occasional gargantuan blast—all called forth various messages of praise and encouragement. But as the uproar continued, the praise turned to scorn as if the speaker could not believe that such tiny mice toots could be launched from such elephantine effort. No sooner said, than the speakers—to prove the merit of their observations—would themselves send a few notes into the air, and the entire score would be replayed from the opening bars.

It seemed to the sergeant that the traditional infantry noise valves were in good operating order, but he noticed that other—usual morning—problems were present. If the sergeant, himself, hadn't gone through such exercises nearly every morning for all his Army years, he would have thought that a crotch malfunction had seized the men. Nearly every one of them was vigorously addressing his groin. One hand, both hands; sometimes with broad sweeping, even clawing motions, sometimes reflectively. The head usually tilted to the side; sometimes pensively as if remembering past glories but always for the purpose of arranging the bodily equipment into comfortable placement for the day ahead.

The sergeant struggled out of his retaining harness, up through a hole in the fuselage, and onto the wing bridge spanning the stream. The sun, on the side of the stream out of the shadow of the cliff facing him across the water, was bright hard. It hit him full in the face, and McCoy came full awake.

He watched a group moving toward the latrine area, thinking of joining them for his morning movement. Many years ago, he had taken to finishing off every day with—when he could get it—a piece of bread or canned biscuit smeared with butter or, preferably, mayonnaise and a thick layer of coffee grounds. Other men seeing him eat this concoction had grown weak, but Wowser held that it was his necessary "roughage" to keep him regular. Something kept him regular because every morning—when events allowed—he moved toward the latrine at nearly the same time.

One of the huts with no roof but three freestanding half walls, well downstream from the main area had been designated as the latrine. After some heavy pick and shovel work, it was in operation.

As the men approached the latrine hut, there was a general discarding of clothing: overcoat, weapon, sweaters, scarves, gloves, and steel helmet were placed upside down with cartridge belt coiled inside. Toilet paper—removed from its carrying place in the top of the helmet liner—in hand, the effort would start.

Those awaiting their turn were vocal in their praise. To a particularly fine effort easily heard, they would proclaim, "Incoming," "Outgoing," "Laundry marking." To a companion shot quickly following, one of the observers would say, "There's a pair I wouldn't draw to." And, so it went. It was all music to McCoy's ears. It was a lullaby heard so many times that he didn't have to listen. He knew the words by heart.

Today, the sergeant was looking for a particular face. Wowser was waiting for Corporal Quentin Hardesty to appear. Hardesty was a good enough soldier. In fact, he was one of the veterans of the company. He had been in the unit nearly five months. He had been lucky with only a modest slash from a mortar shell fragment to mark his time in Korea. But Quentin was not highly regarded by McCoy because Quentin was an irritating presence—frequent attempts at half-mean tricks on others, too many bad-subject jokes, a careless memory, and mouth about bad events that didn't need retelling. Wowser thought him a cheeky bastard and kept him on the sergeant's short list.

Slightly upstream from the latrine hut sat a Sherman tank. It was obvious what had happened. The tank had been charging down the valley, using the stream bed as its roadway, when somehow its treads had been disabled while the tank was in midstream. The tank recovery crew had given up. They had taken out the engine in such manner as to remove most of the rear end of the tank. The armament and other equipment were pulled out. They blew the hatch off the turret and left the tank as a memorial to some now-forgotten action. The stream poured through the tank, back to front, and onward down the valley.

The second day in the valley, Hardesty claimed the tank. From the meager scraps of wood in the village he constructed a toilet seat to fit over the blown turret hole. During the morning latrine walk, he appeared with his new seat—usually singing loudly a few words from his favorite song, "My Romance." He was especially winsome on the line, "My romance doesn't need a castle rising in Spain." When everyone within hearing distance had an eye on him, he moved onto the tank, fitted his seat and proceeded with—as he described it—his morning dump.

This had gone on for three days. Yesterday, the company commander had watched Hardesty then gave an arched look toward Wowser. It was enough. But it wasn't needed. McCoy had already decided that he had had enough of it. Today would be Hardesty's last dump stunt with the tank.

The prior day, Wowser had had a discussion with PFC Harry Princeton—a certifiable nut case but an expert armorer who could repair or remodel any weapon in the company. Princeton was told to make certain alterations in two concussion grenades. These little dandies didn't send fragmented shrapnel, but the boom and flash—especially in a confined area—was quite enough to put the recipients into la-la land for a substantial amount of time. Princeton had delivered the grenades to McCoy the previous afternoon.

McCoy saw Hardesty approaching the tank carrying his toilet seat. It was Hardesty's practice to do a little body work before he got on the tank. This involved several push-ups and then several arm curls using a loaded metal box of machine gun ammunition in each hand. These activities required a flat piece of ground which Hardesty had chosen and was blocked from a view of the tank by a hut remnant.

As Hardesty started his exercises, Wowser started his. With a fierce glare that warned any observers not to reveal his action, McCoy approached the tank. Working from the back, he slid a board to which the two grenades were taped into the tank. Uncoiling a thin, strong fish line, he walked upstream about thirty yards and sat down on the bank of the stream.

Hardesty completed his workout, climbed onto the tank, fitted his seat, slid off his trousers, and sat down. It was Hardesty's further conceit to announce his efforts by yelling, "fire in the hole" as success was achieved, this being the universal cry of someone about to detonate an explosive charge.

Hardesty let out his usual hoop, "fire in the hole." McCoy pulled his fish line. The safety pin and fuse timing in each grenade had been modified to Wowser's specifications. The concussion grenades exploded just as Hardesty said "hole." There was a tremendous thump in the bowels of the tank. Hardesty had only a fraction of a second to wonder if he had set some kind of a new record before a geyser of water shot up the turret. Hardesty disappeared in the rocketing blast and found himself rolling in the stream bed. He came up blowing and swearing revenge on whoever had planted the bomb. He saw McCoy approaching him, but before he could speak, the sergeant waved him to silence.

"I want to tell you something Hardesty," McCoy spoke in measured tones loud enough for most of the company—who had rushed to the explosion—to hear. "I've done you and the whole company a favor, and I'll tell you why. You see this stream," and here he motioned toward the place where the stream disappeared into the earth. "It goes underground. We don't know if or where it comes up. But I do know that about a mile from here, in this same direction, a small river rises out of the ground," McCoy said, noticing that everyone was now assembled continued, "and I know that this small river comes up in the sector of the Turkish Brigade and they use it for their cooking and washing." All present knew the fearsome reputation of the Turks in Korea. Mostly justified, partly budding legend, it was accepted by both sides of the battle line that the Turks were nobody to get on the wrong side of.

"And I'll also tell you that if by chance them Turks find a turd in their soup or a few dingle berries in their wash basins, they may come looking. If they do, none of you will get out of Korea alive." For the rest of the company's reserve period, Hardesty used the latrine in the hut.

◆   ◆   ◆

His disciplinary priorities finished for the moment, Wowser departed for further conversation with Number One. There was much discussion of the assignment list. They made a few changes, but they accepted most of Lieutenant Crayley's previous decisions. They then moved on to other matters: training, equipment status, weapons maintenance, promotions, and other issues of interest. Nothing was said about the position of field first sergeant. That issue had been satisfactorily concluded. Near the end of their conversation, McCoy said to Crayley, "By the way, I got a call from my contact at Regiment"—here he tapped the side of his nose with his forefinger—"that we are getting only one officer. He'll be down, maybe today, probably tomorrow."

"Only one?"

"Looks like there's a shortage of young heroes. Apparently the Army is using them for target practice."

"What's the book on him?

Another nose tapping, more pronounced this time, accompanied Crayley's reply. "Well, his name is Ed Clare: second lieutenant, short-timer, been in the Army just past a year. Been over here about three months. He's been in King Company. He was with them in the Triangle, but King wasn't in the main push up the slot. Word is that he is young, a little too eager, but probably okay."

CHAPTER FOUR

McCoy was sitting on his wing bridge waiting the return of the company clerk, Corporal Trent, who had been sent to Regiment and was due back soon. Waiting for Trent, Wowser scanned the men passing before him on the other side of the wide stream. This frazzled and bruised—but only bruised, not broken—group was listed in the charts maintained by invisible Mandarins at higher headquarters as G Company of a particular numbered Regiment. "George" was a rifle company, one of the basic building blocks upon which the Mandarins' success or failure depended.

While George Company remained in reserve, its duties were not heavy. It needed only to furnish a few details, such as work parties to the Regimental headquarters from time to time, and be ready to help out if things got out of hand in any area where other units of the Regiment were engaged. The company did have one real job to do. That was to recover from Iron Mountain and await the next call for its services. And that was the point: just waiting. Waiting was a condition well known to infantrymen; no direction was required to advise them how to do it. They knew. Whenever the waiting was out of weapon range of the enemy, it took on a luxuriant air of indolence and indifference to all. They just did nothing—and wondrously—expected nothing in the way of unpleasant surprises.

Wowser spotted two members of the company approaching the stream together, chatting about the vagaries of life and how to hold on to it. They were Pope and Mallen, an impossible pair, but to McCoy they were elements of his mental well-being. They, with one or two others, were his company talismans. They had been in the Army since before Pearl Harbor and in George nearly as long as he. As long as they were present for duty, Wowser was attached to an umbilical cord, stretching back well beyond Iron Mountain, well beyond Korea. They were symbols that G Company had a life force greater than the limits of the valley. McCoy was distracted for a moment. When he turned back toward his two friends, there was only one. Pope, in that micro minute, had wandered off and, as usual, could not be seen.

Eric Mallen reached the stream. His objective was a helmet of water for a little facial effort. Like McCoy, from a family of the Old Sod, Mallen was generally known as "Boffo." He had been a stagehand in San Francisco until he signed on in 1937 for an extended engagement with the Army. Retaining an affectation of his theatrical days when he wished to label something "well done" or "first-rate" he would pronounce it "Boffo." He had, in fact, announced the Iron Mountain debacle as, "Boffo! Absolutely Boffo!" The ringing endorsement of this catastrophe had further nailed down the company's perception of Mallen as, "Nuts. Absolutely nuts!"

As usual, Mallen had dangling from his cartridge belt a leather left-hand glove. It was, as always, dripping oil. The glove was important to Boffo. His preferred style of participating in a firefight was to unload his M-1 clip of eight rounds as fast as he could blow them through the barrel. He blasted in all directions with his machine gun trigger finger. When he was ready for this work, he needed to have a ready supply of ammunition, so he carried a full cartridge belt load plus three bandoliers of clips across his chest. And thus ready for serious labor, he looked like an extra in a Pancho Villa movie.

Mallen liked to polish all wooden parts of his rifle so that they gleamed like fine furniture. He used linseed oil by the quart. When he commenced his barrage, the saturated wood got steaming hot and oil oozed out. To protect his left hand from frying in the hot fluid, Boffo wore his glove, which, for his own reasons, he kept with him night and day. His left pant leg under the glove was stained from waist to knee. He looked like a personal plumbing disaster.

Boffo's arrival at any place was made manifest not so much by sight or sign, but by smell. He exuded the aroma of a petroleum supply depot. He excited all the nostrils within a fifty-yard circle. His presence on a patrol several weeks earlier had so confused a Chinese outpost, whose personnel smelled a silent mechanical device approaching, that the patrol had netted one of the very few prisoners to be snagged by George Company. Boffo was a very erratic soldier, but firing madly in the general direction of North Korea whenever the opportunity arose, Boffo plowed straight through all obstacles, and that was quite enough for McCoy.

Wowser's attention was caught by the appearance of Corporal Trent coming into the bottom of the valley. Trailing Trent like a gaggle of apprehensive geese was the group of replacements Wowser had sent Trent to Regiment to fetch back to the company. The new bodies came on, stumbling over small rocks in the dry wash that was their roadbed. They were not talking and joking as soldiers usually did when slogging through an area where silence was not required. There was a collective air of wonderment about them as they entered the George encampment. It had nothing of the neatness and order of their infantry training center back in the U.S. It didn't remind any of them of the smoothly efficient United Nations Army that they had been told was winning the war in Korea. Wowser well knew that the contrast between his people and the freshness of the new draft, smartly turned out in their still new fatigues and with new weapons, was starkly obvious. But Wowser also knew that his men had been tested and found worthy. The appearance they brought to the battlefield concerned him not at all. Besides, in short enough time, there would be no new men. They would all be just George Company.

Wowser looked again at Trent, remarking to himself how much Trent had changed since coming to George two months before. He was a very strange bird to be in the enlisted ranks of a frontline infantry company.

Frederick Trent was a Yale history graduate, who somehow missed getting a navy commission and who declined an Army commission because it meant four years' service and who thought—until that day, two months earlier, when he had been posted to George—that even the Army could not be so stupid as to not recognize his superior intellect and thus assign him to an appropriately important desk job in, successively, the Pentagon, San Francisco, Hawaii, Tokyo, Seoul, Division Headquarters, Regimental Headquarters, and Battalion Headquarters. None of these desirable locations had been available, and Trent had only been saved from death as a rifleman by the fact that the previous company clerk had broken his back in a fall down Iron Mountain on the day when every man of George Company had been attacking up the slopes. Thus, Trent was both sad and happy: sad that he had somehow gotten so far forward in a shooting war and happy that he had not been ordered to take that last, frequently fatal step, of being assigned to a rifle squad—of which there is nothing farther forward.

There was another matter that only Trent and Wowser knew that had the potential to make Trent even sadder than he frequently was. His full name was Frederick Allen Remington Trent. Named for his father and two grandfathers, thus retaining his ties to important ancestors, Trent had made the mistake—only afterwards recognizing it as such—of informing, rather haughtily Wowser thought, the first sergeant a few days after his arrival of his three first names.

Wowser said all those names were just too much, but the first letter of those names might be just about right. After more thought, Wowser said he would probably just call him Trent. But the casual reference to the letters was enough for Trent. He knew—and Wowser knew he knew—that the first sergeant had all he needed to keep Trent in line, socially speaking. McCoy and Trent were the only company workers who routinely saw personnel records. Thus, Wowser had known directly from Trent—as well as his records—what could be a useful leveler if the Yalie got uppity with some of his comrades. However, the sergeant never mentioned his possible shorthand name for Trent, but a

Yale education was good for something, and Corporal Fart cursed himself for bringing his alphabet names to McCoy's attention.

Trent's Army was still at the lower end of the valley, on the other side of the stream when, from behind them, a jeep came barreling along the path that they had taken into the valley. Even without the single passenger being close enough to identify, Wowser knew that their new lieutenant had arrived. He started for the CP to alert Lieutenant Crayley. By the time Horace and McCoy had gotten down to the edge of the stream, the jeep had forded it, and the driver was dumping an officer's bedroll and a few other items on the bank. The lieutenant stood by the jeep waiting expectantly for a welcoming committee. The men in the company were showing studied indifference, but nearly all of them were looking at the new officer out of the corner of their eyes.

As Horace and Wowser approached him, the new man stepped toward Horace, "Hi, I'm Clare. Glad to be here." Handshakes all around, as Crayley spoke, "I'm Horace Crayley. This is First Sergeant McCoy. Happy you joined us. We really need you."

"I've heard about you two. Crazy Horse Crayley, lots of combat time in Germany and here. Wowser McCoy, older than God, more medals than MacArthur. I really am glad to join you two."

At that moment, the first of the replacements sloshed through the stream. Crayley seeing them, said, "We've got a lot to talk about, but it can wait until we get these new men sorted out."

Trent's gaggle was now close enough to be seen as individuals. Wowser called out, "How many of these beauties did you steal for us?"

"Regiment gave us thirty-one." That was a nice number, but they had asked for fifty-six. An infantry company was organized at a little over two hundred men, but none ever got that close. With the number requested, George would have been at about one hundred seventy. Wowser had leaned on one of his old buddies at Regiment, Sergeant Silverstein—a man whose tricks with personnel allocations were well known in the first sergeants' network—to help out. But Wowser knew the game. Nobody got what they were entitled to.

"Only thirty-one! How the hell can I win this war if they keep me short on bodies?" Wowser indicated a relatively flat spot near the CP. "Give 'em a piss break. Keep 'em assembled. Lieutenant Crayley will see them soon."

If the situation allowed, it was a practice of most line commanders to speak to new men. This was especially true of a large catch, such as the thirty-one given by Regiment. Inasmuch as George was in reserve, the situation did allow, so Wowser knew Crayley would speak to the arrivals.

In a short time, Horace joined the group of replacements. Because this was his first command appearance, other members of the unit sauntered to the rookie assemblage to hear their new chief. He introduced himself and told them they could call him by his first name: "Lieutenant." He told them where they were: the blown-out little settlement by the wide stream was Song-Po, about eighty miles north of Chunchon—the large, now mostly demolished city near the center of the Korean Peninsula. He spoke a little about the war and about their Division's place in the big picture.

"The enemy faces us across the river plain at the end of this valley. They are Chinese, and they're very good and very tough too, but we're better. The Division of which we are a part has been in Korea since September 1950. The company has been in action almost all of the time since then. Most recently, we had a bad experience at a place called Iron Mountain, but we survived, and the people you see around you are better for having been there." He told them they were in reserve, and that was why the place was so loose. He said they would not be in reserve long. They would soon get another job.

"Because we are in reserve, we'll have a chance to get acquainted before we move out. During the few days left to us, we'll sharpen up the fundamentals of the whole company. Learn from the men around you. Trust them and give them reasons to want to trust you." Horace paused, lost in thought as to what else it was he wanted to say, then, "Any questions?"

One of the replacements spoke up. "Lieutenant, my question is simple. Why are we here? America is a very long way away, why are we fighting in this place?"

There was an embarrassed slither of boots on the muddy ground, mostly because that was a question not pressing upon the older G-Men who muttered the usual endearing phrases toward the questioner.

Wowser thought. "Another smart-ass. Just like that prick, Trent. I'll watch that one."

Crayley didn't miss a beat. "If there are no more questions, we'll move on." He introduced Sergeant McCoy, telling the men they would later meet their platoon leaders, mostly sergeants, the company having only two officers. He spent a little time extolling Wowser's military record. He ended by telling them their first sergeant had more combat time and medals to prove it than the rest of the division combined. The new troops were admonished to listen carefully to Sergeant McCoy and the noncom's words of wisdom. He concluded by telling them that McCoy would make the assignments to squads. "When that's finished, you'll get some hot food. We don't see that all the time, so enjoy it."

Horace stopped. He seemed to be finished, but then he started up again. He pointed at the man who asked the "why we fight?" question. "You said you had a simple question; I'll give you a simple answer. First you asked why we are here. We're in Song-Po because the Army sent us here. As for the 'why we fight?' part of it, there are many people, going clear back to Washington, who have their own answers to that question. I don't know what their answers are. But I know the answer for the company. Up here there's no one left on our side to debate that question. You can only do that with the Chinese, and they're trying to kill us. So the simple answer as to why we fight is that we fight to stay alive." Crayley turned and left.

McCoy started to move toward the men. He took only two steps before Ed Clare pushed past him. "Now, I want to say a few words before Sergeant McCoy does his business. I am Lieutenant Clare. I just got transferred here from another company in the Regiment. I want to tell you that this company had a hell of a time on Iron Mountain, but they did their job and they pulled through. Now they and the rest of us new people don't expect to sit on our asses while the rest of the war goes by." Actually, Mallen and Pope and several of the longer-serving men who were watching the introductions thought that would have been a very good idea.

Clare continued. "Lieutenant Crayley, who himself has a great deal of combat time, and I with, of course, the fine noncoms who are here, are going to mold this company, which now includes you new men, back into the fine fighting machine it once was. We are here to teach you, train you, lead you, and we will do our damnedest to get that job done so that whatever comes our way, we will accomplish it magnificently." He stopped and stepped back, as if waiting for a loud cheer or at least polite applause. Nothing, except there was peculiar movement amongst the company veterans. Feet began to shuffle as if they had picked up the sound of music and were getting ready to dance. Dance it was, but it was a quick step away. A shuffle off to Buffalo or wherever such kind of talk wouldn't be voiced to jangle their nerves.

"Well," Clare turned toward McCoy, "carry on, Sergeant."

As Clare walked away, Mallen looked at Pope slowly, his right eyebrow climbing into an exaggerated arch striving for a record-high position on the middle of his forehead. His left eye closed slightly as he said, "Uh oh." Pope just nodded and sauntered off toward the latrine.

Crayley who had turned back toward the assembly when he first heard Ed's voice stood transfixed, screwed into the ground. He could only say to himself, "What the hell is he doing? What have we got saddled with?"

McCoy who was similarly frozen by Clare's outburst had trouble gathering his thoughts. Finally, he stepped forward. He looked into their faces, trying to remember what it was like so long ago, but the memory was lost. He reached back, trying to bring it forward. He peered harder at them. To the recruits, he seemed to be glaring at them, almost as if he wished they would go away. But, of course, that wasn't it. He just couldn't grab anything that gave him a bridge to what they were feeling now. "Oh, what the hell," he muttered in what he thought was a comment to himself, but three or four of them heard him and wondered what he meant. After a moment, he cleared his throat with a raspy snort and started.

"The company commander told you who I am. As far as you're concerned, I'm your father and mother combined. If you don't soldier your ass off for this company, my father part will beat the shit out of you." Seeing a few raised eyebrows, which he took as expressions of doubt about his ability to beat anybody, he continued. "And don't think I can't do it just because I'm older than your grandfathers." Actually, he couldn't do it, but he could make life more miserable and dangerous than any poke in the chops, and they were all smart enough to know it. "My mother part will bust my ass to keep you from getting hurt too bad and to return you with most of your parts to a presumably loving family."

"Anything biting your butt, you see me after you've told your own platoon noncoms. Don't go bothering the officers with your troubles. We only have two, and they've got enough to do. Now, here are the assignments." This parceling out took only a few moments. When he finished, Wowser stepped back, looked closely at the group again, searching for something he might add to make sure they had gotten the message. But the best he could do was another, "Oh, what the hell." This time loud enough for all to hear. Abruptly he started up again. "There is one more thing I want to tell you. There will be times ahead," here he stopped, "Oh, bullshit! Just remember, keep a tight asshole." And that was it. End of speech. He turned his back on them and walked away.

This drop-off-the-cliff ending to what many of the replacements thought was shaping as a rousing patriotic oration left several of them clutching for a smoother finish to McCoy's speech. But it didn't come. Wowser never explained to them his curious advice.

As soon as the new men left to find their places, McCoy was in the CP. "Well, Number One, sir, that was an interesting presentation by our new second-in-command."

"Stow it, McCoy. I did think it was a bit overblown, but he's a new kid on the block, trying to make an impression."

"He made an impression, all right. The men in the company are spooked, and the new guys wonder who's running the show."

"I'll take care of it. On your way out, find him and tell him I want to see him."

Being summarily dismissed miffed Wowser, but he put it down to Lieutenant Clare's breach of protocol in taking over the welcoming ceremony after the commander had made his brief speech. He left to find the new man.

Clare pushed through the remnants of the tired tent flap that was guarding the entrance to the CP. "What's up, Crazy Horse? How they hanging?"

"First item. Lieutenant Clare, don't call me 'Crazy Horse.' That's not a label I'm particularly fond of. It's 'Horace' or it's 'Crayley.'"

"Oh," Clare said with a slight lopsided grin. "I thought that was your real name. Okay, I won't use it."

"Second item. I'm real puzzled by your speech out there. You haven't been in the company ten minutes. You know nothing about it, and you're telling, not only the recruits but the men already here how you—maybe we—are going to lead them on the Hallelujah Trail."

Clare started to speak, but Horace waved him to silence. "That was way out of line. Way out. I don't mind enthusiasm, but I won't put up with that kind of grandstanding. We aren't running a political campaign for election as best combat officer. From now on, you stay away from pronouncements about the glory road you want this company to travel."

Clare finally got to speak. "Hell, I didn't mean anything like that, Craz—I mean, Horace. You even said this company had had a hard time of it at Iron Mountain, and frankly, I must say, they show it. They really do look like a whipped bunch."

Crayley, who had been ready to move on, flared again. "What the hell do you know about Iron Mountain? King Company wasn't in on it."

"No, but the knowledge is pretty widespread throughout the Regiment, maybe even the Division, that you guys took a pasting there."

"I'll tell you only this once, Lieutenant Clare. It's true that we took a beating on the mountain, but we weren't beaten. They were able to wear us down because we were used as point for seven straight days. Exhaustion is what beat us, and that can be cured by rest and it is being cured by rest."

"Okay, I thought I was helping."

"You weren't. For now, I've heard enough. You just remember what I said and take it as the gospel according to Crazy Horse."

Crayley waited a moment then took up the business of the company. "Ed, you'll take over Third Platoon. Sergeant Graves, who had it before, didn't come back from Iron Mountain. For the moment, we won't have a platoon sergeant, but the squad leaders are all good. Ortega probably is the one who should advance to platoon sergeant, but I'll wait for your recommendation before filling that slot."

"I'm also making you training officer for the rest of our reserve time. It's a good idea to get them going on some physical activity. See if the new men are comfortable and if they can hit anything with their weapons. See if you can send our mortar crews to one of the companies on line so they can poop out a few targets you pick. Make sure they know which end to slide down the tube." He paused, "By tomorrow night, give me your ideas on a training schedule. That's all for now. I'll see you later when chow arrives."

CHAPTER FIVE

Horace Crayley was born in Montana. His was a ranching and farming family: some cattle, a little wheat. Until the age of seven, he lived in a loving, caring home with his parents and older brother. Then, his father and mother fell victim to a blizzard. The two brothers went to live with an aunt and uncle who were childless. The next summer, Horace became the sole survivor of his family. His brother, Howard, drowned during a swimming party. Horace had been the only observer and had tried mightily to save his brother, but he had been pulled from Horace's grasp by the surge of the river. The events, coming close upon each other, which had taken his parents and brother from him, had driven Horace deep into the worst nightmares of childhood; the protective embrace of blood family was gone.

During the next years while Horace was with his aunt and uncle on the farm, he was pleasant in all things toward them and those few adult acquaintances he knew. He grew toward manhood and became a skilled cowboy and a strong farm hand. He enjoyed work and did it well, never questioning his uncle's orders concerning the farm. But his personal relationships in the farming community did not grow as he grew. Unobserved by others, Horace decided that life had dealt him a poker hand that no amount of new cards would change to a full house. He could only make certain that there would be no more losses as those he had suffered at age seven. Teachers, classmates, and townsfolk were responded to politely as circumstance required, but the "no hurt" armor put on by Horace kept everyone at an emotional distance.

During this period, Horace grew to average height and weight, although he did not reach the bulky stature of his father and uncle. One day when Horace was in high school, the English teacher—attempting to give word examples—called Horace and the biggest boy in the class to stand side by side. She referred to Horace as "diminutive" in making a size comparison. The teacher did it with what she thought was a winsome, appealing, little smile, but which Horace thought was more of a smirk. Horace hated her for it, but politely replied to her further questions.

Later that same day, a large—but not so quick, as Horace knew from watching him play football—upperclassman referred to Horace as "diminutive." Without a word, Horace launched himself and proceeded to pound the taunter into the ground. So thorough was the beating that other members of the football team promptly labeled Horace a "tough little shit." Thus encouraged, Horace went out for the football team, became reasonably proficient, and played halfback his last two years at school.

Horace's football label stuck to him. He continued to be referred to by his teammates as a "tough little shit." The high school year book picture identified him as "Horace (TLS) Crayley." When his aunt asked Horace what "TLS" meant, Horace told her it meant "tough little scatback" in recognition of his football efforts.

In 1943, Horace was seventeen and set in his ways. He felt comfortable in the disciplined, orderly flow of the farm and the community. But within the boundaries of his rural life, Horace had quietly become a flinty loner. His duties were efficiently accomplished with an occasional pleasant word to his working or student companions. Usually the work was done faster than expected, frequently because Horace revealed original creative ways of getting results. Gradually, the community came to regard him as a smart young fellow who would probably do well for himself. Beyond school and work, his life remained closed. Though a young man, Horace had become an institutional conformist while managing to remain fiercely independent.

In the middle of 1943, Horace decided that he was old enough at age seventeen to find out about the war that was going on outside Montana. He did not tell his aunt or uncle or his teachers of his decision. He just went to the recruiting office and said he wanted to sign up. That was fine with the sergeant at the desk, but because Horace was below draft age, he needed the approval of his uncle. Horace's uncle learned of the decision when the enlistment papers were presented for signature. The uncle signed, and Horace was on his way.

Horace had decided on the Army because he had never seen an ocean. He felt that he would not take to sea duty. He had never heard of the marines until Guadalcanal had hit the headlines. Apparently the marines were heavily involved with ships in some way so they were also disqualified. The Army Air Force was not an option for Horace. Those people seemed to lead a life quite different from what Horace thought a war was likely to be. So it was the Army for him.

Although reasonably bright—even quite intelligent by Army test standards—Horace's lot was cast by events. Most young men that year were headed into the infantry, because the big planners knew that Operation Overlord was on the horizon. While these big planners could not discern the entire future, they knew very well that the invasion of Europe would offer suitable employment for a great many young men carrying rifles. After processing at the induction center, Horace went to an infantry replacement training center. The training routine and the hard physical training were pure pleasure to him. He took a keen interest in what he was to learn, and he learned it well. The whole thing was like a honey pot to him. He gorged himself on it.

Following basic training, Crayley was shipped to a replacement depot in England. While there, he took on some specialized weapons training. As usual, he was the star of his class. He was promoted to corporal. He was still in England on D-Day, but shortly thereafter he got a choppy ride across the channel to France.

Six days, later Corporal Crayley, with twelve others, was assigned to his new rifle company. The unit was in the remains of a French village, waiting for tank support to push forward through an apple orchard against the next fortified position. In the small town square, the company first sergeant lined up the new men. The sergeant took the replacement list from his company clerk. "I'm gonna read your last name. When I do, you gimme your first name—loud, so I don't have to strain my balls to hear it."

The roll call started; last name identified and a first name response from the owner. "Crayley," shouted the sergeant.

"Horace," came the answer.

The sergeant peered at the group, then at his clerk. "What the fuck did we both hear?"

"Crayley, Horace," replied the clerk.

"Are you jerking my chain?" The sergeant glared at the clerk.

"No, that's it."

"Okay, Crazy Horse. If that's your name, pick up your saddle blankets and get your ass over to Third Platoon." So "Crayley, Horace" became "Crazy Horse."

In his new calling, Horace became a strong, resourceful, successful fighter and leader. There was ample opportunity for advancement in his line of work, and Horace progressed steadily.

Usually each promotion brought with it a new medal as visible testimony of his performance in the peculiar job he shared with others of his company. Three months before V E Day, Horace at the age of nineteen, got a battlefield commission. Lieutenant Crazy Horse continued to excel for the rest of the war.

It is said about many—usually referring to the semiliterate, semi drunk, semi mean—that they have found a home in the infantry. It is also said very much less frequently about those few who make a stunning adjustment to the infantry life and myth and who embrace and accept all the warts and carbuncles as their own and prosper. It was in this last way that Crazy Horse found a home. So far as he was concerned, he had found his family.

Like any family, the Army takes care of its own. When the war ended, the family eye settled on Horace. He was asked if he would like to stay on. Of course he would, but first Horace was required by his new parent to finish his education. A diploma from the Montana high school was no problem. Credit for his European travels easily satisfied the few credits he needed. The Army then sent him as an ROTC instructor to a pleasant university in Florida. He spent his tour there training bored cadets with ample time left over for his own education. His major was willing coeds with a minor in history. He received his BA degree on June 11, 1950. On June 25, 1950, the North Korean Army attacked south across the Thirty-eighth Parallel, and Crazy Horse was off the reservation and at war again.

CHAPTER SIX

An order came from Battalion requiring the presence of a representative group from the company at Regiment on the next day for an awards ceremony. Several men from different companies of the Regiment had recently been awarded medals, and a general from Army headquarters was to pin the ribbons on the winners.

Ed Clare was in the CP with Horace almost as soon as the word came about the awards ceremony. "Jeez, Crayley, that's great! I'm going to take all of the Third down there. It will be just the shot in the arm that my platoon needs. The new people will be mightily impressed when they realize that their platoon sergeant is a bona fide hero. Oh, by the way, I think you're right. Ortega should get the platoon sergeant's job. Probably move Corporal Hardesty into Ortega's squad leader job."

"Don't do anything with Hardesty right now. We'll get back to that one."

"Okay, well anyway, I tell you that after the platoon hears Ortega's citation, I'll use it to get them cracking. I need to do that."

Horace swallowed Ed's exuberance in small doses. He had gotten in the habit of looking for the below-the-surface meaning of most of Clare's pronouncements. "What do you mean, 'you need to do that'?"

"Well, I just mean it will give them a kick in the ass. It will energize them to get really serious on the training they're getting."

Horace considered taking the subject further, but, in fact, Clare had put together a decent training program for the whole company. Maybe he was right. Ortega's medal could be a good thing for everybody. He decided not to ask more questions. Because the company had its own honoree, Benny Ortega, Wowser was determined to have a good showing amongst the other companies that would attend. So, in addition to most of the Third Platoon, McCoy and Trent picked twenty more of their most presentable and told them to be ready to hike back to Regiment the following day with Lieutenant Clare and his platoon.

Upon arriving at Regiment a formation of sorts was established, and the general began his task. Each recipient was called forward, and the citation for the medal was read before the general did the pinning. George Company's man heard his name. He stepped forward, and a lieutenant started reading.

> *"... On the night of March 14, 1951, near Sung Po, Korea, Sergeant Benficio Ortega displayed daring initiative, aggressive determination, and extraordinary heroism in the completing of his mission and in the leading of his patrol to safety against a numerically superior hostile force. Sergeant Ortega, commanding a patrol of his company, was assigned the duty of ... "*

Sergeant Ortega remembered the outline of the Poppy Bowl very well. The captain had described it with great particularity. This was only the second patrol the sergeant had been given the honor of leading, so he was very attentive. Even though it was not to be a combat patrol, he was careful to listen to all the captain said. The small squad he would lead had only to reach a blocking position so as to be able to assist a roving combat patrol that probably would not even come their way.

The captain had drawn their final mission position and their route to it with a stick in the soft ground, crudely, but accurately ...

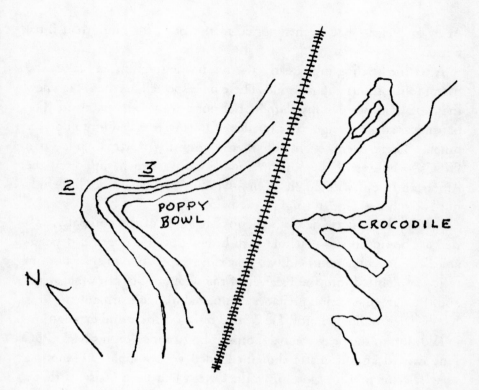

... so that the patrol—their call sign was to be "Dandy" this night—knew the exact route they would take from their present location on the left leg of Crocodile, down the draw to the shattered Kumwha-Kumsong Rail Line, across the tracks up into the Poppy Bowl, and on to Position Two. Then, all they had to do was set up and wait in case the combat patrol, operating northwest of the Bowl, had to return home the long way over the lip at the top of the Bowl, down its terraced inner side—like the seats of a football stadium—and on home to Crocodile.

The captain told them something they already knew, but it made them feel better anyway. The Bowl, because of its open invitation to receive American artillery fire, was almost certainly unoccupied. No positions manned by Chinese Communist Forces—CCF in the official

Army language—had been reported in the Bowl for more than three weeks.

After the briefing in the early afternoon, the sergeant had taken the patrol to the snout of Crocodile. There he inspected his men. He knew them all. They were in his platoon, but none of them in his squad. The patrol was small enough, by any odds, if they were called on to do very much. There were seven of them, counting Ortega, plus two "KSCs"—natives of the Korean Service Corps, which supported the American troops with coolie labor—who were to be ammo, hopefully not body, bearers for the night's excursion.

Ortega, known as "Sergeant Benny" to most of the company, carried a Thompson sub-machine gun: heavy, but effective and dependable. The machine gun held two magazines taped side to side, bottom to top, one fitted into the receiver of the weapon. Six extra magazines and three fragmentation grenades completed his basic armament. PFC Kimball was radio operator. He carried only a carbine and extra ammo in addition to the heavy Signal Corps radio strapped on his back. PFC Fine carried an automatic shotgun loaded with double "O' shot—a very efficient tool for close-in work. Ortega had been insistent that a member of the patrol carry the crowd killer. Corporal Kezar and Private Rollins shared the pieces of the load of a .30 caliber light machine gun that was the principal weapon of the blocking mission. They also had one .30 caliber M-1 rifle between them. The one that carried the machine gun tripod at any time also carried the rifle. It was their signal rifle. If the radio failed, the signal rifle, equipped with a launcher and flare, would be fired—but only upon Sergeant Benny's order. The signal flare would call artillery fire from Regiment's 105mm cannon down onto a point just ahead of the flare's trajectory. The first round in the chamber of the signal rifle was a special blank. It propelled the flare up and away.

Privates Elava and Westfall carried M-1s with two extra bandoliers of ammo each. One KSC carried four boxes of machine gun ammo. The other carried five bandoliers of rifle clips and eight fragmentation grenades. All members carried at least three grenades, either fragmentation or white phosphorus.

After the patrol heard the captain's briefing, they had spent some time in the firing points on the nose of Crocodile looking into the Poppy Bowl and trying to memorize as many of its features as they could. They didn't expect much to happen. They all thought the Bowl would be empty, and they would never see or hear the combat patrol.

After Ortega's inspection, they rested for a few hours; then, about 2200 hours, well after nightfall, they went down into the left draw next to Crocodile. They moved in a generally northern direction through small gullies and ravines for about twelve hundred yards until they came to the railroad embankment. They had not been overly cautious in their movement because their route took them through part of three American mine fields, which they believed pretty well protected their advance.

Then the patrol was drawn up on the south side of the railroad line. Ortega looked at his watch. It was 2310. He told the radio operator, "Eighteen minutes."

Kimball reported Dandy's progress and position quickly and softly into his handset, then said, "We move at 2318."

Right on 2315, the patrol heard the heavy crump of their artillery far behind them. A few seconds later, the sharp explosion of a two-gun salvo hit on the high ground at the top of the Bowl but about a hundred yards beyond the lip. Other shells started coming in one or two hundred yards to the right or left of the initial bursts with the hope that the Chinese wouldn't pick up the direction of the patrol's route from the way the artillery was coming in.

Ortega waited three more minutes, then gave the word, and they went over the railroad embankment, across the tracks, and down the other side. They were in single file, much more alert and careful. The sergeant was in third position, behind Westfall and Kimball. Next came Fine, then Kezar and Rollins. The two KSCs trailed next, followed by Elava.

The patrol moved across gently rising ground. Ortega stopped them at the Bowl's open entrance for a moment but moved quickly ahead. As they walked, they stepped upward, as if from row to row of stadium seats. In this manner the men ascended the terraces and also moved closer to the center of the Bowl's top rim.

Running around the Bowl about thirty feet below the rim was a rock wall, the war-blown remnants of the principal irrigation channel. Ortega had been to the Bowl once before and knew of the wall. He intended to use its shelter for a last look around before taking the patrol up to its assigned blocking position at the top. The men reached the wall nearly at the center of the Bowl and sank down, breathing heavily. Ortega slumped to the ground with the others; all sucking in the cold night air.

The moon was out now, not bright. There was a filmy layer of clouds turning the moonlight in the Bowl to a grey mushiness. But seeing, and being seen, was easier. After two or three minutes, the sergeant carefully removed his helmet and just as carefully peered over the wall up the slope of the bowl. He saw nothing. He ducked behind the wall, moved a few feet to his left and poked up again. This time he was looking at Position Two, a bald lump of ground slightly to his left on the top of the stadium and no more than seventy feet away. Ortega was satisfied. It would be easy and probably safe to camp out a few hours, waiting to see if the combat patrol needed to come their way.

Sergeant Benny gave an order to Kimball, "Tell them we're going up onto Two. I'll report after we're set up."

Kimball spoke softly into his phone, "This is Dandy ... this is Dandy ..."

Ortega motioned to Kezar and Rollins to go first. Rollins had the machine gun. He started to move. Kezar, with the tripod and the flare rifle, moved to follow. Ortega prepared to lead. The rest of the patrol was in a crouch, half on their feet for the move, when there was an explosion of fire—nearly point blank into them. A Chinese heavy machine gun had opened up on them almost from Position Two.

Carefully obeying his directed task, Sergeant Ortega skillfully led his patrol through heavily defended enemy positions toward its assigned objective. Nearing its objective, the patrol was suddenly taken under fierce automatic weapons' fire from a strongly-entrenched enemy strong point. In spite of this surprise assault, Sergeant Ortega maintained resolute command.

The patrol's reaction was instinctive and immediate. They recoiled as one body—down and away from the barrage. The men flopped back down behind the wall and stayed pressed to the ground. The Chinese gun boomed away at them. Only the wall saved the group from destruction. The numbing shock of the surprise attack crept like icy glue through their bodies. No one moved. No one fired back. They tried to ooze into the veiny crevasses of the rock wall.

Ortega's brain turned to cold lard. He couldn't even remember where he was. He was only dimly aware of the arriving of the Chinese grenades when they came in a hissing cascade over the wall. The trajectory carried the little bombs over the heads of the patrol, and they bumped down the terraced slope where they exploded harmlessly below the men.

The Chinese gun continued to beat down about them—locking them to the embrace of the cold rocks of the wall. The patrol was trapped. It was going to die at the wall. It was already dying. A small rock of the wall finally gave way under the pounding. There was a sharp scream, "I'm … I'm hit … I'm hit." It was Elava at the other end of the patrol line.

"Not bad hit," muttered the sergeant, "if you can make that much noise."

Though members of his patrol were wounded and in immediate need of medical assistance, Sergeant Ortega refused to leave his position. Instead, he personally commenced effective counter-fire against the enemy position, while at the same time, regrouping his patrol and directing it to a more advantageous combat deployment.

The scream cleared the leader's daze. He had to so something. "Up. Up. Move to the right," shouted Ortega. He was in a crouch, trying to run while still being protected by the wall. The GIs squeaked to their knees, ready to try a sprint anywhere, any way, just to put distance between them and the CCF gun.

So far not an American had fired. Ortega unlimbered his weapon and, holding it with his left hand only, half pointed it over his shoulder and let off a short wild burst, generally in the direction of North Korea. "Shoot. Fire. Fire," yelled Sergeant Benny. "Fight back, you fuck heads. Shoot!"

At his elbow, Ortega saw Kezar pitch the machine gun tripod away, unshoulder the M-1 rifle and shoot straight up into the air. "Holy shit," thought Ortega, "that's the artillery flare," as he heard the heavy pushing thump of the special cartridge.

> *Recognizing the extremity of his situation in the nearness and aggressiveness of the enemy, but without regard to the safety of the patrol and himself, Sergeant Ortega called his support artillery fire down nearly upon his own position.*

Before the signal flare died in the sky, the distant whump of the cannon sound drifted into the Bowl. Ortega squirmed deep inside his skin. But the shoot was accurate. It carried the top of the Bowl and then some. It exploded, harmlessly, behind the Chinese fire team. And it kept coming. Back at Regiment, the gunners were throwing it into the tubes as fast as they could, and the cannonade beat against the higher ground behind the enemy.

So far, the patrol's only response had been the desperation firing by Ortega. In return, the heavy Chinese gun had turned in their direction, and the sergeant took a couple of small hits, probably from rock splinters. But they were hits nonetheless, so that Ortega had a bleeding hole in his shoulder and a jagged bloody tear in the fleshy part of his side above his hip.

Suddenly, the two KSCs broke away to the left of the patrol. They dropped their loads and ran with great leaps down the stair steps of the Bowl. Breaking through the stubble still remaining on the terraces—falling, scrambling up, falling again. The two Koreans sounded like a battalion in full flight.

The Chinese heard the sound and quickly turned the gun toward it. There was one short wild cry, but still the sound of the headlong scrambling running could be heard. And still the gun followed the sound of the runners.

As the meaning of this reprieve broke through the sludge of Ortega's brain, he gradually realized that there might be a way out. As he collected his wits and tried to get his voice ready for command, the members of the patrol anticipated him. Though each man was thinking only of himself, they each thought alike, and without the sergeant's direction, they all took off, running bent over, close to the wall along the terrace, away from the direction the gun was firing. Ortega moved as fast as the rest, but because he was behind them, he had no control of them.

> *Though now bearing grievous wounds from the hostile fire, Sergeant Ortega displayed great initiative and courage in splitting his force and accomplishing a difficult withdrawal under the cover of his own artillery in the face of a continuing vicious enemy assault*

The lead man, Elava, though slightly wounded, began to hop down the terraces toward the floor of the Bowl. He was headed for the open end. He ran a few steps along each terrace before he jumped down to the next one. The rest of the patrol was close on his heels. At about the middle level, Ortega heard several sharp "thunks"—the sound of mortar shells being dropped into tubes and sent on their way—coming from the top of the Bowl.

Elava was just passing a large outcropping in the side of the Bowl, one of three or four that the patient farmers had not been able to root from the soil over centuries of trying, when the first of the mortar rounds hit the floor of the Bowl. The Chinese were sealing the mouth to block any escape route. Five more bursts came in quick order on the heels of the first. They marched across the face of the Bowl and somewhat up the terraces.

Private Elava caught the edge of the sixth burst nearly full in the head and upper body, but at a distance from the center of the explosion so that he wasn't blown apart—just fatally wounded. The blast deposited Elava backward into the slope under the overhead of the rock outcropping. The others arrived in Elava's footsteps at the rock, but they were shielded from the mortar fragments by the rock. They were met by the bloody bag that was Elava sitting stunned and silent on the ground.

The Chinese weapon was again beating the far side of the Bowl, where the gunners still thought they were on the track of at least a part of the retreating Americans. But the mortars began a slow dance around the inside of the Bowl. There were random hits, just poking around, in search of whatever might be moving on the terraces. To the men of the patrol it seemed safe in the lee of the rocks and, so again, they went to cover.

Elava had collapsed over on his side, still breathing. None of the men moved to examine or help him. It was in this position that Ortega, bringing up the rear—somewhat slowed by his wounds—crashed into the men huddled together under the rock.

> *Reconstituting his patrol within the cover and concealment of an advantageously selected terrain feature, Sergeant Ortega safely preserved the combat integrity of his force against a stunning mortar attack mounted by the enemy against his chosen withdrawal route.*

There was no sound from the beaten men. They hated themselves and each other, but mostly they hated the acid tasted of their crippling fear. The sergeant gave no orders. He was fighting to get control of himself before he could hope to command them. Within two or three minutes, Ortega roused himself, punched Westfall to follow, and moved toward Elava. Sergeant Benny rolled him over. He turned heavily like a sodden sleeping bag full of lumpy liquid matter. Ortega was no medic. They had none on the patrol. He just looked at Elava, wondering where to put bandages—which of several seeping holes to try to clog. It was no use. Elava would live awhile no matter what was done for him. But he wouldn't see the new day.

Ortega turned from Elava to look at his men. Suddenly Kimball, closest to him, grabbed his arm, pointing with his other hand. Ortega followed Kimball's gesture and saw from above them and across the Bowl a four-man CCF fire team carrying a light machine gun coming down from the position of the Chinese heavy machine gun. The heavy gun was firing over the heads of its own men, far down into the mouth of the Bowl. The mortars were also hitting far down the terraced slope. The fire team was going down to finish off what they thought was the pinned-down remnants of the American group, but they were on the far side of the Bowl still on the path of the fleeing Koreans.

As the fire team neared the level of the GIs—but across the Bowl from them, perhaps sixty yards away—Kezar began to whimper, "They'll see us. They'll see us. Oh, please don't let them see us." No sound from the others. No recognition from the Chinese. Kezar moaned, turning his face from the sight to hide behind Rollins' back. The Chinese searched and passed the American's level. No one moved.

Suddenly Kezar, with a soft cry, "Oh, please," jerked to his knees, cradling his light machine gun in his arms. He pushed Rollins out of the way. The Chinese were below the patrol now, about seventy-five yards away. Kezar released a short burst. It hit the closely bunched Chinese fire team full in the back. All four of them went down without a sound except the sliding collapse of bodies and equipment.

Now closely pursued by the following enemy, Sergeant Ortega skillfully regrouped his force and prepared an ambush of his own making. With deliberate care he allowed his attackers to nearly penetrate his position before directing fire against, and wholly destroying, the leading elements of the hostile attacking force

The patrol was revitalized by this piece of extraordinary luck. They were up, immediately alert, watching and ready if the Chinese should somehow regain life. They paid scant attention to the loud booming of the Chinese gun at the top of the Bowl, which had resumed rapid firing generally in their direction but aimlessly moving around the Bowl. They knew they were protected by the rocks if the gun came close to their direction.

The Chinese gun sputtered to a stop. Nothing was heard in the dark cup where the patrol was hidden. Then, they gradually became aware of a series of soft grunts of exertion and pain coming toward them from the direction of the fallen Chinese fire team. The soldiers tensed up and were prepared. Each man was up with a weapon at the ready, set to blow whatever it was right out of the Bowl. Ortega steadied his men, "Careful, careful. Don't fire till I say."

Out of the dark shadows, almost into the patrol before they were recognized, stumbled the two KSCs who had deserted them at the wall. The Koreans thought they had come into a Chinese strong point. They sank in a heap of fear onto their knees with their hands over their heads.

PFC Fine, nearest them, dragged them to their feet. Their relief at seeing the Americans bordered on hysteria. Realizing they were not to immediately die, they clutched each other in a sobbing, choking fit. Ortega gave them only a moment of such elation and then hit the nearest one with a fast swing of his Thompson. The man yelped, but both stopped crying.

The sergeant knew he must move his men if they were to have any chance of escape. He got them pointed down the slope and then grabbed the radio man, "Get them and tell 'em to hit Point Three, starting in three minutes and keep it up till I say stop." Ortega wanted the shell fire to mask their movement that was about to start.

Kimball made the call and got a quick response. Sergeant Benny and his traveling minstrels were about to move, except for one thing. Ortega kneeled beside Elava. As far as he could tell, Private Elava was long gone, but the sergeant motioned the two KSCs to pick him up. They did and immediately started to drop him. Ortega grabbed at the body, hoisted it onto the shoulders of the two bearers and motioned the patrol out. The sergeant handed his Thompson to Fine and took the shotgun with one hand while he steadied Elava's body with the other.

> *Having stopped his attackers, Sergeant Ortega coolly divided his force, made additional artillery preparations and recommenced his orderly withdrawal, taking with him a now fatally wounded member of his patrol.*

PFC Fine led the group away from the rock. He was followed by Ortega and the KSCs and the rest of the patrol. As they moved away from their cover, Chinese mortars again started to hit across the mouth of the Bowl. Thinking about anything was a massive effort for the sergeant. He wanted to chuck it and go bounding down the slope into the mortar explosions. Instead, he held himself in control and in so doing kept his authority and discipline over the patrol. No word was spoken, but there was a perceptible, however slight, release of fear and some sense of a return to life and the thought of escape

The patrol had moved closer to the mortar bursts, which were continuing to strike in random fashion across their route. They came to another small outcropping, not nearly as large as the first rock pile, but the patrol quickly settled into its protective embrace. Elava rolled off the shoulders of the KSCs. His body lumped heavily just where it hit the ground. "That's all, buddy," said Ortega, "but we'll take you home with us tonight."

The Chinese mortars had stopped just as the patrol had sunk into the rocks. There was only the repetitive heavy crash of American artillery shells on Point Three. In between the explosions, there was only the soft sighing of the wind, which told them nothing. The mortars had stopped for some Chinese reason, not just because the Americans had gone to ground. The sergeant knew he had to scout ahead. Ortega motioned to Westfall to accompany him and indicated that the others were to stay. He moved down a stair step trail on the side of the Bowl with Westfall on his heels. The two of them were quickly lost to view in the darkness. The remaining members of the patrol huddled closer together.

> *Still heavily pursued by Chinese small arms and mortar fire, Sergeant Ortega, nevertheless, was able to find protective cover for his patrol while he, at great personal risk, continued to scout, with one other man, for a route allowing him to complete his planned withdrawal.*

Sergeant Benny was moving with conscious purpose. He could only guess that somewhere ahead lay at least one more heart-thudding surprise. It had to be. The mortars must have stopped to allow another enemy interception party to move into the Bowl to hit his patrol.

Ortega rounded a bend in the trail and nearly collided with three men running hard up the path. It was another CCF machine gun team coming up to seal off the Americans' fate in the Bowl. The Chinese were moving up the hill—heads down as they quietly padded upward. The sergeant saw them an instant before they knew the GIs were above them. Without thought and with casual ease, Ortega swung the shotgun, which he had not given back to Fine, in the general direction of the Chinese and pulled the trigger. The weapon blasted its heavy pellets in an expanding pattern. The first Chinese was less than ten yards away with the second close behind. The charge of the gun poured into both of them. Their bodies exploded like overripe grapes. The lifeless forms jerked into the air then into a single sack of garbage on the path.

The third CCF soldier, shielded by the bodies of his comrades, fell into an irrigation ditch beside the trail. Sergeant Benny looked at him with interest, but took no action. The Chinaman didn't move. Then, suddenly he squirmed out of the ditch and started running wildly down the trail. Still Ortega didn't react. Behind him, he heard Westfall pull the safety pin from a grenade and pitch it. The sergeant heard the arming lever pop from the grenade as it sailed over his head. Westfall had thrown hard. The grenade flew, hissing over the escaping man's head and landed scarcely ten feet ahead of him. It was a perfect toss. The grenade exploded just as it hit the ground. The man was engulfed in a dazzling whiteness that floated up, like an incandescent octopus to embrace him. Westfall had thrown a white phosphorus grenade instead of the more usual fragmentation type.

The Chinese soldier fell, screaming, beating at the tiny flakes of flame that ravaged his body. His hair, head, face, and hands were on fire. Insane with agony, the man struggled to his feet and, out of his head, started up the trail toward Ortega and Westfall. Fascinated by the sight of a white fireball lumbering at him, the sergeant nearly waited too long. But, in time, he turned the shotgun toward the Chinaman and blew the burning figure into the stubble where it continued to smolder.

> *During the careful reconnoitering of his chosen route, Sergeant Ortega was attacked by a machine gun unit of the hostile force. Though initially surprised, he seized the advantage and beat off a last counter attack by the remnants of the enemy force. In so doing, he personally killed two of the attackers at point blank range. The rest of the enemy unit was similarly destroyed by a combination of skillfully thrown grenades and coolly utilized small arms fire.*

The rest of the patrol was hastily summoned from their rock haven, and they all returned safely with the exception of Elava who made the trip in the arms of the complaining KSCs.

◆　　◆　　◆

When the lieutenant finished reading, a general, resplendent in oversized stars and a pearl handled revolver, pinned a Silver Star medal on Ortega, shook his hand, and moved on to the next hero.

Sergeant Benny knew that the citation had something to do with the medal, but he had trouble following it, and he wondered who the lieutenant was talking about.

CHAPTER SEVEN

The morning after the award ceremony, Horace's first order of business was the disposition of accumulated paperwork. He kept at it—reading, editing, and signing numerous reports, letters, commendations, and assignments, including Ortega's as platoon sergeant of First Platoon.

After an hour of this desk work, he reached a point where he could push the remaining stack into a folder for whenever he would get around to the next administration session. He left the CP just in time to see the end of Third Platoon exiting the valley entrance.

To Corporal Trent, who was the nearest possibly knowledgeable person, he asked, "Where are they going? The schedule shows them here learning machine gun maintenance and minor repair."

Trent was knowledgeable. He offered Horace a handwritten paper. "Lieutenant Clare gave me this as he headed out. It's a revision to his training activity."

"Read it."

"It says: Revision 0800 hours to 1500 hours—large-unit patrolling. Platoon tactics and techniques, sound and vision signals, advance and recovery routes, etc."

The captain told Trent that Clare was to report to the company commander when Third Platoon returned from its training exercise. Later in the day, Clare bounded up the slight rise to the CP and pushed in. "Hi. What's up, Horace?"

"What's up is, what's going on? I read your revision to the platoon training schedule which"—he stopped to give Ed a long look—"I received after you had left the valley."

"Oh, yeah, sorry about that. But I got to thinking on the way back from Ortega's medal yesterday. If my platoon has an heroic patrol leader, we should build on it."

"Meaning what?"

"When we get a little better, I thought I would volunteer us to Regiment—assuming it's okay with you, which I'm sure it will be—for a platoon-size combat patrol. We can all go out together across the river plain and give some of their strong points a real smack."

"And you assume I would go for this?"

"Good practical training."

"To send thirty men and a boy"—this jab sailed over Ed's head—"two miles or more to hit Chinese positions of unknown strength."

"Sure, why not?"

"Why not? Because it's a bad idea, that's why not. Division's pretty static right now except for some heavy going up north with one of the regiments. If the big cheese wants to move across the plain, I imagine Division will first send small reconnaissance—not large combat—patrols out to sniff around. If we were to get called on for that duty, I'd carefully select a few, very experienced men—maybe volunteers to go with me."

Clare was silent.

"Is this the sort of thing you did in King Company, just charging around like a herd of blind buffalo, looking for a fight?"

"No, no really. Captain Griffith wouldn't let me do it there either. That's one of the reasons I asked for a transfer out."

There was a long silence. Clare was fumbling with his carbine magazine, taking it in and out of the breach of his weapon. Horace just watched him.

"Lieutenant Clare, officers are supposed to try to lead their men to success in combat. Sometimes it may take the last man to succeed. But you are not supposed to start out with a fixed—or dumb—plan to get them all killed."

He looked intently at Clare as if peering through his eyes into his brain trying to see the bumps and swirls that processed the thought to suggest his combat patrol proposal. "Ed, what the hell's the matter with you?"

Clare snapped the magazine into place. "Crazy Horse"—Horace let it pass—"are you RA or a reservist?"

Crayley was taken aback. What did that have to do with anything? He answered, "I guess I don't know. I'm not Regular Army although I've stayed in since the day I came in. Maybe I'll go into the reserves if I ever get out."

"Well, with your record, starting in Europe, you could apply for, and would certainly get, a Regular Army commission. Then, you'd be in for life if you wanted to."

"Yeah, so?"

"You got two CIBs, one for each war plus a pot full of other decorations. I've got one Combat Infantryman Badge. They gave it to me just before I left King, but I can't get another. Not here. Only one per war. That's apparently the rule."

"As I said, so what?"

"So I've got to get into a situation where I can get a lot of ribbons to pin on. I want enough so that when I apply for a RA commission, they'll offer it to me."

"You? Regular Army! I don't see you doing this for a career."

"I didn't say I'd take it. I just want them to offer it to me, so I can tell them to shove it."

"You better tell me the rest of that story."

"I can't, or, at least I don't want to right now. Maybe later."

"'Maybe later,' you say. Okay, until I know where you're coming from, you put that combat patrol in the deep freeze. And, even if what you may tell me makes sense from your point of view, it is extremely unlikely that your training patrol plan will ever be allowed."

"Well, I'm disappointed that you don't see the opportunity here for both of us."

"Not both of us, Clare, just you. And I don't like the opportunities for the Third Platoon. If you can't live with that, put in for a transfer. I'll approve it if you can find a company commander who shares your vision of how to run an infantry company."

"No. No thanks, Horace, I think I'll stick it out here. Maybe things will heat up."

CHAPTER EIGHT

Two days later, McCoy got a call from Regiment. At first he thought it was a mistake; upon reflection, he concluded that it was just the Army's way. He went looking for Crazy Horse.

Lieutenant Crayley was holding forth on the bank of the stream. The newest arrivals to the company were comfortably seated in a semi-circle around him. He was serving up some calm wisdom about how to fill out their dance cards with the boys on the other side of the river plain. As Wowser approached the gathering, he was thinking that the session served a good purpose. He knew that Horace would dish out very little blood and gore, nothing of the romantic foolishness of men locked in deadly hand-to-hand combat, and instead a lot of good, solid advice that might help to get them back safely to their homes and hearth.

Crayley had just finished his sermon when Sergeant McCoy arrived. Taking care to draw himself and his paunch as upright as he could manage, Wowser called out loudly, so that the rookies would know that although First Sergeant McCoy was a man of considerable status for them to obey and fear, he still knew and observed proper military courtesy, "Lieutenant Crayley, sir."

Of course Wowser did not salute as he would have done in garrison. Such a military nicety, maintained in a combat area might, all too often, get the saluted officer plunked by an enemy sniper. Officers were fully aware of this possibility so that any saluting fool was likely to soon acquire a choice assignment, such as carrying a flame thrower up the next high hill.

Horace walked to McCoy's side. Now out of earshot of the disassembling replacements who were on their way to the noon chow line,

Wowser gave him the news, "Well, Crazy Horse, sir, word has come from On High," here Wowser offered a reverent glance upward, "that you're for R and R. You're to be back at Regiment by 1300 tomorrow. Five days of rest and recuperation in glorious Tokyo for our valiant fighting men is yours."

Wowser dropped his paunch a little, adjusted his cartridge belt and continued, "They'll be sixty of the regiment's finest leaving at the same time with you. There are two other officers going, a Lieutenant Buddington from Baker company."

Horace broke in, "Buddington? I know Bud. He and I were in Charlie Company. We were down south together for awhile."

Wowser continued, "The other officer is our own Lieutenant Clare. He will be accompanying you for his first trip to the fun zone."

"Clare? How the hell can they take the only two officers from this company?"

"Aw, well, I inquired of my friends"—another upward look toward heaven—"and it seems that the officer's trip list was made up many weeks ago, one from each of the battalions. Lieutenant Clare was in King Company at the time, and he drew the brass ring for Third Battalion. Once the typewriter key has fallen, nothing can change it short of a spirited call to arms for which the services of the listed celebrants are needed in a location other than Tokyo."

"Who's going to run the show while we're gone?"

"Please, my dear Crazy Horse, we are in reserve. The sergeants will run the show as is usual in well-run organizations. Captain Slade from Battalion will visit us a couple of times a day to see if we are behaving ourselves. If we are required to do anything in your absence, I'm sure some kind officers will be detailed to show us how to do it."

Crayley thought a minute. No reason to suppose it wouldn't work, and after all there was the inviolate typewritten list.

R and R—rest and recuperation—was the Army's tangible expression of appreciation for certain of its Korean happy campers. Perhaps feeling some twinge of conscience as they correlated casualty figures with ammunition expended, the Tokyo stationed planners tried to share their good fortune with the statistical misfits who cluttered up their charts. The idea was that after three to four months on line, a soldier could find himself in one of the bigger Japanese cities for five days of gut-wrenching drinking and frantic coupling with persons of the mostly opposite sexual persuasion.

So the program was put into motion. This shot in the arm—or shot in the ass, depending on how early in the five days the GI got his VD dose—was supposed to do wonders for the spirit of the good young men. But it didn't work just that way. Coming off line, but knowing that it was back to the same work station in five days, resulted in some peculiar antics, all calculated to beat the five-day deadline.

However, no one turned down the trip. The hollow eyes and rancid breath of the returnees simply strengthened the resolve of those whose turn it was to go next. It was only when in Japan that the need to compress five days into a lifetime became apparent. But, by then, the celebrants had a bottle in one hand and nipple in the other, and they were trying to obey the order to get rested and recuperated.

Horace decided immediately that, although they might have to travel to Japan together, he was going to do Tokyo without Ed. Clare's performance since arriving in the company was putting an edge on Horace's attitude toward him. Even though in general Clare's training efforts had been good for the company, he talked way too much about his own path to glory. So much so that Horace was sure he needed to go a few days without hearing more of it.

The next day, those bound for R and R from the four companies of the battalion traveled to Regiment in two trucks. Horace made sure he did not ride with Ed. At the regimental assembly point, Horace was surprised to hear Clare greet him as if they were long-lost pals who hadn't seen each other for a long time. "Hello, Crazy Horse. How they hanging?"

This was a jolly side of Ed that Horace hadn't seen since Clare's first days in the company. Apparently, to Clare, their relationship at the company was left at the company. Now, they were two buddies bound for a new social scene in which Ed would display his good-time party side.

Clare's shout caused heads to turn which hardened Horace's resolve to have nothing to do with Ed on this trip. He had already told him about using the name the long-ago sergeant had given Horace, and here Clare was honking it as if he were Custer just becoming aware of a whole lot of Indians across his line of march. "Damn it, Ed, I told you to forget that name."

"Oh yeah, I'm sorry, but I didn't want to lose you in this round up. I thought we could do Tokyo together, see if we could give it a vote of confidence. Us mountain men should be welcomed with open legs."

"I don't think so, Ed, I'm going to spend some quiet time when I'm over there."

Clare was shot down. "Jeez, I thought that we would have some fun together. I hoped I could pick up a few pointers on how you long-time combats take a town apart."

"I can see you've got fire in your eyes and a mortar shell in your pants. But I'm not committing now to the kind of romp you seem to have in mind. You go do it. We'll probably connect from time to time."

"Well, that's too bad. I hope you think about it. I already got things fixed up. I told my brother about a month ago that I was coming up for rack and ruin and for him to arrange things. And I heard from him a week ago. He's on the project."

"What the fuck are you talking about? Your brother? Where the hell is he and what can he do?"

"Oh, you're right. That's just what the fuck I'm talking about: fucking. My brother is in Tokyo. He's a major, a surgeon at the big hospital there. When I wrote him I would be coming and needed care and maintenance, he said he would help. I think when we get there, Major Dan will have a squad of his nurse friends who will be eager to haul the ashes of the battle-worn, heroic, hard-up infantryman little brother and equally heroic randy friends.

Crayley looked at Clare with interest. Perhaps he was judging this kid too harshly. Perhaps Ed Clare really was a pretty good guy. Perhaps he didn't have to spend all his time taking the high road in Tokyo. Perhaps he should rethink his plans. After a few more questions, Crazy Horse had his priorities clear, and he signed on to the Major Dan Clare project.

◆   ◆   ◆

Amongst the group at the assembly point, there was no trouble spotting Lieutenant Buddington. He was huge: six feet, seven inches tall, over two hundred sixty in weight. Also, his head was shaved. A few thought this to be sort of dramatic affectation, but Buddington's reason was not related to style or ego. It was, he had decided, a sensible precaution. He figured he was tall enough without the extra fluff upon which to perch his helmet liner and steel helmet. So he kept his dome smooth in trying to deny any marksman the extra top inch as a target.

Buddington was from Baton Rouge, Louisiana, had gone to LSU, and later worked in Rochester, New York. Although a southerner, he had spent enough time up north to have lost most of his grits accent and to regard the brutal Korean winter as only achingly fierce instead of with the incredulous awe of most of the troops when first experiencing the icy nightmare of the dark peninsula winters.

Like Crayley, Buddington had been in Europe in the second edition of the Big One. He was an experienced infantry officer, who was a steady player, as Horace knew from firsthand knowledge. Earlier, when together in C Company, Crayley, Buddington, and a now-unremembered captain, who didn't make the round trip, had taken a reinforced rifle company to blow out an enemy strong point so that Army engineers could prepare a river crossing for tanks. This had happened far to the south, where tanks could operate and at a time when the UN Army was just starting its journey toward the Yalu.

Crayley introduced Clare to Buddington. After introductions and a few memories revived, Buddington, when questioned, said he had no special plans. He was quickly briefed on the possibilities expected of Major Dan, and he immediately signed on to the expedition.

◆   ◆   ◆

After the group milled about in a period of appropriately aimless Army fashion, the Regimental trucks arrived, and the carnival and carnal-minded soldiers got aboard. The convoy rattled southward over frozen, kidney-cracking dirt roads toward Chunchon about seventy miles to the rear on the winding road net. Careening around the hairpin curves of the high mountain passes, the trucks blew down the miles to the departure center.

The celebrants stayed overnight and part of a day in Chunchon getting clean, receiving real uniforms, and getting scheduled on flight manifests to Japan. The center was only a waiting room. There would be nothing to do, and they were not to be allowed out of the holding area.

Before the war, Chunchon—somewhat north and about sixty miles east of Seoul—had been an important road and rail junction in the center of the peninsula. As such, it had received enough sincere explosive attention from the Communist armies on their excursions through the South to turn the place into a rubble of rabbit warrens and mole holes. The prewar population had been serially diluted by flowing in and out with the surf of the advancing and retreating armies.

The battle line was now far to the north, and the previous residents, like barnacles brought in on the tidal surge of the most recent UN northern push, had attached themselves to whatever was left in the city. These few were the hardier remnants of the prewar population, determined to rebuild their lives on the bony spurs of the skeletons of their former homes.

On the face of it, it looked hopeless. But the American Army did its best, by mistake or carelessness, to assist their resettlement dreams in this dreadful place. It provided abundant jobs at—and unlimited opportunity to steal from—the many supply warehouses dotting the town. To most of the returnees, with the war far away and the marvelous things to acquire easily at hand, Chunchon was their dreams realized: a greasy pot at the end of a scabrous rainbow.

By the time the convoy approached the town, darkness was skidding down the peaks surrounding the forlorn city. In the dusk of nightfall, the wood fires that provided cooking energy and scant heat were fired up, contributing to a smelly mush haze that squatted on the city.

At the last mountain pass before the road dropped down into the town, the trucks stopped so the convoy could form up. Although the spring winds slicing down from Manchuria like razor wire, getting colder by having skipped off the still icy peaks of the peninsula north of Chunchon, tended to keep the verdant smells, which would ferment to lush flavor in the heat of summer, in check, the city still had a cloying physical aroma.

With the encroaching darkness, the Army generators in the town came alive. They belched, then chugged into a rhythmic meter. Electricity illuminated islands in the rubble. There were too many demands on the power output, so the Army locations could add only scattered pools that dully flickered in the sad scene. Their yellowish, misty gleam married with the smoke and haze of the cooking fires.

From the mountain pass the city was seen in blurred outline. As the trucks proceeded down the grade onto the dimly lighted streets, the men grew uneasy. They didn't like being in any light with dark shadows and black spaces around them. It was dangerous. They were not comfortable in the sound bubble the trucks were making. Such sounds could mask ominous noises from figures they couldn't see. They searched every dark spot on their route looking for the Chinaman with the machine pistol, waiting to take them out. They saw only GIs on their dirty rounds and Koreans scuttling about the shards of their town.

◆   ◆   ◆

The trucks emptied their cargo into the holding pen established to accommodate the vacation-bound legionnaires until their flights to Japan. Their resting spot was an everyday, low-maintenance Army tent camp: forty sixteen-men tents, sixteen Army cots in each; a dirt floor; and two 300-watt light bulbs, pulling about 130 watts from the over-worked generators, strung on bare wires between tent poles. The latrines outside and, as always, several hundred yards away from any tent in any direction. There were also four large fly tents providing places to prepare and serve food, and assorted canvas structures housed various administrative activities.

The camp was completely encircled by barbed wire that sagged and drooped in some places but was sturdy enough to bite and rip the occa-sional ass that tried to hurdle or squirm through the heavy strands. The wire barricade, to the surprise of the inmates who learned its purpose, was to keep the vacationers inside so that they wouldn't, in a fit of joy-ful exuberance, get out and demolish the facilities of the permanent service troops stationed near the departure center. Most of those inside thought that the wire was to protect them from some unstated danger lurking in the town. In fact, the biggest danger was to the town from the tent-city guests. The city residents, and most of the service soldiers, got piss-stiff at the thought of the combat types getting loose and start-ing their rack and ruin tour while still in Korea.

A sighing, soft night wind came up as heavy darkness closed on the town. It quickly became cold. Throughout the city, the fires, already started with wood from the ripped huts and structures and pilfered gas-oline, threw up an acrid roiling umbrella mixing with a descending night fog to lay a murky blanket over the broken city. This greasy man-

tle, pushed up by the hot ground fires, hovered just above the pyrami-
dal tops of the tents in the Army camp. The 300-watt light bulbs on
the outside peak of each tent—the only outside illumination—filtered
their dim effort through the haze to wash the camp in the mushy glow
of a badly lit silent film. The soldiers, actors in the film, moved in
quick half steps jerking from light to shadow in and out of occasional
light spears from an open tent flap.

The energy level of the camp scaled down as darkness came on.
Upon arrival in the later afternoon, what with the general foolishness
of the long truck ride, the realization that they were off line and the
expectation of a blowout in Japan, the horseplay went on for only a few
hours.

After nearly warm showers and a hot meal, most of the men were in
their tents throttling down with light conversation and beginning to
think of sleep in preparation for the next day's plane ride off the peninsula.

Crazy Horse and Buddington left the officers' mess tent. Clare was
already enrolled in a poker game. Continuing an aimless conversation,
the two wandered through the rows of tents enjoying the growing feeling of relaxation now settling on them. Where they had just come
from, darkness brought with it heightened tension, quick movements,
and short dashes from hole to hole. Here it was the soft glow of dim
illumination managed by the gasoline-powered electric generators
chugging away softly at the back of the camp. This was easy
street—sauntering along without weapons, without concerns. This was
the life of big cigars and fast motor cars.

◆   ◆   ◆

In one of the far corners of the camp, farthest away from the sentry
gate, a little business was being transacted. Here the light was a little
dimmer, the traffic on the pathways less, the chance of a hassle by
camp guards less likely. In this corner, outside the wire fence, an enter-

prising Korean family was at work. A husband was pimping his wife, selling her to a line of GIs who, seeing the opportunity, couldn't wait for the fleshier pots of Japan to be relieved of their unwieldy loads.

The cost was two dollars, U.S., an amount of great value to the native family. To earn this, the wife had only to bend over and present her backside to the customer. The wire strands were spaced sufficiently far apart that with care a man could approach and very carefully—really carefully—make the desired entry and flail away. Because they had all been on line a long time, the activity was quite time limited. Usually within a minute or so the love affair was ended. A moment or two for the woman to clean off the wet memory of the most recent transaction, a passing of money, and another romance flourished.

There were, however, certain problems involved. In addition to the barbed wire fence of the camp, designed to keep natives out, but more importantly, to keep soldiers in, that was a substantial obstacle to successfully concluding the liaison, the relative size of the participants frequently caused difficulties. The woman was not large. In better times and in other places she would have, perhaps, been called pretty, perhaps dainty. Some of the soldiers were large, so that now and again she would let out small yelps of pain. She had almost learned by experience not to signal distress after she had found out that the noises seemed to excite the customers. Each time she expressed discomfort, the deep pounding seemed to take on renewed vigor. So, by and large, she simply endured any pain. It was, after all, for the family. And, she, the manager of the family finances as in Korean households, knew many places where dollars could be sold or invested. She was quite satisfied that it was all worthwhile.

Also, a noise suppression system was needed because loud expressions of ecstasy—"Oh, shit! I'm comin' clear from Kansas!" or a particularly high-pitched grunt from the woman as one of the good ol' boys brought it home—had to be avoided. While the camp MPs probably wouldn't interfere, the few permanent cadre officers were less reliable.

If one of them happened to come upon the scene, there could be trouble: for the Koreans, loss of a lucrative venture; for the customers, no R and R and straight back up to the line. As for the officers going on R and R, it was generally thought they wouldn't care, so long as they didn't have to make any decisions. It was widely accepted that the parts of their heads that gave nonstop orders on the line were shut down for the five-day R and R period.

The solution to these many obstacles standing in the way of true love was that after pocketing the money, the Korean husband required his wife to take into her mouth a large cloth gag just as the action was to start. Then, the man would bend the woman over and hold her head firmly in his cushioning lap. Awkwardly, but carefully, he backed her up to the barbed wire. With the bent-over target now in sight, the next lucky GI would guide his cock through the wire into the moist opening. Usually the aim was true, but sometimes because of drunkenness or design, the probe pushed into the wrong opening, which resulted in an explosive yell from the woman. As the soldiers sweated, groaned, and bucked their way to heaven, the husband's lap was the shock absorber against which the wife's head was pounded by the driving lunges of the short time, but earnest, lover.

Despite the fact that the next day would find them in Japan, the sight and smell of any woman's sexual apparatus was too much for many of the men who had been on line for months with nothing but hard memories and soggy pictures to comfort them. The restraining tugs of their buddies—who were more sensibly waiting for the varied, more tasteful, Japan treats—did not slow them down. So the line formed to the right, and the tunnel of commercial love opened to the eager buyers.

From the rear of the line came anxious cries, "I can smell that smoking pussy from here," and "If I don't get to lay my tool in that charcoal soon, all I'll need is a wash rag."

"Hey man, don't shove. You—and that wrench in your pocket—will get your turn."

From the middle of the line, "Jeez, with all this action ahead of me, I'll get into her and it'll be just like taking my dick out in a warm room."

From a departing, highly unsatisfied customer, "Oh, my God, I'm ruined. It feels like a crocodile got ahold of my prick."—this from a lucky participant who forget his withdrawal had to be as carefully calibrated as his entry. After climax, he had hurriedly pulled out—an older brother had told him he wouldn't get VD if he got out quickly—and his still flailing erection had become entangled in a junction of the wire fence.

From near the front line, "I'll be damned. It runs up and down just like back home. All that Asiatic crosswise bullshit was just bullshit."

From the very back of the line, "Oh, I'd eat a yard of her shit just to get a whiff of her snatch."

From next to the speaker, "Buddy, you smell like you've already eaten a mile of elephant shit."

From the active pounder at the point of impact, "I'm in love! I'm in love! I'm in love!" Each one of these declarations was delivered in an even louder voice: eyes and neck chords straining; lower belly above, balls below slapping into the woman's ass with more and more power; the determined husband resisting the slam strokes; the wife, near exhaustion, willing the soldier to complete his task and allow her a moment of respite while the next customer lined her up.

It was the shouts of, "I'm in love" that drew the attention of Crayley and Buddington. The two had been strolling through the tent avenues idly conversing, taking pleasure in the simple act of walking through darkness punctuated by glowing lights, hearing the camp generators thumping away, and the sounds of the camp permanent garrison radios turned to the Army's Far East radio network.

They approached the business corner just as one man delivered his load. There were still six in line. The two officers moved to the fence to see the object of attention. The woman lay crumpled in a heap on a pile of straw mats, trying to restore her energy for the following round.

Next to her was a small girl child of six or seven. The daughter paid no attention to her mother but was busy trying to fit a wood puzzle together in the dim light.

The child had a slight figure; slim, almost fragile arms, small dainty hands. She wore clean, but wrinkled, used quilted cotton blouse and trousers. The pant legs barely revealed the outline of her thin legs. She had a round open face—a beautiful, serene child's face, intent on her world without interest in what was going on around her.

The next man in line looked at the wife heaped on the straw. "Shit, I don't want any of that worn out piece of meat. I'll wait to get to Tokyo." He started to move away then his eye caught the movement of the child next to the mother.

"Now, on the other hand, that prime young stuff might be just the thing to wrap around this tired old dick. Old one-eye here would just love to stretch that little drumhead." This was said to no one in particular, but it seemed to resolve the issue for the speaker. He grabbed the father's arm through the wire. Pointing at the girl, he said, "How much?" The father ignored him. Again, "How much?"

The husband struggled to get his wife in position. "Two dollah," the going price for the woman.

"No two dollah, you fucking gook. How much for the kid?"

The mother now understood. She wrenched herself from her husband's grasp and fell in a protective huddle over the girl. The woman said nothing, but now the husband found his voice. "No sell, no sell. Two dollah," again tugging at his wife.

The soldier was now completely aroused, "You damn betcha, you'll sell, you shit head. I want the kid." He had twenty dollars in his hand. He added another ten and four ones to it. "There, it's more than ten times what the old lady is getting."

The father did not understand the language. He did know thirty-four dollars. He pocketed the money, turned to the woman speaking rapidly. Her face collapsed. She broke into loud wails all the time trying to wrap herself tighter around her child. The father was determined. With two sharp blows, he broke the woman's grasp and grabbed the girl. The child, at first anxious with her father's sharp harsh commands, then apprehensive with the onset of her mother's tears, began to scream as her father started to remove her lower clothing.

The soldier, a corporal, not tall but heavy bodied and beefy, already had his pants down. Others in the waiting line had different reactions to what was happening. Three of the men, disgusted at what was about to take place, simply walked away. The remaining two pushed to the fence, both on the corporal's right side, eager to see the child raped.

Crayley moved to the corporal's left side watching the father's efforts with the frantic child whose lower body was now exposed. The man was struggling to position the girl to the corporal in the same manner as his wife. The child, however, was too small to stand on her feet and still be at a satisfactory height to receive the soldier. The father had his daughter cradled in his arms trying to get her ready to accept the large erection pushing through the corporal's shorts.

"Come on, li'l darlin'. You're gonna do me a whole lot of good." To his two buddies, "I'm going to drive a wedge into that little split tail so far she'll be able to suck on it from the inside." Turning to the child, "Come on, honey, you're going to enjoy this a whole lot."

Crayley moved closer along the wire. Buddington moved back into the shadows recognizing that this was Crazy Horse's play. Crayley, now next to the corporal said, "What do you think you're doing soldier?"

"Who the fuck are you? Wait your turn."

"My name is Lieutenant Crayley. I'm not waiting for a turn, but I am waiting for an answer to my question."

"Fuck off, Lieutenant. This is mine. I paid for it. This isn't nothing to do with the Army."

"Sure it is. I think you ought to forget the kid. Hump the old lady, but leave the kid alone."

"And I think you better the fuck bug off, Charlie. I don't give a fuck if you are a lieutenant or a general. I'm gonna have that kid's ass."

By now, the corporal's shorts were below his hips. They caught for a moment on the barbed wire, but he pushed them to the ground, ripping them against the points of the wire.

The child was subdued or near suffocation with her head stuffed into her father's lap and her bottom twisted toward the soldier. He moved closer to the fence reaching through, carefully, with one hand to steady the girl. With his other hand, he started to guide his stiff penis into the child. To do so, it was necessary for him to bend over slightly.

Crayley, who had not spoken since the corporal's last words, moved alongside the man, himself bending over to get a better view of the event. Crayley's right arm, next to the soldier, appeared to go limp, hanging straight down from his shoulder. As the corporal bent a little lower, Crayley sighed as if washing his hands of the affair, and turned to his left to move away. But it was only a half turn. Then, he spun toward the man with the full force of his turning body. His right arm snapped around and up with the spin, and the back of his clenched fist caught the corporal full in the face. The leveraged blow coupled with the momentum of the soldier's act of bending forward exploded his nose and sent him, first, twisting into the wire, then backward off the wire—with a ripped ear and cheek—to fall heavily on the ground.

The Korean family scrambled together clothes and mats and disappeared into the darkness. The corporal's two friends, startled by the abrupt end to his chances for a really good fresh piece of ass and what for them was going to be a lip-licking show, shuffled uncertainly about their fallen champion. They didn't attempt to help him. Instead they turned toward Crayley. The largest of the two said, "What the hell you do that for? You got no right. This ain't Army crap. This is his private business. You cut my friend out of his punch on that gook kid—bought and paid for." As he heard himself talk, the soldier convinced himself and gained courage. He stepped toward Crayley.

"It don't make no fuckin' difference, you're an officer. He could bring charges against you for hittin' him, and we saw it." He turned to his companion who nodded his head jerkily.

More excited now, the second soldier waded in, "Goddamn it. It's none of your fuckin' worry. I don't care if you're an officer or whatever. You can't do that to us."

They both moved toward Crayley. He stepped toward them. Buddington stepped out of the shadows. The two soldiers seemed to see him for the first time. "Jesus! Where did you come from?" as they saw his size. "Who the hell are you?" queried the largest of the two.

Buddington replied, "I'm the Lone Ranger and"—indicating Crayley—"this is Tonto. Tonight we're on screw patrol, and we've just scored a silver bullet for our trophy case. Tonto here prevented the rape of a young girl child by three U.S. soldiers."

"Wha'd ya mean, three? It was only him going to do it," gesturing toward the corporal who was having lots of trouble trying to get up.

"No, the way I saw it, you two were just waiting for Errol Flynn here to finish then you were going to pile on, and that's what I'll tell them at your court-martials."

"What court-martial?

"The one we'll recommend to the investigating officer who will review your conduct in this affair. I think it's worth five-to-ten in Leavenworth for you all. If you think this little kid was going to get a bore job, wait till the goons at Leavenworth get through excavating your sorry asses. The scouring your butts are going to take will turn them into the Grand Canyon."

"You shouldn't talk like that. We weren't going to screw the kid. We were just watching."

"You've got three seconds to get out of here or some really serious shit is going to start clinging to you."

The two looked first at Crayley, who was inching toward them, then at Buddington. With never a glance toward their friend the corporal, they took off, headed toward the safety of the lighted tent area.

Crayley advanced on the corporal, who was still able to only sit up and hold his head, but it was clear from his eyes that he had been aware of what happened with his two departed friends.

"Soldier, when I tell you this is an Army matter, it sure damn is. Your two buddies got the message. Now, the question is, did you?" Crayley moved closer, "It's still me talking to you cowboy and I'm waiting for an answer."

Nothing.

Crayley knelt by the corporal. He picked up his right arm, placed the knob of the elbow on his own knee and started to apply pressure. "I sure damn want you to understand that when I told you to knock it off, you should have ended it." The backward pressure on the elbow increased. With the increasing pain, the corporal started to come around. He tried to speak through the mess that was the mashed pulp of his nose, but he couldn't get it out. "I'm still waiting for an answer, soldier," said Crayley still pressing on the arm. "You might have trouble in Japan trying to get your pants off with one good arm."

More pressure on the arm. A bubbling moan burbled through the frothy red mush. "It's a pure shame you had to fall down and hurt your face. But the medics see a lot of stumble cases in these badly lighted areas. I think they can probably fix it."

Buddington watched. It seemed to him that Crayley was too pleased with the way the situation was moving. He wondered whether he should step in. So far the two of them were in the clear. They had, after all, stopped a brutal rape. And there were witnesses in the disgusting soldiers who had left the scene early, but if Crayley pushed too far, the event could backfire against them.

"Leave it, Crazy Horse. Leave it." Buddington spoke and moved to Crayley's side. "This scabby piece of shit deserves it, but you've done enough. You need to save yourself for other mercy missions, which you can't perform if you're in the stockade for pulling people's arms off."

Crayley looked around surprised. Without a word, he got up. The corporal, alert now, scuttled to his feet and disappeared. The two officers took a last look around. All was quiet. Their evening walk was over. They returned to their sleeping quarters.

CHAPTER NINE

The next morning, a truck relay started early from the camp to the airfield for the flight to Japan. The DC-4s, flown by air crews bored with their bus-line duty, lumbered up and off the dirt strip for the three-hour trip to Tokyo. Buddington, who was on another plane on the ride over, joined up when they landed at Haneda, the airport on Tokyo Bay. They got their billet arrangements and left in Army busses. The three of them had drawn rooms in the Akasaka district in a blockhouse converted to R and R quarters. The blockhouse was satisfactorily near eating and drinking establishments and reasonably close to the Ginza's flashier and fleshier clubs.

After finding their rooms and stowing their gear, they met in the hotel reception area. Clare had already identified the nearest officers' club. He had managed to connect with his surgeon brother, who confirmed that the club was conveniently close to the hospital and that Major Dan could meet them early the next afternoon to help them plan their lecherous liaisons.

The decision was instantly made to get to the club and its bar as quickly as possible. It was not yet midafternoon when they arrived, so they decided to have a liquid late lunch in preparation for the cocktail hour, which would follow. They staked out a table in the large bar room in a corner almost against the wall. It was near enough to the bar for quick service, yet far enough away not to be in the line of fire in the event that any philosophical discussions ended in disagreement sufficient to cause the launching of flying objects.

The place was half full of infantry officers with a representation of medical types, mostly men, but several nurses and WAC officers were also present. To Crayley, it looked like a noncombustible mix. There was no cause to complain about the medics. Most infantrymen had high regard for them; the conventional wisdom being that they did very good work and were usually willing to make house calls. A general view was also held that it was a bad idea to quarrel with those—wherever they might be found—who controlled the plasma and morphine supply.

As they sat down, Horace recognized that Clare already had a mild buzz on. Ed had found someone in their billet who had a bottle he was pleased to share, and Ed was pleased to be the "sharee."

Buddington motioned a waiter to their table. The waiter was an off-duty GI earning a little extra money. He wore the lapel buttons of an engineer that could be seen through the opening of his waiter's coat.

Clare looked at him. "What's your name, son?" Clare was twenty-three. The waiter was at least forty.

"Minton, sir."

"Minton, what is your rank? That waiter's coat tells me nothing."

"Sir, I'm a corporal."

"Good, now I understand. Corporal Minton, do you know who we are?"

"No, sir."

"Good, again. These two dear friends whose names I have temporarily forgotten are deserving of the best in the house. But, before that, I must ask you if you know what we are doing in this rat's ass town?"

"Yes, sir. You are here on R and R like most of the officers in here this time of day."

"Oh, Minton, that's very good. Now, I ..."

Buddington cut in, "Shut up, Clare. This man has work to do and I'm thirsty." Ed, startled, looked at Buddington as if he were seeing him for the first time. Buddington continued, "I'll set up the program, corporal. Bring us what is regarded as the best bourbon at your bar. Give us each three glasses; have only whiskey—double shot—and ice in each glass. Whenever you see two empty glasses in front of anyone of us, start the three-glass resupply. Got that?" Minton nodded. "Okay, off you go. Don't forget us in the heat of any of your other battles. We depend on you."

The three drank steadily, but conservatively, through the afternoon. They gradually were enveloped in a pleasant glow of comfortable well being. They liked being in the bar, hearing the hum and occasional loud sounds of the city, and observing the civilized behavior of men and women in an agreeable setting. The jolt of being in this place barely six hours after being in the tents in Chunchon was not ignored, it was only suppressed but barely. Although swaddled in the lushness of the afternoon, they all looked at their watches from time to time, all with the same thought: in 120 hours, I'm back in the mountains. Next look—in 119 hours and 20 minutes, I'm back in the mountains.

As time wore on, Clare, more and more, wore on his mates. He couldn't ignore Minton, who steadfastly kept to his refilling task. He kept finding fault with the waiter's performance, which he loudly attributed to Minton's engineering training. The other two paid him little attention, but as his complaints grew even louder and started to personalize Minton's failures, others in the room became aware of Clare's increasingly boorish behavior.

An infantry major materialized at their table. He seemed to have quietly glided up on wheeled tracks. Horace looked at him thinking he was young to be a major. He did not have a uniform coat on. His insignia of rank was on his open collar shirt. Crazy Horse mumbled to Buddington, "Here comes the bouncer. He's bigger than a tank. He's even bigger than you. After his treads crumple us, we're out of here."

"Hi, guys. I'm part of the base cadre. I'm supposed to keep my eyes on the club. How's it going?"

Clare looked him up—from his seated position he looked way up—and decided that the big major was a rear echelon commando not worthy of his respect or concern. "Major, I'm damn sorry to say that the support staff in this club doesn't properly recognize us combat types. I see lots of plump-assed waiters, but they don't jump very high when told to hop to it."

"Well, Lieutenant, quite of few of the service staff have some combat time. Take a walk with me and I'll point out a few."

"Not me, Major. And not with you. I know you've got the rank, but we here"—a wide sweep of his arm to include the table—"are entitled to some respect out of the scurvy crew you have here."

Horace and Bud exchanged glances. So it was Ed's newly acknowledged combat status that was twisting his shorts. They both thought that Clare's big mouth-off to the major was a bad move for all three of them.

The major looked at the other two at the table. He saw that each of them had the device denoting award of two CIBs and, importantly, they hadn't chorused in with the whiny kid. He turned to Clare, "Everybody respects what you're doing on the peninsula, Lieutenant. If you don't see that, I'm sorry; however, I'll appreciate it if you cool off. If you don't, you'll see me again." He glided off toward another developing firestorm.

"Did you see that hang-dog, pussy major? As soon as I pointed out to him the CIBs at this table, he got his sweet ass out of here. Pretty good, huh?" Clare said. He looked at the other two for confirmation but got none, so he turned back to his drink.

In a short while, Minton passed by. Clare bellowed, "Goddamn it, waiter, where the hell you been? Come here." Minton kept going. Clare now fully primed and having trouble staying in his chair, turned toward Crayley to speak.

The big major slid to a stop next to the table. Only now he wore his uniform coat. Clare looked at him and realized he had been seriously outflanked. The major looked like the poster boy for a medal-makers' convention. He had more ribbons in more colors than Clare had ever seen, topped off by a two-time CIB "All right, lieutenant, I've had enough of you. You're not the only kid who ever got shot at. Unfortunately for me, I've got another two months of babysitting idiots like you before my hip heals enough for me to return to regular duty. As for you, I want you to get your ass out of here now. You two,"—motioning to Crayley and Buddington—"take him home. Don't come back, any of you, until this little kewpie doll prick is sober and has had a dose of politeness poured into him." He punched Clare in the shoulder to emphasize his point and said, "And on your way out, you stop by the kitchen door and apologize to Minton. He's waiting."

The three got up and left, giving Clare only enough time to drop by the kitchen. On their way back to their quarters, Crayley and Buddington nudged Clare into a decorative pool filled with beautiful koi. As he sloshed and slipped his way out of the pool, Crayley told him, "You little shit. Your brother better come through or you are back in that pool with Bud sitting on you until you match the color of those fish."

◆　　◆　　◆

Back in his room, Crayley was still mad, then puzzled, then pissed off at Clare's conduct that had got them thrown out of the club and him thrown into the koi pool. Finally, he went looking for Clare. When he found his room, he abruptly entered and, without pause, started. "Ed, I'm wondering what in hell got into you. That was a corporal for crissakes, an old corporal trying to make a few extra bucks, and you went after him like he was some scurvy scab fouling your garbage pit. And what was that shit about engineers?"

"I got my reasons."

"I'm sure you do, but for me, do they make sense? You better tell me something because quite aside from today's bar fiasco, I don't want a nut case in George Company."

Clare considered his options, then he said, "I guess I never told you. Me and my older brother, Major Dan, are the children of my father's second wife. Our father also had two sons from wife number one. The old man and the first two are all West Pointers. All three were Regular Army engineers, and all three were in Europe in the recently concluded shoot-out there."

"Our father had a big-time job in Patton's headquarters; our two brothers were closer to the war. Too close for John, the oldest. He was leading the job of reinforcing the Remagen Bridge when he got killed. Robert got hit a couple of times, but he is mostly okay. The father figure is now a brigadier general at the Pentagon. Robert is some place in Florida redoing the swamps."

"Dan and I don't like our father and his remaining kid. We never wanted to go to West Point, and this made us heretics to our dad. His sons had the same view of us. During the Big War, Dan was finishing med school and I was finishing high school, so we couldn't match the heroics of the rest of the family."

"The old man was—is—a mean old bastard. He made Dan and me pay in every way he could think of: materially, emotionally, and physically. True, he cared for us, but if he had any love for us—and that's open to question—it turned to scornful maintenance when he realized we didn't have, and didn't want, true-blue engineer blood distilled in a West Point beaker. Our mom tried to keep the bridge open between us, but it was no use. He turned on her with wild outbursts about her namby-pamby kids. His treatment of her soured even further—if that was possible—our feelings toward him."

"Dear old papa never ceases to trumpet the deeds of his engineer team as he refers to the three of them. John got Wagnerian horn blasts for his devotion and death. After the war, Dan had to serve some time because of a deferment to finish his medical studies, so he is still in. When I got drafted a little while before the North Koreans moved south, I requested the infantry, figuring if there could be a war some place and if I could be lucky enough to get into some fighting, then I could go to the family gatherings and match the bullshit of Dad and Robert. And, what do you know, I did get lucky. The Korean War started and here I am."

"Lucky," said Crayley. "Did you say lucky? You crazy bastard, you don't need luck to get here. You do need a hell of a lot of it to get out of here under your own power."

"No, you don't understand what I mean. Now that I got my CIB "—he touched the ribbon side of his jacket where was pinned the small, silver-wreathed blue plaque that was his recently awarded Combat Infantryman Badge—"I can stand eye-to-eye with those two. With this,"—again touching the CIB—"I can tell those engineers where to shove their shovels."

"And dear old dad is also the reason I want to chalk up some serious combat action. I told you back at the company that I intend to do something so the Army will take notice of my fearsome skills and ferocious heart, so that the big goombahs with all the stars will see me as a highly desirable add-on to the regular officer ranks and offer me an RA commission. If they do that, and I throw it back in their face, and I tell the old man I did it … why, I'll feel just grand. A bona fide hero who won't join his club even when asked by the member committee."

Crayley just looked at Clare. Of course, Horace had his two CIBs, one for Europe where he learned his trade and one for Korea where he was still perfecting it. He was proud of them, but it didn't energize him to the level that Clare seemed to expect. After a moment, Crayley leaned over, "Ed, we're not heroes. We're here because we're here, that's all. It's the luck of the draw. You play the hand you're dealt. We live in an infected zone. Others aren't exposed to the same disease. If you wear the badge like a leper's bell—to proclaim your deadliness—others not in this particular club will soon regard you as what we all really are anyway: crazy as coots."

"Yeah. I know that, but don't you think I can cram a turd down those engineers' throats?"

Horace leaned back, "Sure you can do that, if you want to."

◆　　　◆　　　◆

The next afternoon, after a less than tasty breakfast of oatmeal and gin fizzes, the three were back at the O-club. Ed was neat, shiny clean, exuding boyish charm, and sober. They found a quiet corner, ordered two beers, and looked around, warily, for the big major. Although he was not in immediate view, the clear memory of his jet-powered glide kept Clare under the watchful eyes of Horace and Bud, who denied Ed even the last drops from their beer bottles.

A short time later, a major was sighted striding purposefully in their direction. But this was not *the* major, the bouncer. Clare let out a whoop, "Dan, over here!"

It was Major Dan, the doctor man. He embraced his brother, pointed at Ed's CIB, saying, "I see you got something to shove up the old man's nose. Good."

Introductions all around followed. Major Dan did a double take when Horace was identified by Buddington as Crazy Horse. Drinks were ordered. This time Ed was allowed a beer. The story of the previous night's festivities was recalled and fully told to Major Dan who was well aware of the big major. "Oh, yeah, that's Major Goetz. He's well-known around town. He's an outpatient at the hospital. He got his hip and leg torn up while chasing North Korean butterflies. He should go back to the States, but he insists he's going back to bag a few more specimens. In the meantime, the Army has come up with a perfect assignment for him. He wanders around two or three of the clubs where you hotshots come to cram a hundred days of fun into five days of R and R." He looked at his brother. "You're damn lucky Goetz didn't take a disliking to you. He's got a couple of thugs on his military police backup that are cat-shit mean. You could have woken up about three days from now, wondering if you had a good time while you were in Tokyo."

"Okay," said Ed, "I won't keep a place open on my dance card for Major Goetz. Now, Dan, what have you got for us?"

"I can get you a few vials of penicillin if you're pissing Roman candles."

"It's too early for that, but don't lose the key to the medicine chest. What I mean is, who, amongst your many eager nurse friends, have you lined up for three brave fellows?"

"Say what? Do I look like your everyday raggedy ass vascular surgeon pimp?"

"But, Dan, I told my friends you could do us some good."

"Tough on them. Worse for you. I can't order anybody to get poked. You should know that this town is filled with GIs looking for someone to take delivery on an overdue load of love. Not hard to find the women to do that, but nurses are not the ones lined up to meet the delivery man. Go down to the Ginza and get a five-day marriage license."

Horace looked at Bud. They nodded in agreement. Ed Clare was a real fuckup.

"Jeez, Dan, can't you do anything for us?"

"Ed, the best I can do for you is to put you within radar range of possible action. There is a place—a lovely Japanese inn—in the hills of the Lake Hakone district. Very peaceful, very soothing to the nerves. Good food, good bar. It gets a big play from the hospital staff when a break is needed from blood alley. Some of the people of our department are probably up there now. It's called the Fuji View Hotel. It's a really beautiful spot. You"—looking at his brother—"could use a little quiet time even if you don't get your tap adjusted."

The three of them looked sourly at the doctor. "Or," Dan continued, "you could try your luck with some of the women here. See that WAC officer? She does medical administration work, not too stressful. Also there are some Red Cross beauties scattered around. Their job is to minister to the needs of soldiers. Look," he directed their attention to a tall redhead ambling toward the bar, "she'd be about right for you, Bud. I heard she used to be a stewardess for Pan Am."

Bud followed the walk, then groaned, "She looks like she was the stewardess on the chase plan for the Wright Brothers."

Major Dan went on, "Take one night at the inn. It will do you good. If you don't like it, you will still have time to deflower Tokyo before you go back." The three were unconvinced. The doctor was still selling, "I can get you a vehicle and a guide to get you there. I've reserved three slots for you." Looking at Ed, he said, "By slots, little brother, I mean three little bamboo rooms with futons and small pebble pillows."

A waiter went by. It was Corporal Minton. Ed saw him first, "Hey, you no-account engineer, bring us some drinks." Minton passed them by. Clare started up from his seat. Three things happened. Horace grabbed one arm; Bud grabbed a leg, pinning Ed to his seat; and the big major bouncer appeared magically on his gliding feet. He braked to a stop and stood looking at Ed. Then he took in the table.

"Hello, Dan. Are you here to do an attitude transplant on this one?" He motioned toward Ed.

"He's my brother."

"He's a pain in the ass. They are all on very thin ice with me. I don't want any of them in here. You'll do them and me a great favor if you manage to lose them for a few days."

"I'm trying to do that, but I'm not winning."

Major Goetz looked at the three and said, "Do it." When he had gone, Horace said to Major Dan, "Thanks Dan, we'd really like to visit Fuji View."

The next morning, a young Japanese man appeared at their billet and told them he was an assistant in the paperwork part of Major Clare's department and would lead them to the hotel.

◆   ◆   ◆

First, they had to go to the hospital motor pool for a vehicle. They walked to the transport lot following closely behind their guide. At the motor sergeant's dispatch office the three officers were told where their jeep would be. They started for it, leaving Mr. Hamanaka to fill out the required forms.

Near the back of the lot coming toward them on the same driving lane were three soldiers. A sergeant as large as Buddington was in the lead. As they passed each other, Ed abruptly halted, "Hey soldier, stop." The three GIs turned and stood looking at Clare. Horace and Bud waited. Clare spoke to the sergeant, "What's that on your uniform?" pointing toward a red badge over two or three general-purpose ribbons.

"That's a combat artilleryman's badge. It's just like your infantry badge only it's red, the artillery color."

Indeed, it was just like a CIB, only a silver cannon barrel on a red background instead of a rifle on blue.

"How did you come by that?"

"Well, sir,"—drawing out the "sir" like it was a piece of food debris stuck in his teeth—"just like you did, by being in combat in Korea."

"And what was your job in Korea?"

"We, all three of us, drive ammo trucks for one five-fives"—a reference to an Army division's long-range artillery.

"I'll be damned. What do you mean, 'combat'? Those big tubes are so far behind the line, the only way you would see a Chinaman is if he was making a home delivery of wonton."

"Now wait a minute, we're just as much in combat as you are."

"Not even close, you dipshit clowns are truck drivers. Take off those pieces of tin. They look like they were cut from a tomato soup can."

"Hold on, Lieutenant. Our company commander awarded us these decorations."

Clare was rolling. "Bullshit. The Army has no such thing as a combat artilleryman's badge. So you three are out of uniform wearing unauthorized decorations. Unless you get rid of those ornaments, the MPs at the gate—on my order—will be happy to take you to the stockade."

The three soldiers, bristling with anger, seemed to be gauging their chances. But it didn't seem to be a good bet. Buddington certainly matched their big sergeant. Crayley outgunned either of the other two, and the windbag lieutenant, while not so big, seemed to be crazy enough to fight all three of them.

Clare stepped forward. "Give them to me, now, or in you go."

The three, with venom streaking from their eyes, handed over the badges. Ed threw them to the dirt and ground his boot heel on them until they were bent and cracked. He turned his back on the GIs and started toward the assigned jeep. The three soldiers looked for a moment at Horace and Bud, then backed away, still facing them.

CHAPTER TEN

They found the jeep, retrieved Mr. Hamanaka, and started out for the hotel. Hamanaka directed them through Tokyo, south along the shore line of Tokyo Bay, past the Odawara beaches. They went through Kamakura but did not visit the Buddha, turned right, and started the mountain climb toward Lake Hakone.

The hotel was midslope on a heavily wooded mountain facing, and on the east side of, Lake Hakone. When they arrived near noon, even though a bright sun overhead gave considerable warmth there were still tendrils of a damp morning fog swirling about. The sunlight where unfiltered by the dark green growth had a soothing, languorous, feeling.

Mr. Hamanaka insisted they experience the serene beauty of the place before proceeding. The gardens of the inn were immaculately beautiful; the essential rock garden was freshly reworked and spotlessly shining. In spite of their early reluctance, the three of them felt better. Major Dan was right. They went to the hotel entrance. They were met by the mama-san who, despite her less than five foot height stood like a formidable centurion blocking the doorway. In passable English she gave them to understand that none would pass through the portals until she made her welcoming speech. She launched into it.

It was less a welcome than a list of "don'ts" and "watch-outs." All this was accompanied by stern looks and stiff finger jabs delivered straight from the shoulder. These mostly hit Bud at belt level with a few in the upper groin area. She made clear that she didn't like "rowdy GI tricks," a term she spoke quite clearly several times and which quite obviously she had seriously practiced. What wasn't clear was what constituted such tricks. It apparently was to be left to her discretion and judgment.

As she was winding down, Ed asked the direct, vital question. It set her off in what must have been a systematic series of Japanese oaths. They poured out of her in a torrent accompanied by flashing arms and bayonet finger jabs at Clare's stomach. Mr. Hamanaka didn't brother to translate. The message was clear. Finally mama-san began to splutter in English "No house girls here, no girls. You no find 'butterfry' girl in this place."

It seemed that every Japanese female between the ages of fourteen and one hundred four knew the *Madame Butterfly* story in which the Japanese maiden is abandoned by her foreign lover. The term was commonly used to explain the situation when no short-term consorts were commercially available.

When she finally calmed down a little, mama-san further explained to them that this lack of courtesy wasn't her idea. It was the edict of the hotel owner, who didn't want to offend the many "U.S. ladies" who visited the inn with the hope of attaining a mystical experience by getting a view of Mount Fuji on a clear day.

When the orientation lecture finally ended, the three arrivals got rid of their heavy boots, acquired the mandatory slippers to polish and preserve the lustrous floors, and started on a tour of the inn.

The Fuji View Hotel had a long central spine, at the front of which was administration, and a large lounge with a bar attached. The far end had a stunning view of the mountains, Lake Hakone, and on the very few days when the forest mists were absent, a magnificent picture post-card of Mount Fuji. There were six wings, three to a side, branching off the central corridor. In each wing there were six rice paper rooms, a small lounge, and a large hot tub at the end of the wing, divided into two soaking areas by a sliding screen.

The travelers dumped their gear in their rooms. Crayley grabbed a bottle from his bag, and they skated over the slippery floors to the lounge in their wing. Bud was the first to express the feeling they all shared, "Well, we're shit out of luck. There's nothing here for us. We might as well start back."

Horace pointed to the darkening sky. "It's going to be dark in an hour. Mr. Hamanaka has already left us for the train station. These mountain roads are narrow even with our jeep. I don't plan to leave my bones anywhere but Korea. I say we stay the night."

That settled the question, and they turned to the duty of the remains of the day. In an hour it was dark, but it was too early for dinner. Ed was half pissed. Horace and Bud were in good shape, but feeling no pain.

Suddenly, Buddington got up and starting shedding his clothes. Horace regarded this exercise. "What the hell you doing, Tarzan?"

"I've decided to have a hot tub before dinner. If the temperature is at the level of live steam, my kinks from the jeep ride may go away."

The three stripped, left their clothes in a pile in the lounge, took their bottled supplies with them, and started for the hot tub. It was right next door to the lounge. They saw painted on the first door in Japanese and English, "Men Only"—another sop to American sensibilities. They pushed through. The vapors arising from the tub convinced them it was more than hot enough. They squatted on the tiny stools next to the tub, took a quick soap wash, and then started to settle into the tub.

"It's hot as hell," were Ed's first words since he had last said, "More ice and fill it to the top this time."

"What is the recommended procedure to get into this lava pool?" was Bud's contribution to the exercise.

"It ain't easy," said Horace, "and don't let your balls hit first or you'll never have any kids." Crayley was easing himself over the side, cheating the approved method. He had filled two small buckets, used for the soap bath, with cold water and was pouring it on his legs and body as he slowly eased himself into the watery furnace.

Gradually they all slid into the liquid brimstone. At first, they were afraid to move because movement, however slight, caused ripples, and ripples explored body areas not yet immersed, with tortuous results. Eventually, they were completely in the tub, keeping just their heads and one drinking arm out of the water. That arm cradled a bamboo cup, which was kept full from their supply bottles that were kept well away from the stone tub.

The water had a wonderfully soothing effect. Their various aches gently disappeared. They stopped talking, nearly dozing, although both Horace and Bud were aware of the danger of becoming so weak in these cauldrons that the eventual rescuers found only boiled beef at the bottom of the tub.

As they quieted down, they became aware of voices in soft tones very near by. It was the occupants of the other half of the tub, separated from them only by a shoji screen divider. They weren't just occupants. They were women. The three perked up. Their languid manner dissolved. They were energized. They looked at each other with questioning glances.

Bud took the lead. "Hello over there, those of you in our swimming pool."

A delay, then, "Your pool? It's our pool. We were here first."

More muted deliberations on the "Men Only" side followed by, "Okay, it's yours. Now that we've given up our ownership rights, how do we meet the new owners? Can we open the gate—both sets of tenants to stay on their own premises?"

Whispered discussions. "All right."

Crayley slowly slid open the screen. There were three women up to their necks in water. A pause as the six heads swiveled to view the occupants, then, one of the two blondes in the tank said, "Hi, sailors. Is this your home port?"

Bud replied, "Only so long as it takes this steaming shop to restore maximum energy and efficiency to our withered parts."

Horace, who had always experienced difficulty when formally meeting young ladies, decided introductions were in order. "This is Lieutenant Buddington, Clare, and I'm Crayley. We just got here," he finished, but thinking he should have said more.

A youngish—all three of the men privately guessed her age about thirty—brunette said, "I'm Captain Radley. This is Lieutenant Sutton"—a smashing blonde, younger than Radley—"and Lieutenant Kaminsky"—another good looking, somewhat darker blonde, somewhat younger than Sutton.

The three men stared at them. Finally, Crayley thought of more clever words, "Hi to all of you from all of us."

Seconds passed—nothing. Then Ed turned to reach the supply bottles to offer the tub mates a drink. He found it necessary to rise out of the water to grasp the containers. His back was to the women as he pushed up on one leg. He started to slip, caught himself, pushed again, stood straight up for an instant, lost it and fell backward into the tub. This created a mini-tsunami that surged the short length of the tub inundating the three women who were crouched neck deep in their end. A loud three-person yelp, a quick jump up, and a faster dip down to neck-high water.

The threesomes looked at each other. Finally, Captain Radley, acknowledging the momentary high jump competition when Ed did his fall-away back flip, said, looking into the depths of the tub, "Nice butt."

Horace, looking to return the compliment, said, "Nice boobs."

This wave episode broke the ice, so to speak. First name introductions followed. First, sake was poured for each bather into small bamboo cups, the only drinking containers allowed for those soaking in the brine. Captain Radley, already thought of as the "big blonde" by the three men, was Barbara. The shorter blonde was Marian Sutton. The smallish, fine-featured brunette was Fran. They were nurses stationed at Tokyo General. To the three soldiers, they were also ravishingly beautiful.

After a few moments, Barbara asked, "Are you guys new doctors?"

"No, we're ground pounders come to Japan for five glorious fun-filled days."

Having established that they were on R and R, Barbara continued, "What do you do over there?"

"We race up and down the mountains chasing—or running from—the bad guys. Why did you ask if we are doctors? Did Ed's stethoscope give us away?"

Barbara answered, "This is mostly a medical depressure chamber. We come here, doctors and nurses, when we need a break from people mending and patching."

Clare spoke up, "My brother told us."

Marian joined, "Your brother?"

"Major Dan Clare."

"Oh, that's the connection. I know Dan. I've worked with him a few times. He's a good surgeon."

Finally, with everyone sufficiently parboiled, the tub party ended with agreement by all to meet for dinner.

◆　　　◆　　　◆

After their evening meal, they returned to the lounge in their wing. Conversation was aimless except for detailed questions as to how Lieutenant Crayley became "Crazy Horse." Clare was noticeably fidgety and was also drinking more than the rest of them. Barbara seemed to be getting along with Bud, but not so much that any of the three hopefuls were ready to declare victory.

Several minutes after the talking had slowed to a stop, Barbara brought from a cabinet in the corner of the room an Army-issue all channel radio receiver. She plugged the line chord of the machine into a power source.

Horace said, "What and why?"

Marian replied, "Sometimes we try it. It usually has very good reception unless the weather is just awful."

Marian turned the machine on and dialed the channel selector until voices were heard. The radio spoke clearly to them. The infantrymen spun to it, their senses riveted to the voice. It was a Chinaman speaking excellent UCLA American English, "*You clowns are finished. We're coming up that hill to sweep your sorry butts off. You better bugout now.*"

Another Chinese voice cut in, "*Well, goddamn you fools, American. You no belong Korea. You no stay. Get out Korea. We know you, Baker Company. We come soon. Knock your ass off our hill.*"

They heard the American reply, "Fuck you, slants. Come up here and we'll send you home as chop suey mix."

"What the hell is that?" said Bud. But they knew. It happened all the time in Korea. In the Communist sweeps down the peninsula early in the war, the Commies had captured so much U.S. equipment that they were still a dial up number on the UN radio net. There were plenty of conversations between U.S. and Chinese forces.

Crazy Horse remembered his battalion commander shouting over his radio, "Quit talking to those fuckin' Chinks and listen to me," to which a calm Chinese voice answered, "*Oh, dear sir, we get not any fucking. Could you send some of your beautiful boys to us for such duty.*"

"It's 'Korea calling,'" said Marian. "Fran has never heard it. We thought she would find it interesting." The mood of the three soldiers instantly changed. From happy fellahs urgently seeking a good time piece of nooky, their tempers soured. "Interesting," said Horace. "Interesting. It may be for you, but it curdles the tempura sitting in my gut."

Fran asked, "Is it real or is it just radio actors?"

Crazy Horse answered, "It's real all right. Those fuckin' gooks clog up the airwaves all the time. It's real, but apparently not over here. Here, it's just theater of the spooky. My hair is crawling down my back into the crack of my ass. I don't like it." Bud and Ed had the same half-wild look as Horace.

Barbara spoke, "We don't turn it on very often, but we wanted Fran to hear."

"Great! Fran heard. Now get out of the loop, please."

Barbara again, apologetically, "Sorry, we don't get many riflemen up here."

When the radio was silenced, the lounge was quiet. The night was slipping away. Fran made small quick movements, picking nonexistent bits of fluff off her uniform skirt. Marian smothered a yawn.

Ed sensed opportunity—if this was opportunity—sliding away. He had been working the bottle since dinner and was by now fairly well oiled. Without preamble, or even a "by the way," and armed with only a fruity smirk, he launched, "LSMFT," he gurgled.

Three of the others said, "What?"

"LSMFT."

"What's that supposed to mean?"

"LSMFT."

"Oh, I know," said Fran. "I remember from the Big War. It's some kind of cigarette jingle."

Horace, who knew what Clare meant, cringed.

Marian picked up on it, "Oh yes, I remember. It's 'Lucky Strike means fine tobacco.'"

Fran, with a puzzled look toward him, said, "Ed, why do you say that?"

"Well," Ed, suddenly nearly sober, swallowed hard, "We're hoping"—a quick glance took in Horace and Bud—"that you're in a position, or will be in a position"—here, a snorting giggle squeaked out—"to help us relieve a very personal pressing need we all have. In a word, to get rid of a heavy anxiety load we are all carrying."

There was silence. Horace thought it was like the silence that would probably precede the end of the world. He had a sliding away feeling. He felt he was swirling down the vortex of a flushed toilet.

Bud was stunned. "Jeez, Clare," then "Jeez," again.

It was Barbara who spoke. First she looked at Bud with what could have been a sorrowing flicker of a smile. "Well, Lieutenant Ed, I've got to tell you that your proposition is different in form than we usually

get. It's certainly direct. You seem like stand-up guys who could probably benefit from a tool adjustment. But, unfortunately for you, we hear
such stuff all the time though not as straight out as yours. We spend
half our time in Tokyo saying 'no,' but that's Tokyo. There it's part of
our duty to listen, to help keep morale and other things up. The success ratio of those attempts is about one in a thousand."

"In a way, we're just as beat up as you are. That's why we're up here,
for our own little R and R. So I've got to tell you, Skippy"—she looked
at the other women—"That you, Bud, and Crazy Horse are sleeping
alone tonight unless mama-san has hot pants for one of you."

The three nurses got up as if on order from Captain Barbara and
started out of the lounge.

"LSMFT," burbled Clare.

Barbara stopped at the door. She looked at Fran. "LSMFT means
'Let's screw, my finger's tired.'"

Fran blushed heavy. The three of them left. Crayley and Buddington turned toward Clare to strangle him.

A few hours later, just past midnight, all six rooms in the wing were
occupied by single sleepers.

◆   ◆   ◆

Bud was jerked, twisting, from a jumbled sleep by a spear-like
shriek. Disoriented and struggling to meet the attack his first reaction
told him was coming, he spun out of the heavy Japanese quilt. By the
time he rolled on to the mat floor, a second howl was filling the wing.
It came from the chamber next to his. It was Crazy Horse. Bud did not
go into the passage way, he simply slid open the thin panel separating
him from Horace.

Crayley was standing, nude, in a corner of his room. His arms were
rigidly extended shoulder high. His eyes were open in a flat, unseeing
glaze. He was a long way from the Fuji View. His fists clinched, and
the muscles of his body clumped into hard mounds. A forefinger

extended from one fist, pointing as a warning to something closing in from the side.

Then, no more screams. His cries must have awakened his nonexistent troops. Now, he is telling them, in startlingly clear commands, how to defend.

"Fosca, machine gun there,"—a finger jab to another part of the room—"Nonowski, get the mortars going, flares up first. Orosco, take your squad down to that spur, not too far. Go! Go!"

He paused to watch his orders being executed. Into this space Buddington—now joined by Clare and Barbara—stepped to Crayley, shook him, and tried to force his arms down. It didn't work. Horace was like a statue: cast and unmovable. Marian had arrived. Fran, wide-eyed and fearful, joined them.

A low growl started in Crayley's throat. It rose to a wail, "Look out, look out, here they come. There they are!" Crazy Horse was back in the mountains in a terrifying fight. His eyes nearly exploded out of his skull. His mouth distorted in a grimace so fierce and severe the others feared his jaw would break. The corded ropes in his arms pulsed. His body seeped fluids. He gave off heat that all of them could feel. Water poured out of Horace.

Bud found a heavy jug of water by the tatami mat and poured it over Crayley. The water, very cold, sliced into Horace's nightmare. He saw—half saw—the others for the first time and collapsed in a heap in the middle of the room. He seemed to be crying, but he was not, he was only pulling great breathy sobs from deep down. He could not or would not talk. He sat mumbling to himself, not noticing the others in the room.

To Bud and Ed, Crazy Horse's episode was of a kind they had seen before. They didn't move to help him because they didn't know what to do after the jug of water sloshed him. But the nurses acted quickly. Marian went to him, removing her bathrobe, which she used as a mop to sluice the water off into a growing puddle on the mat. Barbara gave him—and forced him to drink—more water. Horace commenced shivering, which the nurses took as a good sign. Fran started tidying the room, occasionally reaching out to pat his head as she circled the room. The three women kept up a flow of quiet soothing words—not a message, just words.

Gradually, calm and order returned to Crayley. He realized he was naked, tried to pull Marian's wet rag of a robe about him, but his hands weren't fully operational. He lay down on his damp futon. Marian covered him with the quilt, leaving a side open. She looked at the others. "You can leave now. He'll be all right. I'll stay with him." So saying, she slipped into bed next to Horace and pulled the covering tight over both of them.

Clare and Buddington numbly followed orders and left the room. When they were in the passageway, Barbara took Bud's hand and guided him into her room. Fran and Ed walked together to the end of the hallway to her room.

◆   ◆   ◆

The next morning, all six of them shared breakfast; then, it was time to leave. The men changed into their work clothes: regular fatigues—now clean—that they wore when on line. They planned to drop off the jeep, go to the airfield, and get a ride back to Korea.

There were no lingering good-byes; no clinging embraces. They had enjoyed the stay and each other. There were no promises to call the next time in town. As the jeep pulled out, Barbara pinched Clare's arm, "LSMFT, Junior."

Once out of sight of the inn, Bud turned slowly to face Crayley. By the light of day, Bud had figured it out. "You fuckin' fraud; you lucky bastard. You really pulled it together. I almost believed your crazy 'Crazy Horse' act. It was near perfection."

"Well, you had me worried when you started swinging that water jug around. I thought you were going to brain me with it."

"Your performance was the ticket that got all of us a night of bliss. Ed and I owe you." Bud continued his reflections on the night's events. "The thing that made it work was all that sweat pouring off you. How'd you pull that off?"

Horace waited a moment, milking the question. "The hot tub is never turned off. If you sit in it long enough to steam, you'll keep steaming for awhile even if you get out and towel off. Fact is, I couldn't sleep so I decided on a hot soak to settle my nerves."

They rode on in silence for awhile. Finally, Clare had the last word. "What I don't understand is, if girls are made of sugar and spice, how come they taste like anchovies?"

CHAPTER ELEVEN

Back in Tokyo, they had considerable trouble finding the hospital motor pool. Eventually they located it, but found themselves on the opposite side of the fenced yard from the entrance. They saw the dispatcher's office through a people-sized hole in the fence, but about a hundred yards away, down a long narrow alleyway between three-story black rock buildings.

"Clare, we'll let you off here, if you don't mind. Get the paperwork started at the office. We'll meet you there when we figure how to get in."

Clare hopped out of the jeep and started down the alley. Horace started the jeep around the block—or around several blocks, this being Tokyo—looking for the vehicle entrance to the pool. When still forty or fifty yards from the motor lot, Clare saw three figures exit through the fence opening. As they approached, he recognized them as the three truckers, again wearing their combat artilleryman badges.

As they met, Clare held up his hands. "Stop!" They hesitated, then moved slowly forward. "I told you guys that you're way out of uniform with those pieces of tin. Take them off. Give them to me."

The big sergeant was again in the lead. "Naw, we won't do that, Lieutenant. Our company commander told us we have a right to wear them."

"Bullshit. No U.S. Army officer would tell you that. We'll go see him. But first, give me that garbage."

A corporal, smallest of the three, pushed his bigger buddy out of the way, "Bullshit to you, lieutenant. Our company headquarters is back in Korea and so's our CO. There are only a few of us here coordinating the shipments to our trucking depot. We're going on our way."

Clare said, "That's an order, soldier. Hand over your tin."

The short corporal looked both ways down the alley—no one in sight—then moved face-to-face with Clare. "Fuck you, kiddo. You got nothin' to say to us." He moved to go past Ed. In doing so, he bumped his shoulder. Clare pushed back as he tried to regain his balance. The corporal stumbled back two small steps. He half turned to his friends, "You saw that. This little prick hit me. I don't have to take that, officer or no officer."

Clare turned toward the sergeant, starting to ask the names of the three. It was too late. He never saw it coming. The corporal swung from the pavement and caught Clare above the left ear. He went down to his knees, but bounced back up to grapple with the corporal while he tried to clear his senses and land a shot of his own. Two more quick ones from the corporal, and Ed was down on his hands and knees again, bleeding from his nose and a cut on the side of his mouth.

The little corporal was above him, cursing. He kicked Clare, twice, in the ribs, and Ed toppled over on his side. The corporal stepped back to admire his handiwork. Clare was gasping, clutching at the road trying to get stabilized so he could rejoin the fight. His hand clawed upon a broken piece of the road. He grabbed at it then swung at the corporal's legs. He crashed the broken chunk on the instep of the soldier who howled as he collapsed in the alley.

Clare got up, standing unsteadily and wondering what was next. The corporal, still yowling, was helped to his feet by the third trucker. "Goddamn you, you broke my foot." He swung a looping fist at Ed who stepped aside, but into the arms of the big sergeant who grasped him tightly. Up to that point, it had been one-on-one. Now it was three-to-one. The third man took a swipe at Clare, but barely brushed his head. The corporal, now standing on both feet, drove a power shot into Clare's stomach, which would have doubled him over if the sergeant had not held him up.

The corporal stepped forward again aiming, another fist at Clare. Ed kicked and caught him in the crotch hard enough to lift him off the ground. "Oh my God, you broke my nuts. I'm ruined for life. I'll fix you." A open switchblade appeared in the corporal's hand. He took a step forward. With a swooping slicing swing, he cut through Clare's shirt into his rib cage. Blood spurted onto the alley pavement. The corporal aimed another slice, but it never landed.

Horace and Bud had finally arrived at the dispatch office. They did not see Ed. Looking past the motor pool shack, they saw what was happening in the alley. They sprinted through the fence and closed in—unnoticed because of the focus of the three on Clare—just as the corporal was readying his second knife slash.

To the corporal it appeared that his target had suddenly disappeared. The big sergeant, finally seeing the cavalry arrive, simply dropped Clare and turned to face Bud, but it was too late. Buddington caught him with a full swinging uppercut, and the sergeant took early retirement. The third man, who hadn't seen anybody coming, was watching the sergeant's collapse when Horace spun him around, slammed him with two body shots and a quick snap to the head, resulting in the man's decision for a short nap.

The corporal, now experiencing way too much groin pain to realize he should be thinking of escape, turned to face Horace with the knife twitching in his hand. Crazy Horse had his cartridge belt off. As the corporal feinted with the blade, Crayley spun his belt around it and pulled the man to him. With the pull came a stiff jolt to the jaw. The corporal was out, but Horace held him up and cracked him twice more before he let him fall to the pavement. The sergeant and the third man, recovered from their rest periods, scrambled up and ran down the alley.

Horace and Bud turned to Clare who was struggling to get up. They took off his shirt and wiped his face with his undershirt. The knife wound was not pulsing blood, but he was leaking. They asked him if he could walk. He said he could. They wadded up his undershirt, put on his shirt, told him to hold the wadded package with his arm against the cut, and started back toward the motor pool.

Clare took two steps, stopped, and returned to the corporal still unconscious in the alley. The soldier's head lay at a curious angle to the rest of his body. Ed said, mostly to himself, "That should be corrected." He touched the toe of his heavy boot to the corporal's head, nudging it into alignment with the rest of him. Then, so quickly that Horace and Bud couldn't react, Clare launched a swift, hard kick to the head, which shot violently sideways from the thrust of the blow. There was a crack sound audible to all three. The head lolled on one side on the top of the corporal's left shoulder.

They all had seen enough dead men to realize that the corporal was stone cold gone. "What the hell, Clare," said Bud, "this guy's dead."

"He was trying to kill me with his fuckin' blade."

"But, for crissakes, he was out of the fight. He was sleeping it off. Now he'll never wake up."

Clare replied, "He said he was a combat soldier. He got dead. There's a lot of it going around in that line of work." He started to move toward the motor pool office.

Horace was thinking. Ed had sure as hell killed an American soldier. If it had happened in the wild, swinging melee, it might be called self-defense, especially if the corporal was, at the time of the kick, using his knife. But self-defense probably didn't work if the guy was already out of the fight. Still, it had to be reported. There was a Provost Marshal's office nearby. They could shade events a little: maybe that the blow had happened when the corporal was crouching low for an upward thrust with the blade. But, his mind racing, Horace remembered the two truckers who had fled the scene before Ed had drop-kicked their friend. He knew that, although they hadn't seen it, they would make up a hell of a story. And, if that happened, they could all be stuck in Tokyo for many months, or years, if their story wasn't the winning scenario.

Clare's conduct at the company and during R and R had convinced Crazy Horse that Ed was unstable, maybe dangerously so. And, now, his bizarre and fatal act over a few pieces of decorative tin would, as soon as Crayley could arrange it, close the short career of Clare in George Company. But, even with all that had happened, he couldn't bring himself to initiate the process that could lead to Ed being put away for a very long time.

"Come on, Crazy Horse, let's get out of here." It was Ed, already several feet down the alley and moving away.

But Horace wasn't ready to go yet. He was rooted to the spot, still seeking an answer that did not come. He looked around. No one in sight; no activity in the motor pool. The buildings squeezing the alley were all industrial with windowless walls. Crayley looked at Buddington. "We can't do it, can't just cut and run."

For the first time, Buddington spoke. "Yes, we can. Let's get out of here."

Crayley stared at Bud, who stared back. Then, Bud gave an exaggerated shoulder shrug, which told Horace that it was his call. Horace did nothing. Bud waited a moment and then started toward Ed. Horace hesitated, still looking at the dead soldier. No one was in view. "Come on, let's get out of here." They moved quickly, without running, to their jeep, which had not yet been turned in. Bud and Clare stayed back while Horace finished the return paperwork. Then, all three rode in the jeep to the back of the lot, where Horace cleaned out its first-aid box. Hidden back among the vehicles, they packed Clare's wound with World War II sulfa powder and bandaged it with the heavy cotton pads that were in the aid kit. Clare put on a clean fatigue shirt and jacket.

They went to the airfield, got a flight back to Korea, and were in Chunchon well before nightfall. They found transport heading north and hitched a ride. After two vehicle transfers, they arrived at their regimental headquarters and went to the medical tent.

Crayley announced loudly as they pushed through the tent flap, "Hey, hey, medic, we got a wounded man here. Need help."

A sergeant came over. "Who's hurting?"

Bud helped Clare out of his jacket and together they opened his shirt. The Tokyo bandage was soaked. "This one is hurting. He's got a puncture."

The orderly looked at the slice, now showing a gnarled knot of blue black, and led Clare to a cot where he eased him down. "Rest easy. I'll get a doc."

One of the Regiment's surgeons appeared, moved Clare to an examining table, looked at the wound, and said, "You'll live. You've got enough sulfa packed in here to cure all the clap in Korea." He looked at Crayley, "I know you. You're Crazy Horse. How did it happen?"

"We,"—indicating Bud—"don't know. We were at Second Battalion when they brought Clare in. He got this pig sticker on patrol last night"—at this Ed gave a weak confirming nod. "The Battalion aid station said he wasn't terminal, and they were behind in their repair work. We were coming back to Regiment so the Battalion doc asked us to haul him here."

The surgeon who had no idea that the three were in widely-separated units said only, "I didn't hear about any heavy activity up at the Second, and we don't get many bayonet cuts. Are you sure"—to Clare—"that you didn't get this falling on your can opener?" Clare said nothing. "Oh well, what the hell. We'll fix him up and wait for the rest of them to come down to us."

The doctor quickly stitched up Clare, plastered new bandages on, gave him a couple of shots and some pills for pain, told him if he had any problems to see his Battalion aid station, and then he left. The three officers followed him out.

CHAPTER TWELVE

The company command post was in the rubble of one of the small dwellings in the stream valley. What was left of the roof had settled heavily and unevenly on the stumps of the supporting walls. From a short distance it looked like a stone mound. The place had been living quarters for a family, but now Horace had decided to patch it over with canvas, rope, and rubber ponchos to serve as his CP. The entrance was canted at an angle to the rest of the structure. It was short, narrow, and cramped by stone blocks. To use this entrance, it was the usual practice to enter or leave butt-end first. By doing so, the eye was not confused by trying to align body position to the slanted entrance. Frequently, however, such traveling posture resulted in the moving party falling flat on his ass in or out of the rock hut.

Sergeant McCoy had been called to the CP in the early dawn. Trundling across his wing bridge in the half light, he had nearly slipped off twice. The thought of a spill into the cold stream had caused his balls to cringe upward, seeking the comfortable fold of fat overhanging his crotch. Despite a full night of sleep, the sergeant was not in good shape. It had been a bad night. He had been "out among them," his phrase for knocking back large quantities of booze while noodling old tales and new lies with friends.

Wowser left the CP in the usual way. As he exited the doorway, he peered around his rump, looked directly into a searing flash of sunlight slicing through the usual heavy overcast. His eyes slammed shut. He took another backward lurch and sat down with a heavy thump. On the ground, eyes closed, but still streaking with light splinters, McCoy considered his situation. His butt and legs were quickly getting cold. The slick dirt surface felt like an oily ice cube. He could fell the chill moving through his body. He decided to get on with the day's work. He half rolled onto his stomach, grunting as he did so. In that position he teetered for a moment trying to balance his body on an overlarge beach ball. Resolutely, he swallowed and heaved himself to his knees. He was aided in no small measure in this maneuver by a bugling belch and immediately felt much better. He got to his feet and turned around to face his world.

Corporal Trent was looking at him. McCoy glared at him. There would be no recovery time in the crystal palace. "Aw right, clerk, what do you want?" Trent continued to regard him, finally saying, "I wondered if you were ever going to get off your ass. You looked like a fat water bug scuttling for the stream."

The sergeant stared at Trent. His eyes scanned the immediate area. No one else had heard the corporal. McCoy thought on it. What had gotten into this kid? He had not been at last evening's blowout. Maybe he had a stash of something Wowser didn't know about. McCoy took a few steps toward Trent, "I'll give you a little advice smart ass. You might even call it survival training." McCoy paused, "I've been thinking we may need a new company clerk. What do you think of that new kid, Hillman? He seems bright enough. Then, Corporal Fart, you could get some straight duty in one of the squads. Maybe I could arrange it so that Number One would let you carry the flame thrower on our next outing. What do you think of those possibilities?"

Trent said, "No. I don't want to do that." His point made and his life and death hold on Trent again established, McCoy looked at him for a long minute. "Okay. We'll see what develops. Now, as I asked you before, what's up?"

"We got a call patched down all the way direct from Division. Koppleman is on his way to see you." Out of the corner of his eye, Trent saw movement. "In fact there he is now," indicating with the muzzle of his carbine a lanky figure just turning into the mouth of their valley.

Bernard Koppleman was another of the switchboards in Wowser's network of long-known friends. Back in the late twenties—when both were springier of step and hornier of outlook—they had been together at the Presidio in San Francisco. In the thirties, they had spent a long time avoiding Gila monsters at Fort Huachuca in the blistering desert sands of Arizona. Based on the great skills learned there, they had savored the sunny pleasures of Patton's Desert Center in California searing their bodies on the incandescent metal of the lumbering tanks. But Patton didn't fit their style. They were infantrymen, not tankers. They had last seen each other in Europe, and for the first time, they had been in the same company—a subset of the Twenty-Eighth Division—in the Bavarian forests, where the red keystone shoulder patch of the Pennsylvania Division had been renamed the Bloody Bucket.

Bernie, now a master sergeant, as was McCoy, was a good man to know, and McCoy found reason to consult with him on various matters from time to time. Koppleman was the chief clerk in the Division's personnel section.

Whereas Wowser usually looked like a mobile mound of dirty laundry, Koppleman looked like a recruiting poster. He was tall, erect, stiff-backed, and his face was stern and his step purposeful. Sergeant Koppleman's uniform fatigues were clean—even starched, which impressed Wowser mightily—pressed to an edge so sharp his legs cut a swath like a scythe through the brush on the path. He even wore a few of his best combat decorations on his shirt. This he did, he had earlier told McCoy, so that the candy-ass short timers who clotted up at Division Headquarters would know that he had not spent his Army life pushing people down the path without knowing what was at the end of the line.

Koppleman had entered the valley trailed by two soldiers. Before reaching McCoy, Koppleman motioned the two to divert toward the kitchen tent to see if anything was left from breakfast. Bernie arrived at Wowser's spot. He towered over McCoy as they stood toe-to-toe. He shot out his right hand like a karate jab. "Hello, Gleason. How are you?"

McCoy looked at the outstretched hand as if it were offering him a buffalo turd. He looked up at Bernie, but spoke to Trent who was loitering nearby. "Well, Trent, the goddamned war must be over. The tourists are starting to arrive." That shot at the rear echelon launched, Wowser took Koppleman's hand and vigorously pumped it. "What brings you to the war zone? Are you lost?"

"No, you old fart. I found what I'm looking for. As soon as we entered the valley, I said to my two trackers, 'Just point me toward the worst monkey shit smell your noses can catch. That'll be McCoy, and here you are.'" The ritualistic greetings thus accomplished, the two sergeants continued.

"Good to see you, Bernie. It's been awhile."

"You too, Wowser. It's been way too long."

"To what does my raggedy-ass company owe this honor? You haven't come down here to kidnap some of my boys have you?"

"No, I'm not takin' anything from you. Actually, I'm here to help you."

The nerve ends in McCoy's scalp generated a buzz. He wasn't going to like this. "Why would you be so generous?"

Koppleman looked past McCoy toward the corporal standing looking at them. Wowser said over his shoulder, "Trent, I'll be busy for awhile. Why don't you find something to do."

"You know, Gleason, I haven't seen anything this peaceful and pleasant in a long time. This valley, aside from the junk left behind, is quite beautiful. Green weeds almost like grass, a few trees starting to leaf out, a pretty stream, a little sunshine starting to poke in, of which none of us have had much of late—very nice indeed." These smarmy sentiments set bells jangling all through McCoy. "What do you want to tell me, Bernie?"

Koppleman slowly surveyed the scene. His eyes fixed on Wowser's airplane. "Oh yes, we've heard about your splendid roost, even back at Division, in the other world. Your bridge," indicating the wing, "looks sunny and maybe even comfortable. Why don't we find us a spot away from the crowd." The two moved toward the wing bridge, which was still marginally slippery. They clung to each other like a couple of old drunks negotiating an ice rink as they tiptoed to the center of the wing. McCoy called for Army blankets. They were delivered by one of the new men who arranged them on the cold surface. The two sergeants sat down facing each other.

McCoy had already noticed that Koppleman was carrying a bulky musette bag over his shoulder. Why was this? he thought. Bernie never carried anything heavier than a stub pencil.

"Why the bag?"

"I didn't eat this morning. You probably didn't either. I thought we could have an early lunch." Bernie started to unload his lunch carrier. "What is going on?" mumbled McCoy, so softly that Bernie didn't hear it. Wowser was getting very jumpy. To Koppleman, he said, "What the hell is this? Are we celebrating a wake, and if so, who is it for?"

"We'll get to that, Gleason. Let's have lunch." A terrible thought ignited McCoy's head; Bernie, his good buddy, was here to tell him he was finished. They were going to transfer him out of the company because he was too old for the grind.

Koppleman's lunch spread was extensive. Arranged on an olive drab Army blanket was a huge salami, a large hunk of cheese, Spam slices fresh from the can, half loaf of bread, two onions, a dozen crackers, and—in small bottles procured from the medics—mustard, catsup, and olives. A carbine bayonet, honed to exquisite sharpness, almost completed the buffet. The last to appear was a plastic Army canteen set with a thumping flourish on the wing.

Bernie swished the bayonet. Indicating the salami, he asked McCoy, "How much of this donkey dick do you want?" Without getting an answer, he swung into action. Soon the towel was littered with food pieces. "Hop to it, old son. Eat up." Wowser reached for the bread, but was stopped by a wave of Bernie's hand. "Wait. Before you get into the chow, lay your lip on a little of this," pushing the canteen toward McCoy. Wowser took a short pull. "Damn, that's good. What is it?"

"Cherry schnapps. We traded some items to some Belgians, who were wandering around in our area, for a few bottles of this." They leaned into the lunch and the canteen, and in short order Wowser was feeling much better. He looked across the stream at his men. Today, they didn't look like much to him. "What a grand sorry lot they are," he thought.

Turning to Koppleman, he said, "Look at them poor, dumb, runty fucks. They don't have a rat's-ass idea about which end is up." Koppleman looked across the stream. They looked okay to him: infantrymen marking time doing nothing, waiting for somebody to tell them what was happening and what to do about it.

Wowser renewed his musings, "You know, if brains were dynamite, and you lumped all of them in the company in one head, you couldn't get an explosion big enough to blow your nose." He took another large swallow from the canteen, "But, you know, it's really okay. It's part of the magic of the system."

He and Koppleman had had this conversation many times. But periodically they liked to remind themselves how wise they and the Army were. Bernie jumped in with his lines, somewhat more warbling than usual because he was slightly farther into the canteen than Wowser was. "Well, look at it this way. The smart ones enlist in the air force or the navy. So, right away, the Army's sucking hind tit. After most of the obvious talent is drained away, there is left at the bottom of the barrel a thin scummy residue. This is what the infantry gets. They are us."

It was Wowser's turn. He came in on cue. "But,"—and here he looked owlishly at Bernie—"this is the pure genius of the system. If the infantry had the top of the barrel, there'd be a riot everyday and a panic every night. With all them brain cells working, any order given would be just an invitation to a debate. And, at night, those same brains cells really go into overdrive. They imagine that every sound, every flare, every shadow is the start of an enemy attack headed for them. I tell you, Bernie, smart guys have too much imagination. If they hear two squirrels fart, they think it is a mortar barrage. Too much imagination makes you unfit for this line of work."

Koppleman interrupted McCoy's train of thought in a rich plumy voice like a lawyer greasing a deal, "Imagination which doth make cowards of us all." Then, after waiting for effect, continued, "Who was it said that? Was it Shakespeare or somebody else?" Answering himself, he said, "I think it was Eisenhower."

Wowser, ignoring the fruity observation, took up his line again. "Most of our guys learn to use the weapons okay. And they couldn't imagine a train wreck even if they were standing on the tracks. If they get an order, they just do it for as long as they can. Then, like toilet paper—used when needed and smeared with shit—they are wadded up and tossed in a hole and covered with dirt."

They had done this pontificating exercise before, sometimes with like-minded friends. But it needed doing from time to time so as to reassure themselves, together, that they understood and were part of the grand process that, in spite of itself, generally delivered the right people to the right place.

As they talked, both had become aware of friendly artillery fire coming from far in the rear, hitting on the lower slopes of the Chinese positions across the river valley. The fire had started to the east of them, but it had been working its way toward them for reasons unknown. As the whistlers came closer, Koppleman got increasingly jumpy. Finally, the shells high up were going right over their heads. No one in the area paid them any attention—except Koppleman who had taken to swiftly shifting his carbine knife from hand to hand and who ducked slightly each time shells went over.

"They're outgoing, Bernie," said Wowser.

"Of course they are. I know that."

"What is it? This stuff doesn't rattle your cage, does it?"

There was a pause while Bernie closely examined his blade, "Yeah, it does, Wowser. My nerve lines seem to have run out. I don't see how you do it up here with a rifle company, for God's sake."

"That stuff isn't for us. It's got a Peking address on it."

"I don't just mean the artillery. It's the whole picture. Doesn't matter if it's theirs or ours, us or them. It just goes on and on. It's like wiping your ass with a barrel hoop. There's no end to it."

Wowser busied himself with picking up the remains of lunch. For several seconds he packaged pieces of food, secured them in the musette bag, and took a last gulp from the canteen. Then he turned toward Koppleman, "What is it, Bernie? Did you come to tell me I'm out of here?"

"What? What? Oh, hell no. You're a fixture in this company. You do what you want so far as Division is concerned." Bernie reached out, gently waggled Wowser's forearm. "There's no top your age on line. You shouldn't be up here, you old fart. Give it up. I'd give you a job back with me, but I know you wouldn't take it." He paused a moment, waggled the forearm again, "Nobody's gonna take you out—except maybe the Chinks." Bernie shook himself a little. "No, I'm not here to take you away from all this splendor. I'm here to give you a present—a present which may come in handy in short order."

That was enough for McCoy. He hadn't heard what he dreaded. He wasn't being washed out. He pushed the packed lunch bag aside, picked up Bernie's carbine blade, tapped the point against his chest, "Well, Koppleman, what's this shit about a present?"

Bernie straightened his back. "Okay, kiddo. The word is that this Boy Scout troop is going to vacation on Monastery Ridge. Very shortly, your boss is gonna get an invitation to dinner and dance from my big general. At that time, your boss will get the marching orders for this band of thieves. It must be an interesting job because the Old Man is bypassing Regiment and Battalion to go direct to your guy."

"Why are we going out there?"

"Don't know. Don't know exactly when, but soon."

Wowser thought for a moment. "That kind of news flash doesn't seem to me to justify your coming all the way down here for a lunch box social and a present."

"Oh, yeah it does," said Bernie. "Something's going on in that river valley and it's got a bad smell about it."

"Why us?"

"Well, you been sitting on your ass in this Garden of Eden way too long. It's time you earned your keep. So you caught the brass ring."

"Is there any plan that goes with this move, or do we just set out there until the Chinks want to play Monopoly for that piece of real estate?"

"Don't know. As our new general says, it will all be revealed in the fullness of time."

"How is this new star?"

"He's okay, but he's ambitious, and that is always trouble for those of you"—Bernie swept his arm in a circle to encompass the company—"who are the spear point of that ambition."

"The real problem is, he gets hot flashes, and there's nobody to tell him he's off course. His operations officer, the G-3, is a West Pointer who made it to his job way too early. He buys into a lot of loony ideas the general floats. When the Big Cheese asks his opinion, the G-3 is lost. He doesn't know whether to shit or go blind. So he cuts it down the middle; he closes one eye and farts. The general thinks the rumble he hears is applause, and he's off and running."

Wowser thought for a moment. "I knew something was brewing. We got way more than our share of replacements out of the last batch that came into Regiment."

"Yeah. I know. I put my thumb under the scale for you."

"Okay, so what's the present?"

"You see them two I brought with me?" Bernie motioned toward the two young soldiers who, having finished their meal, were setting quietly—apart from the company men—on the bank of the stream. They had their boots off and their feet in the ice cold water. Their rifles were at hand, propped against their steel helmets, which were on the ground at their sides. Both were honing short throwing knives with small rocks from the stream bed.

"Yeah," Wowser focused on them for the first time. "Who are they? What are they?" The last question came because McCoy saw that each of them had a bun of black hair twisted into a rope strand coiled on top of his head. Looking closer, McCoy saw that they were nearly identical. Short, almost squat, powerful bunched muscles corded their fatigues. Their faces had a swarthy sun-cooked cast with deep black lustrous eyes like looking into a deep cool shaft, he thought.

"Who are they? What are they?" he again inquired. "With them pigtails perched on their heads, they could be Chinamen. We do our own laundry. Why do we need them?"

"No, they're not Chinks. They're Indians. Full-blooded Apaches." Koppleman waited. "Ring a bell?" McCoy looked blank. "They're the twin sons of Hector Cruz."

"Cruz—Sergeant Hector Cruz! I'll be damned. I haven't seen or thought of him for years. Not since Fort Huachuca. How the hell is he? How the hell you end up with these two?"

"A year or so ago, I got a letter out of the blue from old Hector. He's retired, feels fine, lives in Santa Fe. Anyway, he tells me he's got a couple of sons—twins—already in the Army. Been in since they were fifteen—Hector still has friends in the right places. He says they're comin' up for a Korea tour. He wants them to stay together, and asks if I can help. I've still got buddies at the Pentagon. The rest is, as they say, history."

"I've kept them with me. For awhile they were in our recon outfit, where they were in a few dustups that ended up with a supply of Chinese dog meat. At present, I've planted them in the communication section. And, now, I've brought them—or, at least, one—to you."

"One of them is George Washington Cruz. The other is Abraham Lincoln Cruz. I don't know which is which. I call one of 'em Geronimo, the other, Cochise. Even though I probably insult them by giving them wrong names from the wrong tribes, they haven't scalped me yet."

"And what am I supposed to do with them?"

"Well, it's at this point that I show how clever I am. Remember how we had some of these guys with us in the Twenty-Eighth in Europe? We used them in radio traffic. It drove the Krauts nuts. Those Nazi hotdog translators had no idea what they were talking about. I figure when you go up on Monastery, your ground wire commo net will get blown to hell in about the first five minutes, and you might want to use your radio with Cochise, the one I'm leaving with you, to talk to your friends. Seeing as how the Chinks got as many of our radios as we do, it'll be a party line connection when we talk. Here's where the Cruz boys come in. When they talk Indian family talk, no one can understand them. The Red Menace won't know what the hell is going on."

Wowser was thinking that this excursion was shaping up as real bad. "Well, Bernie, thanks for thinking of us."

"By the way, Wowser, these two boys are the toughest mothers you or your crowd will ever see. They are strong, quick, and fearless. Leave 'em alone, and they'll be calm and pleasant. But if any of your drag dicks get smart with Cochise, there could be very big trouble very fast. And, speaking of trouble, keep Cochise close by you up there. You maybe can use someone keeping an eye on you when the shit hits the fan."

The early lunch was over. Wowser and McCoy sidestepped off the now dry wing bridge. Bernie waved to the twins to join up. He introduced them to McCoy, told them his communication plan, and designated Cochise—Abraham Lincoln Cruz—as the man for the company, telling him he would send up his duffle with the next supply column.

While the twins compared notes and good-byes, Bernie and Wowser shook hands in parting.

"Thanks, Bernie, thanks for everything. I'll see you around."

"Sure, Wowser. It's good seeing you and we'll have lunch again real soon." Koppleman turned to leave, took a step, turned back, waggled McCoy's arm again, "Be safe, Gleason. Be safe."

CHAPTER THIRTEEN

"I tell you, you're fuckin' out of your heads. There ain't going to be no fuckin' good come out of that call." PFC Veloz was adamant as he glared at the others in the company communication hut. Three other men had crowded into the hut, and they were all discussing the call that Veloz had just received over the wire net. The call had come through the Regiment's switches directly from Division Headquarters to George Company. That, of course, was the worrisome part—a shout straight from Division to them. The word from Division was that their boss was to report—as an overnight guest, yet—to the Division commander, Brigadier General Krill.

As PFC Veloz thought more on it, he got very agitated. "It just ain't right. No division chief calls straight to one of his line companies unless somethin' hot is going on, or"—he paused ominously—"somethin' big is about to happen to that company. Anytime a lowball first lieutenant gets the 'come up and see me' from the head cheese, it's goin' to be trouble for that looey and his sad-ass followers. You just wait and see, numb nuts,"—this directed toward Corporal Hardesty—"you'll see I'm right."

That call soon made a lot of people in the company very skittish. The only time a company commander might expect to get the personal attention of a division commander was if his company had badly screwed up in some monumentally stupid way. In such event any conversation was completely one-sided and in the nature of a termination interview.

But that could not be the case with this phone message, so the company could only wonder. And, from wondering they moved on to worrying. Those in the communications hut, joined by others who had heard the news,—announced loudly by blowhard Hardesty to those passing by on their way to the breakfast chow line—finally and unanimously agreed that it was bad news. Just how bad had not yet emerged as a consensus, but bad was firmly settled upon.

A large part of their concern was based on institutional wisdom. Nothing good ever came to a junior officer out of a conversation with a general. This conventional knowledge was heightened in the present situation by the reputation of General Krill. It was a matter of dogma that he was called Killer Krill by his subordinates. Those close to him knew that by so doing, particularly when the reference got back to him, they were ingratiating themselves with their boss. All infantry generals liked to be called "killer." Many of them were—frequently of their own men—, but when one had a name like Krill, so that the label and the name slid easily off the tongue, it was a winning combination.

But, interestingly, Krill was also referred to as Killer by his peers and some of his superiors. Their use came not from his present command status but from his earlier exploits as a regimental commander in the early days of war in the Pusan perimeter.

In fact, he had mellowed as a division chief. Having firsthand knowledge of what havoc his orders could create for his men, he was, generally, thoughtful in what he required his units to do. But, if the moment called for it, he was no posturing paper tiger. He could push his people into wild, hair-raising, teeth-clinching situations.

The senior men in the company knew most of the Krill story, but—and this also worried them—he was a one-star general in a two-star job. They knew that such a man was always looking for ways to pick up an additional star or two. Now Krill was going to favor their boss with a personal interview—even an overnight—and the company didn't like it. They very much wished their man wasn't so favored.

♦   ♦   ♦

Horace arrived at Division in the early afternoon. He reported to the G-1 section, and after a few minutes' wait, he was met by a Lieutenant Kohler, one of Krill's aides. Kohler told him that the general would meet him at 1500 hours. The lieutenant continued, "The general has invited you to bunk in his complex tonight. I'll show you his layout." As they walked, Horace took notice of the headquarters' area.

Big squad-size tents were carefully laid out along well-defined paths bordered, by rows of white-painted rocks. Flood lights were mounted on poles next to the paths. Wires ran from the poles to each tent. There were many large trailers in use as offices and functional command centers. A short distance away he saw the canvas spread of the medical facilities. Well beyond the hospital, he could see eight heavy 155s, the Division's biggest artillery. Two guns were in action. The big boomers were on a slow fire mission; every twenty seconds a round would blast out of one of the tubes. Crayley guessed they were interdicting—harassing—a Chinese position or road junction. Far past the artillery, he could see the airfield for the Division's L-5 spotter planes. Moving through the area were many young Koreans—KSCs—doing various housekeeping chores. They clearly were not supporting combat operations. They were servants for the Division's mandarins. Crazy Horse knew that the headquarters hadn't moved for nearly two months. Everyone had heard of the extensive layout, but he was not prepared for the cityscape he was in. A gleeful snort—covered by a hasty cough—escaped him as he envisioned the Keystone Kops drill that would take place if the tent town ever had to move out fast.

Kohler was still talking, "As I was saying, the general will meet you at 1500 hours. At 5:00 P.M.—I mean 1700 hours—he has invited a few people, you included, to meet the members of a small USO troupe that is here for a performance tonight. You know," he looked at Horace for confirmation, "these USO shows don't usually get this far forward. Mostly they do their thing down south at the big logistics bases. My God," again he looked at Horace, "we're only nine miles from the front line. That's pretty damn close." Crayley didn't answer.

The general's billet was an eye-opener. It was eight ten-by-twenty foot trailers laid out in the shape of the Cross of Lorraine: a central corridor with two cross members near the top. Horace looked at it in amazement. It was the biggest intact building he had recently seen in Korea.

Kohler again, "Pretty swanky, eh? It works real well and suits his purpose just fine."

"What's his purpose?"

"Well, it has his office and a staff operations room. Next to the OPS room is a general—purpose area like a lounge, where he sometimes invites a few of us to ease the cares of the day. There is a small kitchen, an above-ground latrine for all the occupants, and his bedroom, plus two others for overnight visitors like you."

Kohler led him up the steps at the end of the long central spire. After several steps down the corridor, he opened a door. "This is your room." It was not quite square. The walls and floor, painted the same muddy green, were the flat panels of a trailer. There was one small window high up on the outside wall. Furnishings were Spartan: two thinly upholstered chairs, two small tables with lamps, a hanging bar for clothes and—the wonder of it all—a small double bed with clean sheets appearing at the top edge of the olive drab Army blankets.

"Well," Kohler was waiting for a reaction, "what do you think of it? Isn't it neat?"

Horace said nothing, but he wondered to himself if this was part of the same war the line companies were in.

"Well?," Kohler was still waiting.

Crayley thought of several smartass responses but decided against them. He turned slowly to Kohler, "Is there a shower in the latrine?"

There was, and it had hot water and a big bottle of non-Army issue liquid soap. To test the performance of the plumbing and the output of the hot water boiler, Crazy Horse stayed in the shower for twenty-five minutes.

◆　　　◆　　　◆

Horace was back in his room in clean clothes when a corporal appeared at the door. "Sir, we just received a radio call. The general is on his way back. He'll meet you in the operations room in fifteen minutes. Follow me, please."

In the short walk down the corridor, Horace wondered what to expect. He had never seen Krill. They walked into one of the trailers that he easily identified as the general's private war room. Maps, charts, and logistics statistics covered the walls. Six telephones and two small radios were in easy reach of a long conference table that was flanked by steel folding chairs. There was one huge, soft, leather chair that did not need to be labeled as the chief's resting place. On an end table next to it there was a lamp, its body fashioned from a small artillery shell. Also on the table was a miniature tank, which took Crayley's attention. He decided it was a lighter. He pushed down on the turret. Fame belched from the tank's cannon. Horace wondered what the general smoked that required a two-foot blast to be lit.

General Krill strode in with measured marching stride, his highly polished combat boots pounding the floor. He was in clean, freshly pressed fatigues, and each point of his open collar sported a massive single star of his rank. A modestly billowing scarf covered his throat. As he came through the door, he took off his steel helmet and helmet liner, which he dropped onto the conference table with a heavy clunk. He was shorter and stockier than Horace had imagined he would be and had a fair complexion with rather high cheek bones, intense, deep, nearly coal black eyes, bushy hair somewhat in need of a trim, which Crayley thought would surely be available in a barber shop someplace in this military city.

"Hello, we haven't met. I'm Krill." He stuck out his hand. "Thanks for coming." As if there were a choice in whether or not to see the division commander. Horace gave his hand a vigorous pump and offered appropriate subordinate's replies.

"I've informed Colonel Bozoni"—Crayley's regimental commander—"that I've asked you here so he won't get his shorts twisted in a knot with my going direct to you. You'll get your field orders through the usual channels, but it's just you and me here this afternoon."

"I've asked you here because I want you to understand about the job you're going to do for me. I know you're new in your job at the company. And I checked you out before I brought you here. I heard you did good work in Europe in our most recent rain dance. Bozoni tells me you're on the ball here. Your credentials are good for a youngster." He broke off that thought. "Somebody told me you have an Indian name. Are you an Indian? You don't look like an Indian." Before Crayley could answer, the general was off again. "Hell, I don't care what your name is or what you are. The main thing is, I'm told you're the right man for this job, so"—mixing metaphors—"I'm letting nature take its course, and you're the guy who drew the short stick."

The general moved to the little table beside the leather chair, extracted a ten-inch cigar from its drawer, and prepared it for ignition. He punched the tank turret, and flame shot halfway across the room. After a few chest heaves, the tobacco plant was afire. Then came an enveloping cloud of smoke aimed at the ceiling, and the general was almost ready.

He looked around the room, spied his favorite aid—a two-foot long swagger stick capped with an empty .30 caliber shell. Now he was ready. He walked to the wall where the largest map in the room was mounted. "This," he announced with a slam of his swagger stick—*thwack!*—"is Korea."

Indeed it was. Crayley saw a large scale map of the peninsula. On it was a purple line marking the Thirty-Eighth Parallel. This was a straight line, long ago dictated by the positions of the earth, sun, and stars. The political dividing line between the two Koreas was also marked. It was not a straight line but was close to the Thirty-Eighth purple line. The current battle line was on the map. It did not exactly track the purple line, but it was fairly close, especially on the western edge of the peninsula.

The general moved to a more detailed map. "Now here we are"—*thwack*—Krill located their approximate place on the map. "Your company is sitting behind this spur ridge right on the edge of this big dry river plain. Right?" He looked at the lieutenant for confirmation. Horace nodded. "Okay, now it's this old water course that's got everybody on our side, and, we think, probably on their side also, so very interested."

"Look at this line. See where it runs. It's a major freeway across the whole country." He traced with his shell-nose stick the line of the river plain, starting near the east coast far to the north and descending in a southwesterly direction across the peninsula toward the Han River estuary and Seoul. Not waiting for this geography lesson to sink in, the general continued.

"Now, you know the peace talks started up again awhile back at Panmunjon. There has been no cease fire, no armistice, but since the restart, there have been none of the massive sweeps up and down the length of this land that we were in before. There's a lot of vicious fighting going on all over the place—your company was at Iron Mountain—but it's localized. Sometimes it's only a company fight, sometimes a whole division gets into it, but the objectives are limited in time and area. We don't see the Chicoms,"—the word frequently used by one-star generals, and up, for the Chinese communist forces—"so far at least, putting together another grand plan to try to push us off the peninsula. And it sure as hell doesn't look to me like we're going to try to push them back into China."

"The battle line"—trace, *thwack*!—"now cuts across Korea mostly within shooting distance of the Thirty-Eighth Parallel. The UN is above it on the east coast and slightly below it on the west. I don't know when, or if, this thing will end, or where the final line will be drawn. But, if it ends close to where it is now, there are some attractive pieces of land in the middle that both sides would like to have."

"Within the last few weeks, the smart boys at Eighth Army have developed what they call an appreciation of the situation. Look at these locations,"—his stick lashed out at the map; *thwack*! Seven times he belted the board in a descending route on the river plain toward Seoul. "Each one of these places," he gave an unaimed *thwack*! for general good measure, "is or could be, a strongpoint on this route," he paused. "For example, like Monastery Ridge, which, as you know, just happens to be on the other side of the spur from where your company is sitting right now."

"Now, if the Chinks think the war will end with everybody where they are now, they may want to hold the river plain highway in case they decide to vacation in Seoul in the future. If so, they don't want any obstacles in their way, so they appear to be taking them out now while the fighting and the political negotiations are still going on."

"Four of them are north of Monastery; two are southerly toward Seoul. Two months ago, the UN held them all. Two of the four spots to the north were held by Americans and two by the ROKs. All four of them are now owned by the Chicoms. Of the two south of Monastery, one is held by ROKs, and the last one up river from Seoul is held by the First Marine Division."

"Each one of the four roadblocks up north"—*thwack, thwack, thwack, thwack*!—"put up a hell of a fight, but the end result is that they are Chinese territory." He paused, spewed a big cloud of cigar smoke, then another. He fixed Horace with a fierce stare. "Now, Monastery Ridge is not going that way. I'll be goddamned if I'm going to lose a blocking position and have the Marines keep their cork in the bottle. I'll never hear the end of it." Horace noted that he didn't say such result could effectively end his chances for a second star.

"I don't know if they will hit Monastery. But I think they will and soon. If they do, you're the Dutch boy that is going to keep a finger in the dike." He glared at Crayley. "You clear on that, company commander?"

"Yes, sir."

The general was off again. "By now, you can see my handwriting in the sky. Your company will relieve the boys up there now, and you'll be there for awhile. Have you ever been up on Monastery, Lieutenant?" Horace shook his head. "Okay. Well, I have. I was there about four months ago when we were last in this area. It was ungodly cold then; warmed up a little now, but not much."

General Krill was reciting to himself, but he rejoined the war and picked up on his description. "You've seen what it looks like from where you are now. It's a hell of a fortress. All rock and straight up, except on that south side. That's where they'll have to come. There is a narrow slit in the tower on the side facing the Chinks. Maybe some of them could get up that way—if they're mountain goats. But I don't think you'll have to worry much about that route."

"Yes sir, Crayley, the only way to the top with any force big enough to do any harm is up that smooth south slope. Of course, you can see that, and so do they. The Chicom tactics at those northern outposts"—*four quick thwacks*!—"have not involved a general advance on a wide front. They just hit hard at the spot they want. They seal off any UN units close enough to be able to support the outpost. Then, they put all their attention on the objective. They bring whatever it takes, a company, a regiment, or a division."

"Now, for Monastery Ridge, none of our companies are close enough to help you, and I don't intend to send a lot of people to your rescue. The division artillery heavies are already zeroed in on the south ramp. But, hell, it's only about forty yards wide. It's very tough, even for our guys, to hit that narrow roadway from nine, ten miles back. I can cover the whole place with proximity fuse shells,"—air bursts—"but that will spray your company. Even if you're in your rock holes when that mail arrives, you could get hurt. So I won't do that, unless the place is about to be lost. In that case, I'll fire so many air bombs the weeds won't grow for fifty years. And, if that happens, your boys better be hunkered down deep in that stone castle because even the spiders won't survive what I'll send your way."

"Of course, the smaller tubes in Bozoni's regiment will be on call, but the problem with all the artillery is that it can't hit any of the Chinks as they get close to you from their side. The rock spire is too tall. None of the artillery has the trajectory to clear the tower and land close to it on the far side. We can punish them for a fair distance as they cross the plain, but when they get cozy with you on their side of the rock, we can't do much to them. It's only how good our gunners are in hitting the south ramp that can give you any close-in artillery help. It's only the mortars, yours on top of Monastery and those of nearby companies that can clear Monastery in a high arc that might be of help. And they don't carry much of a load."

The general stopped. He seemed to be finished. "Any questions, Lieutenant?" Crayley made no response. "Nothing at all, eh? Okay. I'll give you anything you can carry up there. What do you need?"

"We don't need anything. We're all right."

Krill squinted at him then started up again. "I know the ground. It's pretty small on top. A heavily armed, well-emplaced rifle company is a nice fit for the area. And that's you and you're gonna hold it for me, my boy. You're gonna keep it on our side of the ledger."

"If we can get 'em as they start across the plain, it would be Pickett at Gettysburg all over again." He considered what he had just said, then continued. "I know there wasn't any Monastery Ridge at Gettysburg, but it's the thought that counts. If the Chicoms had a general like Pickett—he was last in his class at West Point, you know," he looked at Crayley who didn't know but nodded anyway, "we might hit them out in the open. But they don't, and we won't. If they want to get Monastery, they'll get there. but that doesn't mean they'll get up on top."

The general moved toward Crayley. "You're damn sure you don't need to carry something extra up to the top with you?" He tapped Horace's chest with his stick all the while looking intently at him. "All right, then." The general moved toward the door placing his formidable pointer on the table. "Come with me. I think our guests have already arrived." He moved to the central corridor, Horace trailing behind, walked five steps and turned into his lounge.

◆   ◆   ◆

The feel and smell of the room was much like the others. Its decorations were what set it apart. There was a rug of Korean design and make on the floor. There were four comfortable chairs, a fifth like a large overstuffed leather pillow—obviously reserved for the general—two large puffy leather couches, and four small tables each bearing a tiny lamp. Two stand-up cabinets stood against the wall, and there was a small wooden bar at one end. On one of the cabinets, an olive drab GI issue radio was tuned to the music station of the Army's Far East Network. It was Krill's private officers club.

Five people stood up as the general and Horace entered. A sixth, an Army corporal, was at attention behind the bar. Three of the five were women, young or at least fairly young. A civilian wearing Army fatigues was borne aloft by a searchlight set of dazzling white teeth. At first glance, he looked young enough to be Krill's son: a beaming face, an incandescent smile, carelessly but artfully tousled hair. The fifth person was an Army lieutenant colonel in clean sharply pressed, but regular, fatigues.

"I want you all to meet Lieutenant Horace Crayley. He and I have been having a serious tactical discussion." The general's arm twitched as if he wanted to thwack something to give emphasis to his announcement. But, without his pet stick available, he satisfied himself with a sharp handclap. The sound jerked the barman corporal to attention once again, and he began to fill glasses with chipped ice.

"Lieutenant Crayley is going to perform a valuable service for me and for this division." He thought more about it, "For the entire UN Army." The others in the room looked at Horace with more interest, seeking to find in him the Hercules that was going to do a job for the whole Army.

The general turned to Horace. "These charming people are part, a large part, of a small USO troupe that has favored our division by being here tonight to put on a show for our war-weary men." Horace thought he had seen no war-weary men during his stroll through the complex. However, he thought it best not to offer the general his views on the subject. Krill continued, "You know, Lieutenant, it's very rare that the USO gets this close to the front. But this brave troupe has expressed its willingness to come up here and show us a little of what we're fighting for." The general went on. "I mean, these people are going to bring us a part of America right here in Korea with their presence, their songs, and their spirit."

Crayley thought Krill had fallen off the deep end into a tub of bullshit, but the others were looking at him like he had a USO phonograph needle up his ass, and he was spouting the USO recruiting speech.

"Now, Horace, if you will permit me to call you Horace."—Crayley thought of telling him not to be so familiar, but decided against it—"I already know these charming people, so I'll introduce you all around." He turned to the tallest and oldest woman—but by old Horace thought maybe thirty, thirty-five—"This is Celeste. Next," not having his swagger stick, he motioned at a substantially younger, almost beautiful brunette, Horace guessed probably twenty-four or five, "this is Melody. And last, but certainly not least in any way, "a finger wave at the third charmer, a red head, very nice looking. Horace estimated her to be about the same age as Melody, "this is Nancy."

"So there you have it. This is the troupe." Then, seemingly for the first time, seeing the golden boy civilian. Krill picked up, "Oh, I mean there you have it for the ladies. This, of course, is the head man, Chicki

Legrande. Chicki is a veteran of this work. He's traveled with Bob Hope's military shows"—There was a palpable moment of silent appreciation at the mention of Bob Hope—"Chicki does it all. He sings, he dances a little, sometimes plays his sax, tells jokes. He keeps it all moving."

With this expansive introduction, Horace took another look at Chicki. The smile was still fixed, not a wisp of hair had moved, but the handshake was flaccid, and it looked like nobody was home behind the eyes. At Horace's second glance, he decided that Chicki might be old enough to be Krill's father.

"The military contingent is Lieutenant Colonel Blakey, the Division's chief medical officer." Crayley thought it odd that the head sawbones would be on board, but he had noticed that Chicki and the doctor had been in earnest conversation during part of the general's introductions so he decided that they were old friends, hence Krill's courtesy in inviting Blakey.

"Well, on to more important things. Give your liquid requirements to Corporal Vincente." Drinks were delivered along with a large tray of snacks: cheese and Spam slices, bread, crackers, canned beets, onions and beans with bits of allegedly fresh fruit stacked haphazardly on the platter.

Krill was on again. "I'm told you never eat much before a performance so we have only a little to hold you over until after the show. This isn't, I'm sure, the kind of repast you ladies are accustomed to. But when you are this far forward in the combat zone,"—he stopped, his eyes searching the room for the missing swagger stick. He needed a thwack to jump start his next thought. Finding nothing, he clapped his hands loudly, exploding a nervous giggle out of Chicki who had the doc cornered against the wall—"you have to endure some of the privations we are used to all the time."

During the general's remarks, an informal pairing seemed to occur. Celeste was hovering within easy grasp of Krill. The Division surgeon had abandoned Chicki and clamped on to Nancy. Chicki was halfway

across the bar admiring Corporal Vincente's dancing pectorals as he
shook a beaker loaded with Krill's favorite. Horace found himself zero-
ing in on Melody.

Melody fixed Horace with what she thought was her most endearing
look, especially featuring her eyes which she blinked rapidly several
times to give them a lustrous dewy look. Horace caught her flapping
eyelids and wondered if she was slipping into a spell of some sort.

"Well," the damp eyes rolled in his direction, "you must be something. Chicki already told us about you. He heard it from Doctor
Blakey earlier. He said you have to do a job for the general, and the
general just said the same thing." She took a swallow of her drink to
clear her pallet after scarfing a dainty morsel of Spam. "What's the big
deal?"

"Not much. A bunch of us are going to go sit on a tall rock for
awhile."

"That doesn't sound so dangerous. Why does Krill make so much of
it?"

"Well, if the Chinese decide to increase their real estate holdings in
this part of the peninsula, we would be in the way, and the negotiation
could get a little boisterous."

"Oh really? That's too bad. Anyway, good luck." Having thus disposed of Horace's potential catastrophe, she again turned her attention
to the platter. Three pieces of Spam, two of cheese, and a bit of canned
beet disappeared as if they had been fired from a machine gun. A
dainty gulp from her glass, and she was again with Horace. "Now,
Lieutenant Crayley, the doc also told Chicki that they all call you
Crazy Horse. Is that true? Are you an Indian? You don't look like an
Indian."

"I'm not. It's just a name that got attached to me."

"Well, if you were an Indian, you could have a powwow and smoke
a piece pipe with those bad Chinamen." She giggled, started to take
another swallow of her drink, hiccupped, and decided against it. The
conversations of the group dwindled into trivial chitchat until sud-

denly Chicki slammed his glass on the bar, splashing Corporal Vincente who leaped backward hitting his head on the wall light. "Omygawd, girls, it's late, late, late. We've got a show to do for these brave fellows. We must get to it." With a wave to the general, a nod to Blakey, and a bright, hopeful smile toward Vincente, he led his three troupers out of the room.

◆   ◆   ◆

By the time Krill, Blakey, and Crayley arrived at the makeshift theater area, the sloping dirt area was fully occupied. Of course, there was a front-row location reserved for the general, and as he and his party went forward, the soft din of the waiting soldiers died out. They knew that Krill's arrival meant that the show was imminent. Horace felt way out of place taking one of the comfortable chairs next to the general.

A beefy major—the Division recreation officer—took the stage to introduce the entertainment. He spent several minutes lauding the Division, the Division commander, and all the men of the Division, and then the USO for being willing to put its performers into the combat zone, and last, but certainly not least, as he assured the crowd several times, the daring entertainers themselves. Eventually, he finished with a flourish by introducing the "biggest Hollywood star to ever be this close to the fighting front." A whoop went up from the assembly—who is the star? Nobody recognized Chicki as he bounded onto the stage and took three quick bows as the three-man band launched into a peppy number.

Horace thought the band—an out-of-tune accordion, a drummer with the biggest head Horace had ever seen on a life form of this planet and who couldn't maintain a beat for more than three bars, and an absolute wizard guitar player, who Crayley was sure must have been under sentence for some musical transgression to have been so unfortunate to have ended up with Chicki—needed lots of help. But he was quick to notice that Krill seemed to like it a lot, so Crazy Horse smiled a lot and mimicked the general in jerking his head to the erratic beat generated by the bulb-headed drummer. Horace applauded, laughed, and snorted when the general did, although he did it a second later so that it sounded like Krill was doing a two-step with his exclamations of approval.

Chicki introduced the cast and told a few jokes—"We were out walking. I told him to look at the dead bird." (pause) "He looked up"—kaboom came a rim shot that the drummer nearly missed. The three ladies danced a bit. Chicki warbled through a song, the three ladies danced again, wearing a little less than the first time out. Chicki told more jokes, and the guitar player picked a really nice set. Chicki hit a few sour licks with his sax; the ladies looking younger and wearing even less danced a long number revealing spry bodies and beckoning gestures. There was a grand finale with the whole troupe—interrupted once when the drummer fell off the stage during his attempt at a virtuoso skins performance. Chicki thanked everyone. The general spoke a short appreciation and the show was over.

◆　　　◆　　　◆

"C'mon Lieutenant, good things are in store." said Krill as he headed toward his caravan. Horace trailed along wondering what other good things could possibly happen. Back at the general's quarters, the bar was stocked with fresh ice, clean glasses, and bottles of his "good stuff" as Krill pronounced it upon entering. Corporal Vincente was not present, nor was Chicki. It was a do-it-yourself set up.

Krill filled three glasses with ice and bourbon neat. As he set the last glass on the bar, Doc Blakey walked in, nodded to the general and Horace, and picked up a glass and drained it. He immediately topped it off, no ice, and poured it down. He looked at Crayley and said, "Well, Crazy Horse, it will be a rough gallop tonight so we better get ready. I think I'll have a drink." But before he could turn his suggestion, of which he thought very highly, into action, Krill put his hand lightly on his arm. "Wait a bit, Doctor. You may need your great skills. I don't want my chief surgeon flat on his ass this early in the evening. Casualties haven't started coming in yet. I know you've got good doctors, but your personal touch may be needed to sew up a hole or two." Blakey gave the general a sour glance, but he moved away from the bar.

Horace regarded the lieutenant colonel with curiosity. Why was he here without Chicki, he wondered. And who the hell told him that Horace was a.k.a. Crazy Horse. Before the question left him, Blakey waggled his empty glass at him. "Oh, I know. You wonder where I came across your Indian name. Well, kid, everybody in the headquarters here knows that the general"—another glass waggle in Krill's direction—"has given you the shitty end of the stick. So people talk about it, and names come out. I think one of the corpsmen heard it from a sergeant in personnel, name of Koppleman."

The general said, "Aw right Blakey, sit down and shut the fuck up. Keep your hand filled with that empty glass the rest of the evening." The doc sat down in one of the hard chairs and glared at the floor.

There was a long silence. Horace was thinking he didn't need any of this. Just at the point of asking the general if he could be excused, pleading the necessity of returning to his company in the early morning, there were footsteps in the corridor and Lieutenant Kohler marched in with the three ladies. The female troopers were freshened up in clean tailored fatigues.

Kohler looked around, hopeful smile on his face, eager to join the party, seeking an invitation to drink up. What he got was the jerked thumb "out" sign from the general. Sadly, he sidled out the door.

Horace thought the women were a welcome addition. They really were quite pretty. Celeste moved immediately to Krill's side at the bar and proceeded to prepare drinks for the new arrivals. The general's attention to Blakey evaporated as his workmanlike focus fastened on Celeste. Nancy was behind the bar, where she found the snack tray now loaded with the same savories as had been available before the show, only this time thin beef slices competed with the Spam for main course honors.

On the next round, Blakey managed another water glass of the general's best for himself and was ignored by Krill who, by that time, was telling Celeste how he and Eisenhower had won the recent war in Europe. There were several references to the Battle of the Bulge, which Celeste thought referred to a weight problem he had conquered.

Nancy was still positioned behind the bar sailing Spam and crackers down her throat while trying to avoid—not strenuously, Horace thought—Blakey's attempts to check her pulse halfway between her neck and her midsection.

Melody and Horace were seated on a couch. Although together, they were not a couple in the party sense. Neither spoke. They watched the others until, eventually, the general included them in the recitation of his crusade in Europe.

In a very short time, Nancy had conquered the food tray. Blakey had scored two big glasses of his favorite beverage. Killer Krill had finally won World War II, and Melody had again asked Horace if he were an Indian.

The general, still without his swagger stick, crashed his empty glass on the bar. "Well, ladies, it's been very charming, but we must move on. The lieutenant and I have more business to attend to and,"—seeming to notice Blakey for the first time since the girls arrived—"our medical chief has to prepare himself for some very exacting surgery." Blakey signed a wobbly okay at the general, turned toward Nancy and gave her a silent wave-off, ignored Horace, and stumbled out.

The general turned again to the three women now gathered in a protective cluster in the center of the room. "Again, ladies, thank you for your great kindness and courage in coming to my division. I do hope we meet again in more pleasant circumstances. Good luck in your future endeavors and good-bye." He turned to Horace. "Come along, Lieutenant," and left the room. Horace hurriedly shook the hand of each of the women and followed the general to the operations room.

◆ ◆ ◆

Krill found his swagger stick and, as Horace came into the room, he was swinging it at the wall map. "Here we are, Crazy Horse at Monastery Ridge once again"—*thwack!*—"I want one more go at you before we're finished. I've been thinking maybe I was a little bleak in our earlier discussion when I said that the Chicoms will come to Monastery if they want to. But, my God, at what price to them? You haven't been up on top, but when you get there, you'll love it. I mean, you'll just love it. You'll stand there on that pinnacle and look out at the field of fire you have. There they are, running across open flat ground for a thousand yards, and you're on top of a shooting gallery lookin' down their throats." The general swallowed hard and continued. "By damn," he speared Crayley with his bullet pointer, "it'll just make it run down your leg, it's so good. Crazy Horse, it'll just be great."

Horace noted that he was now Crazy Horse to the general. They must be pals. But he couldn't bring himself to address the big boss as 'Killer.' There was no amount of booze—and neither Krill nor Horace had had much at the post-theater party—that would save his ass if he got that chummy with the head cheese.

"Well, sir, we'll do our best up there. We're a good bunch. We'll hold our own."

"Damn it, Lieutenant,"—*thwack!*—"I don't want you to hold your own. I want you to hold Monastery. And, by God, you'll hold it. That is a key piece of real estate for our side. We must control it." He thought more, "Besides, I won't have some Marine general laughing behind my back."

Horace cared nothing about what amused generals. He was concerned that at least some portion of Krill's plan involved an ego battle between the Army and the Marines. But Crayley also recognized that the general's roadblock theory had sound tactical justification. Anyway, he thought, what the hell. If the general said they were for Monastery, that's where they were headed, even if Krill was certifiably nuts.

"General, we'll do it. We'll do it."

"Good. That's what I want to hear. By the way, you'll be a captain when you go up on Monastery. The paperwork is already in the mill." The general laid his swagger stick carefully on the desk. Horace understood that the discussion was over. He waited to be dismissed.

"You'll get your orders on this in a couple of days through the usual channels. I won't see you tomorrow. I've got an early call at Corps Headquarters." He reached to shake Crayley's hand. "Good night, Crazy Horse." He paused, "Good luck, Captain."

Horace entered his room. One table light near the door was on. It was a low wattage bulb offering only a dim light in a pool around the table. The bed was in the dark at the back of the trailer. His eyes still dilated from the bright light of the operations room, he did not see Melody sitting up in bed until she spoke, "Hi Lieutenant. How ya doin'?"

Crayley spun to the sound. Only then did he see her. At first, he thought she was just perched on the bed. But as his vision sharpened, he saw that she was sitting up against the trailer wall with her legs under the blanket. Her fatigues were neatly hung on the clothes bar. She was wearing only a T-shirt with an Eighth Army insignia on it and the text, "Ready to go all the way."

Crayley was startled, then immediately very confused. "Hi, Melody. Did one of us get in the wrong room?"

"No, honey. This is your room, and I'm in it."

"So I see. What's the occasion?"

"I thought the big cheese would have told you. It's his idea."

"His idea?"

"Yeah, Chicki told me the general wanted to give you something because you're gonna do a tough job for him. And I'm the something."

Crayley was mystified. Then it dawned on him. This was a joke by Krill. Soon Killer and the whole troupe would come pounding in for a big laugh. He listened for noise, feet shuffling, whispers in the hall. It was silent. Melody seemed straightforward enough. He also thought she was not enough of an actress to carry off the joke he thought was coming.

"And what am I supposed to do with the something?"

"What's the matter with you, cowboy—Oops, I forgot, you're on the Indian side. What do you think you're supposed to do?" With that, the T-shirt came off. Two perfect, firm breasts with nipples like Buick hood ornaments were aiming at him.

Horace may have been surprised, even wary, by what had happened so far, but he wasn't an idiot. "Well, lady, I sure as hell don't know what's going on, but so far I like it." His clothes were off in an instant, thrown on a chair. He slid into bed next to Melody. To hell with Krill. If he came in now, he'd have to pry Horace off with a crow bar.

Horace was farther into bed than Melody. His head was even with her breasts. He put one hand on her hip and turned to swallow one of the gun turret boobs.

"Wait," said Melody.

Here it comes thought Crayley. Now the joke is on and the room will fill with people.

"Wait, me first." With that Melody slid under the blanket and took Horace in her arms. One hand briefly caressed his face then moved slowly down across his chest to his groin and rested there. Horace heard a little yelp as he came to the full ready position.

"I don't know if you're crazy or not, but you're a real horse. This is a real beauty." What sounded to Horace like singing seemed to be coming from under the blanket. Melody was softly singing the words of a current pop hit. "Cal-donia, Cal-donia, what makes your big head so hard?"

Horace waited, exhaled deeply. Her next comment from the bed pile could not be understood. There was an indistinct mumble: a gargled, "um-um" like a child seeking more dessert with an already full mouth. Horace could only wheeze, "arguh-uh," but finally managed a weak "fire in the hole" as he exploded.

After a few moments of quiet reflection, Horace pulled on his shorts. Melody salvaged from a large purse a black silk robe blazing with red dragons, and they moved to the two thinly padded chairs. Horace saw a bottle, glasses and ice on one of the tables. Melody poured into two glasses, and they sat looking at each other.

By now, Crayley knew that Krill was not going to be leading a laugh-tour through his door. This realization only confused him more. It had been great so far, but why had Melody been waiting for him? "Melody this is the best thing that's happened to me in Korea. But I would like to know what lottery I've won."

"You really don't know?" She searched his face, "I guess the big old general didn't let you in on it. Well,"—she paused for a dainty gulp—"it's sort of complicated and it starts with Chicki and ends with Chicki—and Doc Blakey."

"Chicki is a guy with a long history of hanging on. Originally he was on Broadway. He got work in a succession of third-rate shows. Along the way, he became friends with Dick Powell, the singer. When Powell went to Hollywood, Chicki was part of the baggage. He did odd jobs for Powell, which led to odd jobs for others. He got to know a lot of people a little bit."

"When the big war arrived, he managed to do some of the stage setup work for the camp shows put on by the Hollywood gang. At first, they were local shows around California. He kept at it and eventually went big time working as a property man for a few Bob Hope tours."

"When this war started up, he conned the USO into giving him a troupe of his own whose purpose was to go closer to the front than the big shows with real stars. So here we are, within the sound of shot and shell, as Chicki likes to tell the reporters whenever he gets a chance."

Horace thought on it, then said, "So that explains Chicki. But it doesn't explain Blakey and it doesn't explain ..."—he gestured toward her.

"Oh yeah. Well, my ambition is to be a Hollywood personality. Not a star or even a celebrity, but a recognized personality. To become that, you need an "in" with the right people. Chicki is a semi acquaintance of a lot of the right people. I know two or three girls who have been on tour with Chicki and done what he asks of them, and they're on their way to becoming personalities. One of them even had two lines of dialog in a Cary Grant movie. So that's why I signed on with the creep."

"I seem to be closer. But so far I don't know why you were in my bed, grand as it is, and why should Chicki set me up just because Krill may have thought it was a good idea?"

"Oh, its not just you. Celeste is humping the general, and Nancy, if she can get the drunken doctor's dick up, is doing Blakey."

"Okay, so all three of you are getting laid. Why?"

"Chicki, you probably didn't notice earlier because he was comfortably loaded today, is a junkie. Not a raging maniac, but he loves to float lightly. The way he does it over here is to get friendly with the medical officers. Those who go along with it, provide him a bundle of those morphine kits that the front-line medics, like those in your company, use to send the badly wounded to la-la land while they get wrestled around on their way to an aid station."

"In return, Chicki tries to provide real, live American dream girls to his suppliers. We don't have to do it if we don't want to, and it doesn't happen every place we go. But if the guy is reasonable, or nice like you are, some of us occasionally help Chicki out. Our pay off is that Chicki helps us back in the States, like the girl in the Cary Grant movie."

"That's a pretty good parlay," said Horace. "A six-way scratch my back, I'll scratch yours."

"Well, it's scratch something. Speaking of scratching, let's see if you can locate an itch of mine that needs attention. We really should get to it because the troupe must leave at daylight."

Back in bed Horace, as ordered, got to it. Lying full length next to Melody, his right hand explored the area beneath her stomach. Her body became rigid. Suddenly, with a hoop that Horace thought would wake the gun crews slumbering on the perimeter of the compound, she let him know he had found the place to scratch. "Yeow, Chief Tomahawk, you found the spot. Go for it."

Horace earnestly worked at it until Melody, between sharp intakes of breath said, "Okay cowboy, or Indian, or whatever you are, climb in the saddle and let's see if we can buck our way off the reservation."

◆   ◆   ◆

An hour later, Horace was jostled from sleep. "C'mon, honey, let's do a nightcap. It'll help me sleep. Only this time I get to be on top. I've got lots of dancing to do in the next several days, and I'd like to keep my hips lined up so that everything moves in the same direction."

Horace muttered, but it sounded like a groan to Melody. "I think I'm okay for sleep now. My ammunition locker seems to be empty."

"Naw. All we did was blow a little dust out of it. If we work at it, I bet we could do it again, and it would be better." In short order, Melody was astride him exhorting him to "keep it up and keep it going." Horace winced that he was doing his best. Melody replied, "Not good enough, Indian Giver."

Horace tried harder, and finally with a war whoop of her own, Melody let him know that her happy hunting ground had been reached, and she collapsed on his chest. It turned out that Melody was right. They could do it again, and it was better. Horace went to sleep thinking what a great guy Bob Hope was.

When Crayley awoke in the morning, Melody was gone. She left him a note on the table, "Thanks for the ride, Sitting Bull. It was great. See you in the movies."

Horace was the only officer in the general's complex. Corporal Vincente prepared his breakfast featuring the Spam remnants of last night's banquet, eggs, potatoes, and a splendid Bloody Mary.

Transport was arranged, and Captain Crazy Horse went back to his company.

CHAPTER FOURTEEN

It wasn't a monastery, and it wasn't a ridge. Ten thousand years ago, it had been an undistinguished bump amongst small hills and valleys. Then came a cataclysmic wrench of the earth that created the soaring spines that terraced upward in a northern march to the Yalu River border with China. A stream, which had wandered through the area, became a powerful, scouring river. Over the millennia, the earth was gradually molded by the river as it found the easiest path on a southwesterly course toward the Yellow Sea.

Although the river processed the land to its desired shape, one piece resisted. Other mounds, hills, and even peaks gave way, but this erratic lump did not. It had a granite core, which stood fast against the water surge. It refused to be moved or whittled down. When the river, after scouring a broad expanse for its purposes, finally decided to move elsewhere, a granite pillar was left on sentry duty nearly in the middle of the broad dry flat river plain.

Eight hundred years before Crayley's time, the rock tower attracted the attention of a small group of monks who were searching for a refuge where they would be safe and could quietly study and contemplate the greater celestial meaning of their beliefs.

They took the rock spire as their own. Over time, they fashioned a wide path from their cultivated fields in the river plain up a gradual slope on the south side of the column. On the nearly level top, they built a simple place of worship out of stone quarried from the interior of their stone shaft. They gradually expanded other structures, all constructed out of stone, to cover almost all the usable area. They found room for a small herb garden, carefully tended and watered from two wells they managed to chisel through the rock to find water deep in the hard column. Their haven became a monastery: a place of teaching to those desiring to learn the truths known by the monks.

They built not only on, but in the tower. The spaces were connected by corridors, arched bridges, and concealed walkways. There were different levels inside the stone pillar. Floors, rooms, and secret compartments had been hollowed out and fitted to meet the monks' needs. There were hidden passage ways, avenues, and dead-end avenues. These were means to move to and through much of the interior of their granite monolith without ever being forced to move in open, unprotected areas. These measures were necessary because, as the years passed, myths that attracted roving bands of outlaws grew, concerning great wealth hidden in the monastery.

More than two hundred years had passed since the last few monks had gathered their meager belongings, no gold or treasure, and left their ancestral home. Abandoned by its owners and of no use to the farming communities around it, the tower and all it had been became just a landmark in the long river plain.

All that changed after June 1950. The tower came to life again, but not as a monastery. It bore no resemblance to a place of meditation or religious contemplation. The stubbed walls outlining the boundaries of the monastery were a jumble of weathered grey rock shards and broken, cavity-drilled fangs, jutting up to snag the occasional low fog cloud that scudded down the plain.

From the hills on either side of the river plain, the stone spire seemed to be breasting the current of a long-gone turbulent river with a basaltic knife edge on its north eastern side. The south side had a manageable slope that led up to the lower rim of the column. There was one narrow rocky trail up a cleft on the side of the tower facing the Chinese. Other than this trail, the only way to the top was the wide earthen ramp leading up the south side.

On the top, the pillar was just over two hundred yards long and just over seventy yards wide. The height above the flat river bed was known exactly, because the UN Army had pounded it with artillery and heavy mortars every time the Chinese were in residence. When the Americans were firing, their range-finding equipment had the top at 336 feet, but on their maps the notation was 103.4 meters.

With the efforts of each successive tenant, the pile had been turned into a formidable defensive position much admired, particularly by the side that didn't have it. Manned and armed, it was a massive roadblock to any push up or down the flat river course. Sometimes the Chinese, or the North Koreans, held it. Sometimes the Americans, or the ROKs, or the Canadians, or the Turks. Whoever was in possession denied passage to anyone not wearing the correct uniform.

At the moment an American unit, one of George's brother rifle companies, was securely in place. They had been there three weeks and were due for rotation. Their stay had been peaceful. Although they had received almost no attention from the Chinese, they were glad to be leaving because they were, after all, nearly two miles from their closest friends.

CHAPTER FIFTEEN

As soon as the tall sergeant and his buddy had cleared the alley and turned a corner around a building, they stopped. They stood for several minutes, examining themselves and each other and commiserating together about what they had done, what was done to them, and what they should have done.

Finally, it occurred to the sergeant, Carlo Fanelli, that only two of them were discussing the highlights of their day; their little corporal buddy hadn't made the trip with them out of the alley. He peered around the corner. He could see Luther more than fifty yards away, still flat on his back with no one in sight. He lightly punched his companion, Orpheus DeBow, "Luther's still sleeping. He must have taken a real shot. We better go back and pick him up. Them prick officers are gone."

He got no response. Orpheus still had a pleasant, somewhat bemused expression on his face, as if he were recalling other places and better times.

"Come on, get with it. We gotta go get him." He pulled DeBow around the corner and they started walking, unsteadily back to their latest battle ground.

As they both got closer to Corporal Luther Potts, Orpheus was the first to say, "He looks kinda funny. His head don't look at all good."

Fanelli, ignoring that Luther's head seemed to be coming out of his body where his shoulder should be, just said, "Move! We got to get Luther moving and go after those bastards."

Orpheus, again probing his own battered head gently, looked at Carlo. "Go after them? I don't think so. Let's just get out of here."

"What do you mean, 'no,'? They attacked us. They can't get away with that."

DeBow was staring at a knife lying on the ragged pavement. It was the knife that Luther had brought into play; it's blade was covered with Ed Clare's blood. He looked at Fanelli. "Are you out of your fuckin' gourd? Whose blood do you suppose that is on the knife and in the street?"

The sergeant could see that DeBow had a point. He thought more about it. "Well, maybe you're right. Let's get Luther up and move on." They turned their attention to Luther, and, in the flick of an eye blink, they recognized that he was no longer present for duty, any duty. "Holy crap, he's dead."

They circled, tentatively, around him with little shuffling steps, their eyes locked on his still form. They looked closer at his oddly placed head. Finally Debow said, "Yep, he's dead. One of them lieutenants broke his neck," with a look at Fanelli. "And you wanted to go after 'em. Shit, they'd pull off your legs and feed them to you. Oh, boy. They're in trouble now."

Debow cocked a weary eye at the sergeant. "Start thinking about us. Quit pulling your pud and start thinking. We have an earlier blowout about these made up red badges we're wearing. Later, we meet one of them again. The three of us jump him—an officer at that—and one of our guys pulls out his favorite cleaning tool and slices him up. You and I get flattened. When we get up, we bail out. Neither one of us knows who did Luther, 'cause we're both gone down the street. Now, Corporal Potts is dead. If we start a racket, the only thing I'm sure of is we'll spend a lot of time talking to a lot of officers and not just about them lieutenants. There'll be lots of questions about what we did, when we did it, and to who. There might be other questions, too, like why do we spend so much time around this motor pool. Then, our own captain might get interested in what we're doing." He paused—"And your first thought is we 'go after them.' You got a brain cramp the size of Tokyo Tower." He turned from Fanelli, thoroughly disgusted.

Carlo took a moment to ponder on all the good advice he was getting from Orpheus. He realized it merited extensive consideration. "All right, Debow, we're in this now. Let's get our story straight before we put this thing in motion. First thing we do is stick our badges in our pockets. I don't want to start all this explaining while wearing these things." They both unpinned the red badges and lost them in their deep fatigue uniform pockets.

"And," Fanelli continued, "you pick up the blade. Nothing we can do about the blood splotches in the street. Just throw some dirt and grind it in with your boot."

"While I'm cleaning up, what are you doing?"

"I'm thinking of a good story to explain poor Luther's death."

The next day, the Provost Marshall's office finished the first sessions of questions with Fanelli and DeBow—and by which time the Army coroner had reported that death had been caused by a broken neck, almost certainly when Luther was already on the ground and quite possibly by the kick of a booted foot. The story the PM had to go on was that the three truckers, minding their own business, had been taking a shortcut through the alley; five GIs—at least they thought they were GIs, they could have been Marines, even the Navy, perhaps foreigners—all of them at least a little drunk, had been moving in the opposite direction. A small discussion arose about who had the right-of-way; which led to a spirited fight, during which the three truckers had more than held their own. At least two, possibly three, cut faces and bloody, possibly broken, noses had blossomed during the confrontation, causing blood to fly. Then, being gradually overcome by superior force, Fanelli and DeBow had become somewhat separated from Luther; both Fanelli and Debow had, at the same time, been cowardly attacked from behind and rendered temporarily unconscious. When they revived remarkably at almost the same instant, they saw Luther dead on the pavement. They had never seen their five attackers before. They were just average-looking guys. Not too tall or short. Not fat or thin. No bald heads, no facial hair, no noticeable tattoos, or any other remarkable features. They heard no names called during the fight—except the terms of endearment, which usually lead to a fight. They had, unfortunately, been blithely sleeping when Luther received the fatal blow, so they could not help the investigators on who and what had done in poor Potts.

So, with that story, the investigation started. The Provost Marshal, a pudgy lieutenant colonel who had been an Army cop all his military life, didn't believe much of the story, except the part about the five attackers. Given the number of U.S. Army, Marines, and Navy, plus soldiers and representatives of over fifteen other United Nation countries in and around Tokyo, such types of confrontation were regular entries in the office log book of events. The PM recognized that the situation, on its face, presented a remarkable, if not unsolvable, problem. There were fifteen to twenty thousand or more U.S. military personnel in the Tokyo-Yokohama area. In addition, military visitors and transients from other areas of Japan such as Kobe, Osaka, Sendai, even Sapporo, also troops rotating to and from duty in Korea, floated through Tokyo all the time. Other United Nation troops were not uncommon, and, of course, there were always many hundred party goers on R and R from Korea at any one time.

The PM turned the investigation over to the criminal investigation department—his own CID This group was heavily staffed with former civilian police type from various jurisdictions in the United States. Sergeant Aaron Levinson was one of them. A former investigator for the district attorney's office of San Diego County, in California, he had been in the Army—and in CID—since he had been drafted in 1943.

Sergeant Levinson looked at the Fanelli-DeBow story. For the attackers, he had no names, no descriptions, no unit designations, and he was not even sure what branch of service. He knew he was looking for five guys out of, probably, more than thirty thousand possibilities. It looked monumentally impossible. But he started. He had two helpers: one a former beat cop from Phoenix; the other GI was an Hawaiian-born Japanese American, who spoke some, and understood, Japanese.

The three of them decided that the first place to start was the area in which the homicide had taken place. The ex-Phoenix cop, Corporal Billie Dogget, and Corporal Takashi Matsumoto started canvassing the area for any possible observers of the big alley fight. After four days of "Were you here? Did you know? Did you see? Did you hear?" to every person, Japanese, American, or other that they could find in the area, they drew blanks. No leads.

During this time, Sergeant Levinson was checking out Fanelli and DeBow in their unit. The story he got was reasonable. They and Luther Potts had been close; they were always together, clearly liked each other, and were somewhat cocky when making the rounds, but all in all a tight threesome of pals. No one could even imagine anyone of them ever getting mad enough to swing at another member of the trio, much less break his neck.

The more he thought on it, the firmer Sergeant Levinson's feeling was that the Fanelli-DeBow story didn't wash. It was too finely scripted. Neither one of them lost a beat in the telling and retelling of the attack in the alley. Levinson decided on his "first through the door" approach, which he had used many times. It seemed to him that DeBow might appreciate the first chance. Fanelli and DeBow were still in Tokyo, detained as material witnesses in the case. They were not under arrest, but they had to check in three times a day at the PM's office, and they slept in one of the military police barracks.

Only Levenson and DeBow were in the room. "Corporal, I've spent a lot of time thinking about and looking at this case from every angle, and I'll tell you what I think. I think you and Fanelli haven't even come close to telling me what happened."

DeBow looked at him, completely at ease, unconcerned. Levenson continued, "I've been talking to some guys at your unit about your sideline business." This wasn't true, but Levenson continued. "They say the three of you had a falling out about a deal that went bad."

"What deal?"

"I haven't got the specifics yet. I'll get them when I need them. I may never need them. You know what it is, but the deal itself is not important to the events of the murder; it's just background. But I'll tell you what I think. You guys were running a trucking business on the side, and you arranged to make backdoor deliveries in Seoul directly into the black market."

"What the fuck's the matter with you, man? A black market in Seoul for 155mm artillery shells—she-e-e-t." Drawing out the last word so that it bounced around the room.

Levenson thought he was not leading the discussion in just the way he had planned, but he plowed on. "There's lots of commodities floating around the rear area where your unit is headquartered. Lots of good stuff that needs to find a home and not necessarily in the Army. You three were a small cog in the distribution system to get the goods where they would be most appreciated."

DeBow, changing the subject, "How you get to talk to any of my buds? They a long way from Japan."

"Orpheus, the Army has real good communications in this Asian theater. I was, at different times, on both telephone and radio. And your buds tell me that you and Fanelli had a hard-on for Luther, a real big one."

Not a twitch from Debow. "None of my pals, not one, would say anything like that. You're trying to string me, Levenson."

"I think you and Fanelli did the job in the alley and have made up this fight story to cover up a murder. And I'll tell you just one reason why I know your story is bullshit. Both of you have a pat description of a wild fight with your five attackers, with blood flying everywhere. But there's no blood anywhere on your uniforms. A few scrapes on the face where two of the attackers slammed you and Fanelli, but no blood. We did get a couple of blood spots out of the cracks in the pavement, but it is a blood type different from both you and Fanelli. It is curious to us that it is the same type as Luther's, but he doesn't have any cuts to account for the splotches found in the alley." Orpheus said nothing.

"So, if you want to tell me who did Luther, tell me now and tell me all of it. If it was Fanelli, and he's the one that takes the biggest hit at the court-marshal, maybe I can get you a lesser charge, or a lesser sentence. You might even get out of Leavenworth in twelve to fifteen years, still a young man."

DeBow got up, stretched, twined his arms over his chest and pulled, stretched again. "You know, I wonder sometimes about you people. The story's out and around that you guys wear different uniforms—even civilian clothes if you want to. For all I know, you could be a private or a colonel—what are you?"

No answer from Levinson.

DeBow strolled through the door, stopped and turned around. "Well, fuck you very much for trying to pin poor Luther on us. You got nothing that says we did it, and we didn't." He left.

Sergeant Levinson went into the Provost Marshal's office late that afternoon and told him of the DeBow interview while the PM drummed fat drumstick fingers on a thick blotter. Levinson finished his story, and the PM finished his number at the same time with an imaginary cymbal taking a slashing swipe from Colonel Gene Krupa, who then looked up from his drum rip, "So, did these two do it?"

"I don't think so. I've got nothing. No deals gone south, no bad blood between the three of them. Some evidence on the two of them that supports a gang fight ..." his voice trailed off.

"So, what's the next step?"

"I picked DeBow for the weak one. I may have been wrong. I'll let DeBow carry the story to Fanelli, and we'll see what happens."

Levinson had been wrong, very wrong, about DeBow. Even before Orpheus finished telling the story of his interview, Fanelli started to vibrate. By the time the recitation finished, he was in a state of near panic. "Listen, Orpheus, listen. These guys will do us for Luther. They're trying to hang you and me, and 'why,' you ask?"—Carlo fastened his eyes on his pal who hadn't answered—"I'll tell you why. Because they got no one else to pin it on that's why. As far as they're concerned, we'll do as well as anyone, and they can say they solved it in quickstep time."

"Listen, Orpheus, listen. We got to tell them the truth, get them to look for those three bastards who did it."

DeBow looked at his friend, "Oh, yeah. We should tell them everything. They'll really like the part about Luther cutting up that little prick lieutenant."

Carlo was taken aback. The knife attack had escaped him. "Well, not everything, just everything but Luther's work with his shiv. We won't tell them who did Luther, cuz, honest to God, we don't know. Maybe when we're finished, we'll get a little bump for being out of uniform with our artillery badges. Maybe we get a bigger jolt for fighting with officers. But that's just time in the local stockade. It sure isn't Leavenworth, and it sure as hell isn't a noose."

"I don't think so. That CID cop, or whatever he is, didn't look so smart to me."

"Are you kidding me? These people are twice as smart as us, and they don't like soldiers murdering other soldiers—unless, of course, it's enemy soldiers."

DeBow looked closely at Fanelli as he started to think about Levinson's offer to him. Carlo continued, "We just tell them the important parts. Come on, let's think this out together."

The next day, Carlo and Orpheus arrived unexpectedly at Levinson's office. He was wearing his regular sergeant's uniform. "Well, Sergeant, we've been thinking about that affair in the alley,"—Fanelli speaking—"and, what with us getting knocked around pretty good, maybe we didn't remember so well for awhile. But it's come back—the last few days—so we decided to help you out."

Levinson put away the file he was working on. "Okay, tell me what happened."

When he heard their story, he dismissed them and headed for the PM's office. As he arrived, he heard the last staccato thumps of what must have been a virtuoso drumbeat performance.

"Who did it?" The colonel stared, still dripping perspiration from his recent hot drum licks.

"Well, I still am partial to these two, but I can't find the string to tie them to the recently departed. But it seems their past scenario wasn't exactly how it happened. Now, they want justice to be done for Luther's murder." His eyes rolled heavenward—"So they have now given me the complete, final, absolute truth."

"And?"

"I'll give you the shorthand version. It seems that a few days ago, our three truckers met three young lieutenants in that alley off the motor pool. One of the loots was real big; another was a little over medium height, but very tough; the third, the youngest one, was the smallest and the loudest. I've got better descriptions in my notes, but to proceed—the small, mouthy loot stopped our boys, pointed to a red badge, which our three said were combat artillery badges, whatever the hell that is supposed to be, which mightily upset the little loot who, as well as the other two, was wearing a combat infantryman badge. He got even more upset when he learned that our guys' jobs are hauling big shells to the big guns, which are big miles back of the front. He demanded that they surrender their red badges. More loud talk, but finally our guys gave in, and the groups went their separate ways."

"On Luther's day, the same two groups met in almost the same place, three on a side. Our guys are again wearing the red combat artillery label. The littlest loot goes ballistic and, without even a cheery hello, charges Luther. The other four decided to be spectators. Only when Luther was getting the best of little louie, the big lieutenant hog-tied Luther to keep him off the little lieutenant. Our guys couldn't abide such an unfair act, so reluctantly, very reluctantly, they stepped in. But it turns out they miscalculated. The middle-sized loot put DeBow to sleep almost immediately. Fanelli lasted only a few seconds longer against the big one. When they awoke, the three lieutenants were gone, Luther was dead, and they had no idea how it happened."

"Do you believe any of it?"

"It doesn't play too well with me. The part about the three loots just charging them without a word smells way too ripe. Also, I'm sure the two survivors have left out some interesting filler material. I still like Fanelli and DeBow as our killers. But for the moment nothing points that way." Levinson continued, "If there were three loots, where did they come from? stationed here? passing through? on R and R from Korea? Who knows?"

Levinson waited for the colonel's response. It didn't come, until finally the colonel looked at him and said, "So?"

"Let's play it out a little. Let's say there were three loots here from Korea"—again he looked at the colonel, who didn't acknowledge. "Why Korea, you say? Well, why not, I say. There's lots of them in the streets of Tokyo these days. They were young, wearing only their CIB as decorations. They meet three soldiers who are wearing a funny combat badge. These guys are really truckers who only learn about combat from the evening news. The effrontery of this,"—another quick look at the colonel—"pisses the loots off very highly. They warn our guys the first time. Two, three days later, the loots are back in the motor pool area. Unfortunately, again, the truckers are there, which is a very bad coincidence. The three loots have their hormones really clanking. Maybe they haven't managed to get laid yet; hard to believe, I know, but it happens. They simply charge our guys. One of our three gets dead. None of our guys saw it happen, so we don't have the killer. The three loots are gone, and here we are."

This time the colonel jumped in immediately after Levinson finished, "So?"

"So I think we should go a little further on this. At least three lieutenants narrows it nicely from the thirty, forty thousand who were possible suspects yesterday."

"And you're going to do what now?"

"I'm going to check the motor pool records for a start. If these were three loots, one really big one, a medium size, and a loud shorty, they were at the pool a couple of times within a few days. I see them checking out or trying to check out some transportation for some purpose. So I'll start there. How tough can it be?"

CHAPTER SIXTEEN

The inmates of the asylum in which Harry Princeton carried on his life's work tagged him as weird, very weird. For anyone to be so thought of in G Company required a substantial quotient of nuttiness. Harry's appearance was of a man peering out at the world from inside a fog-filled bottle. His face was usually scrunched up, portraying deep thought as if he had just been asked about the origin of the universe and he was working out the answer. Harry was always making an effort to link up with the passing parade, but he generally missed his connection. His world was fantasy driven, occasionally slashed by spikes of reality. His favorite scenario was his Hollywood fantasy and his treasured portfolio.

McCoy and Princeton had been together, off and on, for many years. Wowser was well enough connected to have many friends in the sergeant's network in several of the right places, so that as McCoy moved around he could usually make arrangements to get Harry transferred to his care. So it had happened in Korea, and Harry had joined the team about eight weeks after McCoy made his arrangements.

Harry was, from time to time, and sometimes quite inadvertently, a very funny fellow. But that wasn't why he was wanted. Wowser had no need, or little use, for a company jester. He suffered Harry and his antics because Corporal Princeton was a steady performer when the fighting started and, more importantly, was a superb armorer.

The armorer is an important cog in the infantry machine. He cares for and repairs the company's weapons. And Harry could do it. He was a master hand at keeping the ordnance in working order. He could fix anything having a killing purpose. So McCoy always had a place for Harry.

The thing about Harry that, sooner or later, put most people off was his portfolio, and the elaborate wackiness that he wove around it.

In 1945, as World War II was ending, Harry was in the States, having been transported home on a hospital ship to recover from a grievous hip wound acquired during the breakout from the Remagen Bridgehead across the Rhine and for which his participation had earned him a Silver Star medal and promotion, again, to sergeant.

Sergeant Princeton was recuperating in grand style at a hospital in Van Nuys, California. The place was close enough to Hollywood that assorted female types, proclaimed "starlets," frequently visited to hug and kiss "our boys" while flashes sparked over public relations cameras. In one such heart warming episodes, just after Sergeant Princeton was presented, in a splendid hospital gathering, his newest medal, Harry started talking with one of the studio retainers shepherding the starlets. Phone numbers were exchanged and promptly lost by Harry. But to his surprise, nine weeks later, Harry, now an ambulatory and nearly discharged patient, got a call from his bedside friend, who told Harry that an Army colonel—technical advisor on a slam-bang war movie—needed some explosive advice. But it was needed the next day. With no time to go through Army channels, the film producer wondered if Harry could show up for a few days at the studio to help the colonel. Could he? Damn sure bet he could. Harry was going to Hollywood. He would be part of the bright lights, and he would get paid for it. Paid more per day than he made in a month. He was at the film factory the next day two hours before the gates opened for business.

Harry's first job led to another and another and many others. War pictures were in vogue at the studio, Twentieth-Century Fox, and there was much work blowing things apart. Harry had a little trouble at first getting it clear that he wasn't supposed to kill anybody. But nobody was seriously hurt before Harry learned that make believe meant that the same people had to show up the next day to continue the story. Harry became so sufficiently proficient that the studio arranged for Harry to be on detached service to it while World War II was being rewritten and refilmed on the back lots.

Sergeant Princeton was in hog heaven. He wallowed in it. He was a big medal wearer and that helped. A few of the prettiest men asked Harry if they could swap stories with him, but Harry barely noticed them. His eyes and everything else he could unlimber were on the ladies, who came in all sizes, shapes, and persuasions. Harry did his best to accommodate them all. He had a hunting license in a game preserve. He fired everything he had, scoring many direct hits and only a few near misses. His appetite for the delicacies available gradually brought him a modest back-lot fame. As Harry's status rose, so did the stature of the dollies admiring his skills. He worked his way upward through the extra ranks, bit players, some featured actresses, and, said Harry, several real stars.

During this upwardly mobile progression, Harry fixated on three of Twentieth's ranking ladies: Betty Grable, Alice Faye, and Linda Darnell. Harry never got close to this level of star power, but by the time he was in Korea, Harry had convinced himself that he had serviced them all, sometimes all in the same session, and they had loved it. Harry was at Twentieth for more than four years. It was during this exotically pleasurable period that Harry compiled his portfolio. The word "portfolio" was unknown to Harry until one of his starlet partners showed him her portfolio; it being a cook's tour of the people and places she had encountered on her way from Festival Princess of the Armadillo Rodeo to her present exalted position in the chorus line of a Fox musical. Harry heard the word and upon learning its meaning adopted it for the photo review of his conquests that he was putting together. The portfolio, according to him, was to be personal and candid shots of the ladies he had loved and left to cry over him.

Except for a few young beauties eager to try anything to push themselves upward and except for the big time stars who were featured only in face shots obtained from the studio PR department, Harry's collection was mainly a rogue's gallery of baggy old broads: whores coupling with studs of enormous specifications in various poses of sexual gymnastics.

Near the end of his stay in Hollywood, Harry got crosswise with the wrong tycoon. He had been banging a young starlet new to the studio. He had—to use a phrase Harry liked—wormed his way into her confidence. Or, so he thought. When he suggested a photo shoot with the starlet and a small pony, the young lady was momentarily fascinated but ultimately outraged. She blew the whistle on Harry just after she blew the studio head. Harry's detached Army service to the film business was undetached in short order.

In June 1950, seventeen days before North Korea started its march south, Harry was ordered back to regular duty. He carefully gathered up the very many pages of his portfolio and left his playground. As soon as the shooting started, Wowser, who had kept track of Harry called the right people, and Sergeant Princeton was soon exercising his military skills for the company.

Harry missed the good life. The portfolio was his tie to those glamorous years. The split-tail dossier was always close at hand available for a quick refresher course whenever Harry was nostalgically moved and he was frequently greatly moved. The collection regularly appeared, helping Harry to relive that grand period.

In the early days of his return from Hollywood, Harry, himself, had star power. His portfolio was eagerly sought. His lurid exploits were seriously evaluated. Harry sucked it up. He was a big time guy greatly admired by his peers. He was not just a clownish old timer who had one useful specialty. But after repeated viewings, the sexual splendor of the portfolio lost its ability to interest Harry's achingly horny buddies.

As interest waned, Harry's tales of his exploits as he displayed the portfolio became even more flamboyant. It turned out that not only had Harry skewered all the meat in the book, he had accomplished it with such skill that all those in the pictorial line-up adored him. Even the true stars all agreed that he was one of the great Hollywood swordsmen. Harry informed his listeners that his fame was due to the Flexible

Flyer acknowledged by all of Hollywood to be the most magnificent riveting machine in movie history. Harry never explained why he referred to an infrequent erection as his Flexible Flyer, but the Flyer took on mythic proportions as he pounded the drum for its virtues.

As Harry exhibited the portfolio—particularly to the replacements who now constituted his only audience—he would occasionally clutch the Flexible Flyer and ask it a question in a loud voice so as to be sure he was heard through the many layers of clothing he wore to ward off the spring chill. He did this when it was necessary to refresh his memory about a particularly rousing episode. The company very well knew that the only purpose of Harry's terminally flaccid penis was to connect his bladder to the outside world, but such universal knowledge didn't stop Harry's strong endorsements.

Crazy Horse was aware of Harry's picture book and accompanying commentary. He had let it go on for awhile, but there came a day when he decided that Harry was spending too much time in Hollywood. He had a discussion with McCoy—once again—about Sergeant Princeton. Wowser, too, had been observing Harry's increasingly strange behavior and had decided that it would have to be toned down. He also knew that he couldn't just take Harry's portfolio. And he also knew that Harry would be needed in the days ahead.

On a pleasant afternoon with the valley receiving a few spears of sunlight on the little river burbling its way toward the Turks, McCoy invited Harry to sit with him on the wing bridge leading to Wowser's sleep quarters. As was his style with his long-time companions, McCoy got directly to the point.

"Harry, you're fuckin' up the company with your Hollywood shit." Here Wowser lapsed into his formal English mode—"You are inflaming passions that are already aflame"—back to first sergeant—"These guys are so hard up they'd take turns screwing a water buffalo if they could find one alive in these hills—or even if it wasn't alive."

"But, Wowser, you know I got to keep my Hollywood memories fresh."

"I don't give a shit what you got to keep fresh. Just keep it to yourself."

Harry puzzled over those instructions; then decided that they needed clarifying. "What the fuck you talkin' about?"

"I want your portfolio to take a long intermission."

"Like what?"

"Like, give it a rest. Put it away. And quit talking to your prick all the time. Lieutenant Crayley thinks you're crazy. I know you are, but I need you."

"You can't take my portfolio. It's mine."

It was here that Wowser brought forth the scheme he had been hatching. "Harry,"—this with a serious look at Princeton—"you're too good a man for me to lose. I know you from way back, but right now you are too balmy even for me."

Harry looked at Wowser sidewise, denying the suggestion that his drum beat was not keeping time in anyone's orchestra.

McCoy continued, "I know how important the portfolio is to you. I even think"—he lied—"that it is important to the company as a record of what could be done by one of our better men. So I'm thinking, I'll ask Number One to make the portfolio part of the company's records. We'll put it with the company clerk. Trent can keep it safe. Whenever you want to see it, you can get it out and review if for yourself."

Harry thought, "Would the record say I had done all those broads?"

"Absolutely. It will be recorded as 'Sergeant Princeton's Hollywood Duty.' We'll put it in big letters on the cover."

"Okay. I'll go for that."

So the portfolio passed from company view, but its pictorial garden was frequently reviewed by Corporal Fart as part of his clerking duties.

CHAPTER SEVENTEEN

When Captain Crayley returned from Division, his first observation, which he kept to himself, was a sense of increased tension—a twitching virus that clearly had infected the majority of the men in the company. The knowledge of Horace's promotion, which had been phoned down, amplified the twitch. No orders had come with the promotion, but his move up in rank validated the company's conviction that no good would come to them as a result of Crazy Horse's night out with Killer Krill. PFC Ulgado Veloz reminded all within hearing distance that he had earlier predicted bad things to come when he had received the direct call from Division requiring Horace to report to General Krill. "I told you it would be bad," he fixed a fierce stare on Corporal Trent, "I don't know what will happen, but you'll be sorry." Trent, who was already thoroughly sorry about even being in Korea, said nothing.

Horace told the company nothing, but he did give a few orders that were quickly recognized by the old-timers as signaling a move. Two days after Horace returned, G Company orders came rolling down the chain of command from Division, Regiment, and Battalion. They were to move to Monastery Ridge three days later. The day after receiving the orders, Crayley, two of his platoon leaders, McCoy, and two men from communications section went to the ridge for a firsthand look at the outpost and to discuss the relief procedure with the E Company occupants. They went in broad daylight, and the small group encountered no opposition in crossing the plain to Monastery.

When they returned, Crayley assembled the company and informed them they were going to Monastery Ridge. He told them they had two days to prepare. He said he didn't know what they were going into, but they might be very busy. He told them that General Krill was pretty sure the Chinese would try to knock them off the ridge, and that Krill had made it very clear that they had to keep it.

As soon as Horace finished, two days of preparation began. Everyone got very interested in their weapons. Individual arms, rifles, carbines, pistols, and automatics were field stripped. Each part was carefully, even delicately, attended to. About this, there was no horse play. These were the tools of their trade. Then, their attention moved to other equipment. There were many more carbine bayonets than there were carbines in the company. These short stabbers were great favorites. Now they were methodically being honed against sharpening stones. Not withstanding the extravagant claims about their utility in close combat, these knives were seldom, if ever, used against people—way too messy—but in sudden, deadly panic they sometimes had to be used for their intended purpose and, of course, they were handy implements to have when it came time to eat. Here and there, a man had a heavy trench knife: a fearsome thing, devilishly sharp with a handle that had wicked metal knuckles to enclose a fist of crushing power. Though much admired, these miniature broad swords, as with the carbine blades, were principally used in attacking the boxes, cartons, and cans of the food rations.

Two of the new replacements were in a huddle with Hardesty, who was teaching them a forbidden black art. After first tightly, very tightly, taping the safety lever to the grenade, they were removing the safety pin. He was showing them how to lightly polish the pin with an emery cloth before inserting it back into its hole. It was then secured only enough to barely stay in place in the arming mechanism. In this way, Hardesty had assured them, when the time came, they could easily pull the pin even, if they wanted to, with their teeth just like the Hollywood heroes. Without the pin being prepared for such withdrawal, an attempt to pull it with the pin pull ring clamped in the mouth would result in losing several valuable front teeth.

Harry, who was wandering about the area, mentally preparing his list of items to take to Monastery, came upon Hardesty. He needed a light for his cigarette. He asked Hardesty, "Got a match?"

"A match? Sure, my ass and your face. That's the best match you'll ever see."

Harry grunted, "Ho, ho, you always were a flatterer." By then, he had seen what was going on. "But your trick is dog shit. Goddamn, Hardesty, I told you—everybody told you—that's fucking stupid, you could kill us all."

"Screw you, Sergeant Princeton," a formal rebuke, "it so happens that Lieutenant Clare, our platoon leader, thinks this is a damn fine idea. He wants us to be prepared to act quickly"—he struggled with the word "definitively" and ended up saying "quickly" again—"when the time comes. So I'm teaching these new men how to do it; so get your sorry ass out of here."

Turning to the recruits, Harry said, "Can't you dumb clucks see that those slick pins can slide out while you're running around the hills? If they do and that thing is in your pocket, you'll hear the safety spoon pop off, but you'll never get it out in time. You just killed yourself. And, if your pocket is loaded with a couple more of these, a lot more of us could get blown up with you. Those who are left will send your bits and pieces back home to your mama in a canteen cup."

Hardesty fumed, "Don't be such a pissant weenie, you tub of shit. It works okay, I've been doing it."

"You ain't been doing it, you lying sumbitch. You're trying to get these little virgins dead."

Projecting as best he could his mostly sternly superior expression, he said to the rookies. "I'm the armorer of this company. Any weapons modifications are done by me. No one else." Hardesty snorted, but the two youngsters didn't take their eyes off Harry. "Give me those things, and do it carefully. I don't want to blow my ass to kingdom come saving your poor sorry souls." They looked at Hardesty, not liking what they were hearing. Princeton's warning had an ominous—one might even say deadly—tone.

Hardesty glared at Harry. "Okay, asshole. You and me are going to see what the Lieutenant says as soon as I can find him." He started to stalk away.

Only one completed grenade lay on the ground at their feet. The tape was off. The slick pin was loosely holding the safety lever. Both the new men started to hand over the grenades they had been working on. Their hands collided. Both grenades dropped, one hitting the altered one on the ground. It started a slow roll down a slight slope. On the second roll, the pin slid out. The spoon popped, giving the grenade a slight jump, and the five-second fuse ignited. Hardesty jumped backward, fell down, and started crabbing away on his back, hands and feet flailing the ground. The two replacements, each with both hands tightly clasped over their ears, stared at the sputtering grenade, only a few feet away.

Princeton reacted instantly. With a hoarse cry, "Grenade!"—alerting all to get to cover fast—he pushed the two young men flat and jumped on the grenade, now two seconds through the fuse. The stream, which cascaded into a deep hole, was only twenty feet away. Harry lobbed the grenade into the pool, where it exploded at the bottom without any damage.

Crayley and McCoy, who had been watching preparations, came at a fast trot, demanding from Harry an explanation. After he told them, Wowser took off after Hardesty. Horace went looking for Ed. But he was intercepted at the CP by PFC Veloz who told him that Major Andrus, a Regimental surgeon, was on the wire. Horace diverted into the CP, picked up the field phone, and heard "Hello, Crayley. This is Andrus."

"Yes, sir."

"A few days ago, you,"—Horace heard papers being shuffled—"and Buddington brought in,"—more papers—"a Lieutenant Clare to get a cut patched up. Well, two days ago,"—Horace thought, 'the day I went to Division'—"he came in and started badgering one of my men. He said the paperwork for his Purple Heart had somehow not been filled out when he was in, and he wanted it done. Said you had sent him down to get it done. When the corpsman didn't react fast enough, this Clare guy,"—another paper rattle—"gets pretty demanding and, eventually, pretty obnoxious. Eventually, he left, but not before making an ass of himself."

Horace started to reply, but Andrus cut him off, "What I want to know, Lieutenant—the surgeon not having heard about Horace's promotion—"is, are you putting Clare in for the wound medal, and do you want me to sign off and send it up through channels, and, if so, in the future do it right. And, in the meantime, teach your Lieutenant Clare some manners."

Crayley thought a moment. "No, not right now, Major. It's somewhat premature. I've got to check on a couple of others,"—he lied—"who were with Clare. I may send up a few more at the same time. For now, you can just trash the paperwork. I'll pick up on it at a better time."

Andrus paused, "Okay, I'll do that, but I don't think a manners course for young Clare should wait too long."

"Thank you, sir. I'll take care of it."

Now, Horace really did want to see Ed. He strode out of the CP, nearly bumping into Clare. "Come with me, Lieutenant Clare."

"Sure, what's up?"

Horace was silent as he lead Ed down by the stream bank. Away from the men working in the area, he stopped and turned abruptly with his back to the company area and with Clare facing him with his back to the stream, "Goddamn it. What the hell's the matter with you?" Before Clare could speak, Horace continued, "I've got two things. The first is that Hardesty teaching your boys to kill themselves."

"What do you mean?"

"This stupidity with the grenade pins."

"Oh, that. That's a little trick to make them feel like swashbuckling hotdogs. It's just part of the training program I've been doing with the whole company, but this part is for my platoon only."

"You know, it's stupid and dangerous. You could get them and others killed."

"Yeah, well that's what combat is: stupid and dangerous and people get killed."

"That's close to what you said about that corporal in the alley."

"Yeah, so it is."

Horace backed away, took a long look at Clare, thinking, then deciding. "Enough. No more of it. If you've got any more of those modified grenades in your platoon, get rid of them, and don't make any more—and pass the word to that lunk, Hardesty."

Ed paused, "Okay, we'll find another way to liven them up." He started to walk away.

"Wait, we're not finished."

Clare stopped, looked around, "What now?"

"I got a call from Major Andrus."

"Who, he?"

"Regimental surgeon. He spent some time telling me of your visit to his place on the day I went to see Krill."

Horace was surprised at Ed's reaction. "So ...? He told you I went back to make sure they put me in for a Purple Heart. What did you tell him?"

"To forget it. It was a mistake in communication between you and his people. What the hell did you think you were doing?"

"Listen, I told you in Tokyo, I'm out to load up on that shit. I want lots of fruit salad. That little prick that knifed me in Tokyo thought he was a combat soldier. Well, in a certain sense, I got sort of a combat wound." He waited, half turned away from Horace. Then, abruptly, he turned to him head on, his face only inches away, he spit out his next words. "Anyway, it's all baloney, what difference does it make to you? You could have moved it along, instead you torpedoed it. What a pal."

"What a pal? What a pal? You miserable shit. A lot of good men, a lot better than you, have died in real combat, and the only thing their families have to show for it is a Purple Heart. That was a cheap, despicable stunt."

Then it came to Horace. "The medal attempt, it's all part of the same scenario; your training program, your push for patrolling, the grenade modifications, the Tokyo alley—the big picture to you is a lot of people getting killed, and you don't care who, just so you get a lot of medals to show to dear old dad."

Clare, savagely, "Well, that's part of it. But the other part is that I'm willing to take my chances to get it. As for you," he paused as if searching for something. "I don't know about you. Before I came over here, I got the book on the 'Great Crazy Horse,' and I was glad to come to this company because you're a certified basher and slasher. But I get over here and I see a young guy, but really old, over the hill, nearly as pathetic as that old fart, McCoy, going through the motions with a burned out dead-in-the-water bunch of lead weights waiting for something to happen and hoping it doesn't. I see none of the piss and vinegar in them or you that matches your reputation."

"If anything ever happened to you, and this company was mine, I'd get rid of McCoy and those derelict misfits he carries with him, and I'd turn this unit into a real fighting machine."

Horace took a long moment before he spoke. "It's really too god damned bad, that we don't measure up to your vision of what we should be. We've been in a healing period here, recovering from a situation you know nothing about. I'll also say, we're ready to move on, and that's what we're going to do. I also say, it's unfortunate that I must take you with us. You're dangerous to yourself and everyone around you. But let me tell you, you little bastard, we're not here to fight your war with your father and brother." He punched three short, two-fingered jabs into Clare's chest, causing him to bounce back a few quick, short steps. "So you're on a damn short leash with me. If you sneeze up there without me telling you which way the wind is blowing,

I'll drop you over the side." Horace turned and left, leaving Ed standing by the water.

Crayley went back about his duties, seeking to turn his mind to the task at hand. He searched for Harry and found him. "Do you need anything to take up on that rock pile?"

"I been thinkin' we should take some extra barrels for the lights." This was a reference to the .30 caliber machine guns of the company. "I've got only three spares. We're supposed to have three guns, and we got seven, so we should take seven or eight more barrels. We got a few new boys. If one of them gets on a gun, he's liable to get excited and just spray nonstop. That'll burn out a barrel pretty quick, and who knows what happens next?"

"Okay, Harry, what else?"

"I can't think of anything. We already are lugging enough ammo to start our own war."

"That's all right. If the party starts while we're up there, we won't get any resupply." Crayley thought more, then, "I want you to load up with WP, both mortar and grenades. The Chinks are very limited in white phosphorus and, to coin a phrase, it burns their ass. If we can spread a few flakes of that stuff on them, they'll come out of their holes and start dancin' across the landscape like it's the spring prom. We'll mix a little HE in with the phosphorus, and the high explosive will clean 'em off the dance floor faster than a scraper blade."

"Okay, Captain. I'll get things organized." Harry skittered off yelling for the supply sergeant.

Wowser had told him that Princeton would snap to when the time came. Now was that time, and it seemed to Horace that Harry was pretty well plugged into the plan.

◆   ◆   ◆

Moving day came, and Horace gave the company their instructions. He told them they would move into the lines of F Company, which was in place in front of their reserve position, on the other side of the spur that faced the river plain. After dark, they would move down the slope through F Company's barbed wire and onto the flat river course and make their way to Monastery. They would move up Monastery's south ramp into the E Company position. E would leave the Ridge, and it would be all theirs. He told them he expected no trouble on the way out. The Chinese had been fairly quiet for several days. Patrols from E and F had seen no unusual activity. He called to their attention the amount of artillery shells sailing outward the last two nights. The firing—sporadic and not heavy—would continue tonight. Its purpose was to aid in masking the sound of their movement. Even with such sound cover, he especially emphasized the necessity of maintaining silence during their movement.

In addition to his normal load, each man was to carry one machine gun ammo box of two hundred fifty rounds and one mortar shell. Traveling with them would be fifty KSCs—who would depart as soon as the company settled in—each packing about eighty pounds of equipment and supplies.

At the conclusion of his instructions, Crayley asked if the musical instruments were packed and ready to go. They were. McCoy had earlier told the players to bring their musical equipment because they might have a chance to give a concert for the Chinks. There were four or five trumpets, two trombones, three bugles, and air raid siren ready for the trip.

As dusk started coming on, Horace contacted the E Company commander by wire net and told him they were on the way. Then, the company moved out in a loose column of twos. They went up a slight rise to F Company's position, then stopped and waited for deeper darkness. There was a drop from there to the river plain that was steeper and longer than the walk up the back side. Slowly, they made their way to the wire at the front of F Company and passed through it with a minimum of noise.

Once out in the open, Crayley sent a few of the most experienced men out in front and to the sides of the march line and waited for them to get into position before moving forward. While the other men waited, they ditched their loads and sat down. A quiet signal on a short-range, handheld radio told Horace that his flankers were ready, and he, at the front of the column, passed the word to saddle up. "Sling arms." The word went softly down the line, "Sling arms. Sling arms," from front to back.

Near the end of the column, Corporal Frederick Trent was waiting. Sergeant McCoy, still somewhat pissed at Trent for his remarks to Wowser at the time of Sergeant Koppleman's recent visit, had told Trent to help one of the sixty-millimeter mortar squads. As the newest helper, he, of course, got the shit detail: carrying the heavy mortar baseplate.

As the word came down the line, the corporal bent over to pick up and sling the baseplate onto his back. Next in line to Trent was Private Stanley Binder—who had a hard-on for Trent because he thought Trent had prevented him from being selected for officer candidate school. This was a joke to those familiar with his complaint, because Stanley could not be counted on to load his rifle, for which reason Wowser had put him in a mortar squad, where he could be reasonably relied upon, after many hours of practice, to place a mortar shell in the tube with the propellant end down.

As Trent bent over to get the plate off the ground, Stanley laid a stiff middle finger into the crack of Frederick's straining ass. Trent felt a gentle finger flutter in his butt, then a sharp prod. It was, all in all, a magnificent goose. The corporal expressed his appreciation with a giggling whinny. As Binder's finger moved insinuatingly down his fanny split, Trent's whinny rose to a high-pitched yell. "Sling arms, sling arms, sling arms," shrieked Trent as he clean-and-jerked the base plate and took off on a dead run for Monastery. As he passed Crazy Horse and Wowser, he was still exhorting the world to "sling arms."

The company broke into roaring laughter. March discipline was gone. The rest of the trip was made as a convivial, even jovial, group of soldiers out for an evening stroll.

The Chinese took no action to spoil the mood.

CHAPTER EIGHTEEN

The last of the men labored up the south slope just before dawn. With their arrival, Monastery Ridge was occupied by two rifle companies, but only for the day. As night fell on the first full day, the departing company was glad enough to leave. For although its time on top had been a pleasant vacation, free from demands of the line companies behind them, it had an institutional sense—a persistent crawling itch on the back of nearly every man's neck—that it was getting out just before the balloon was scheduled to go up.

The next day, the men of George Company got acquainted with their new outpost position. They probed the structures and cavities of the monolithic rock. They gave careful attention to the rooms—most small single monk cells—on the circumference perimeter of the massive column. The monks had lived, worked, and carried out their religious obligations in these Spartan cubicles. The backs of the compartments were on, or nearly on, the edge of the tower. Most of them had openings to the fields below, some of which had been built in place by the monks. Others had been blown out by previous military occupants to get a better field of fire. The former thin slate roofs were now timbered and heavily sandbagged.

There was a principal passageway down the center axis. In the monks' time it had been mostly covered by a mat of woven reeds so that the affairs of the monastery could be comfortably carried out regardless of the weather. Now, the path was open to the skies. Wooden ricochet-battered sign posts at each end identified it as "Main Street" with many cross bars showing mileage to several U.S. and world locations. Main Street made it possible to move speedily the full length of the company's position without exposure to enemy fire. It also allowed quick movement between the monk cells, now fortified bunkers, which faced outward from Main Street.

The men much admired the work of the previous tenants, whether United Nations or Chinese, who had turned the once serene monastery into a formidable fortress. The consensus view was that this was a place from which their business could be very effectively carried out.

Captain Crayley's first order was to establish the areas of responsibility of his platoons. This was quickly and easily done: three rifle platoons in line, north to south. Next, his weapons platoon was distributed around the tower rim. His seven machine guns—the company was authorized only three—were placed to take advantage of the best fields of fire. Three were pointed down the south ramp. The weapons platoon's three sixty-millimeter mortars were set up in a former herb garden almost in the center of the tower. The company command post went into what had been the monks' assembly hall. It was well situated for control of the platoons and the support weapons. Also, it was closest to First Platoon, which was positioned above the south ramp. Ground communication lines were tested, radio contact established, and the company was open for business.

◆   ◆   ◆

As Wowser exited the CP, he found Harry Princeton out for a stroll on Main Street. "Come along, Harry, we'll see what we've got here."

A short distance down the passageway, they bumped into Boffo Mallen, who was just coming out of one of the bunkers on the Chinese side of the tower. "Oh, there you are," he said. "Two of the best. Come with me into my new apartment, and I'll show you a boffo sight." They followed him into the bunker and to a firing step in the front wall. "There you are—nothing at all. But there are enough Chin-ee boys out there to cook up pot stickers for the whole UN Army."

In front of them the river plain was completely without human activity. As far as they could see beyond the river plain into the surrounding hills and to the mountains beyond, there was nothing. Of course, none of the three expected to see Chin-ee boys moving about. The Chinese did most of their work at night, unless there were large troop movements by either side or unless a specific objective required unrelenting short-term pressure.

"Well, naturally you won't spot anything now. But I know they're out there and so do you."

"Chin-ee boys" was a Mallen label. He had fastened on it during his "stage career"—as he liked to call it—in San Francisco. Mallen had been in the Army a lot of years, but during one of two very short periods as a civilian he had, for a limited time, been the lowliest stage hand in a theater crew. Unable to excite any of the female theatrical performers to his version of Bohemian pleasures, Boffo had taken to visiting the main city library, posing as a serious researcher with the hope—and very limited success—of hitting on lonely librarians, who would be persuaded by his celebrity status. From one such book custodian he had to suffer through several nights of discussion about her historical literary specialty: Chinese laborers who had worked on the western end of the first great transcontinental railroad.

Out of that ultimate—but sadly unrewarding—conquest, Boffo had developed his own shorthand, "Chin-ee boys." He wasn't sure he would ever use it, but then Korea engaged his services, and he found much opportunity to discuss "Chin-ee boys."

Boffo turned again to gaze at the view. He struck a "lord-of-the-manor" pose, surveying his domain. Wowser admired him for a moment then, "Move," as he pushed Mallen out of his observation post. McCoy moved as far into the firing port as he could go. He shoved a discarded ammo box forward so he could step up for a better view. Craning his head up and over the lower edge of the opening, he could look down the sheer cliff side of the tower. As he did so, he saw the cleft in the rock that Krill told Horace about. Wowser looked at it closely. He thought it might be a possible route right into the middle of the company's position. It was a rocky, nearly vertical, trail. It would be damn difficult for anybody to scramble up, but maybe it could be done. If so, it couldn't be ignored.

"C'mon you two. Hoist your lard asses up high enough to take a look at this." Harry and Boffo each took a long look. "Well, what do you think? Can it be done? Can those gook clowns get up here?"

Boffo, "No way. It's too fuckin' steep. Besides we'll be shooting their asses off as they come."

"Not from here or from the other side of it. Anybody coming up would be too deep in that notch to get hit from either side. What do you think, Harry?"

"Maybe some of 'em could make it all the way up, but I don't think so. Just in case, we'll have to attend to it."

"You do it, Harry. I'll leave it to you."

Wowser steered the three of them down Main Street. A short distance from Boffo's vista point, they turned off the path and went down a steep wooden staircase. At the bottom, they were in a rock chamber, which continued in a slight decline farther into the heart of the shaft.

The power room, a small cavern drilled ten feet into the rock below Main Street, had been pointed out to them by members of E Company when they arrived. It was in operation with one generator—two on standby—to provide power for radio and some illumination for the dark spots inside the rock.

As they proceeded, they came to side tunnels leading into other spaces: some tiny, but three bigger than any of the structures on the surface. They found two wells of clear, very cold water, ample for their needs. They came upon rooms filled with food and ammunition, each prior occupant bringing to the Ridge more than was needed and leaving behind everything not used. Continuing downward, they entered a bitterly cold chamber. Thin frost covered two of the walls.

Harry stopped two steps inside the entrance. "I ain't goin' into this fuckin' tomb. There's something weird in here."

"Only you, Harry," said McCoy.

"Screw you, Wowser. This place is to stack the stiffs, not me."

Boffo chimed in, "You're probably right. I bet them monks planted their dear departed in this mortuary until they carved a permanent hole some place."

"Could be, and it might come in handy for us," Wowser observed.

The other two looked at him, but he was already out of the room. Standing outside the mortuary, they could hear voices from a long distance down a curving tunnel leading to the south end of the tower. Coming to them out of the dark, they could make out their captain and Corporal Trent.

"Oh, McCoy. I was looking for you topside and you too, Harry. Come with me." They turned back down the tunnel with Crazy Horse leading. "I couldn't find you Sergeant, so I commandeered Trent from his typewriter, and we headed down. I want to see what we're mining down here." Crayley led them all into a large, well-lit room, nearly as cold as the mortuary. "Here it is. See what we have."

Harry was the first to speak, "Fuck me. It's a goddamn engineer explosives depot."

They counted what they saw. Stacked along one side were twenty-three shaped charges, each with forty pounds of TNT molded in such a way that the direction and force of the explosion could be specifically focused. On another wall were thirty-seven fifty-five gallon gasoline drums. In the center of the room were plastic explosives, fuses, and detonating cords of several types.

"Looks right, Harry. This must have been an engineer supply depot for units moving forward from here. When they left, this stuff stayed behind in this refrigerator."

Trent asked, "Why plant gasoline here? It belongs in a POL depot."

Harry moved to one of the drums, unscrewed the bung cap, sniffed, stuck a long finger in, then said, "Because it ain't gasoline. It's napalm. They already put the napalm mix in. This stuff is almost like jelly."

They continued their look around. Finally, it was Boffo who said it for all of them. "Damn me, there's enough shit here to blow us all to China."

"Do you guys realize where we are?" Crayley asked.

They all looked around. Finally Trent replied, "No, we've come a long way in the tunnels. Where do you think we are, Captain?"

"Look at that wall opposite the entrance. It's dirt, not rock. We've come out of the stone shaft. We're under the south ramp. I estimate we're about fifteen feet below the surface."

"Well, Crazy Horse," Wowser speaking, "If that's so, I'm happy. I wouldn't want something to happen to these fireworks if they were directly under us when we're on top tending to business."

"We'll see, McCoy. We'll see."

When the miners returned to the surface, Harry went off to attend to the notch trail next to Boffo's bunker. He gathered his material, grabbed two men who he believed were resting too easily, and started off. He stopped at the CP to explain his plan to Horace. When the captain heard Princeton's description of the trail, he went with Harry to Boffo's bunker. When he saw what any attackers would have to accomplish, he decided that Krill, and Boffo, were probably right, there was only a very slim chance that anybody could come up that route and do them any damage. But he told Harry to get on with the job.

The task required Princeton and his two assistants to be out on the cleft. It also needed three more in the bunker to secure the ropes tied around the three cliff climbers. By going through the firing port and clawing their way along the outer wall of the bunker, Princeton and his assistants were able to reach what could be the end of the trail for any Chinaman good enough to get that far.

Harry and his helpers began to weave a lattice work of thin ropes on the sides and bottom of the nearly vertical trail. On this frame they strew mines, booby traps, and other assorted flash-bang devices. Princeton's work was undoubtedly under observation by their enemy. But neither Harry nor Horace cared. If the Chinese had any idea of coming up the notch, they certainly knew that the Americans could see them and would take steps to deny them entrance to Monastery by way of the cleft route.

◆   ◆   ◆

By the second day, the company was prepared and ready; Crayley, through the ground communication net, was wired into both Bozoni, the regimental commander, and Krill. The company had been detached from its battalion for this job, so Horace didn't have to concern himself with his battalion commander.

Crayley cranked the phone. "We're all set."

Krill answered before anyone else. "Tell me what's happening up there." Crayley gave a quick recap of their short time on top.

"Anything I can do for you?"

"If Div. arty has its sights right and can avoid hitting us, it might be a good idea to show the rice eaters what that means. Give them a small show."

"Okay. I'll think on it. Bozoni and I will put something together. We'll get back to you."

Forty minutes later, the field phone gargled. "For you, Captain," said Fisco, a new man who had joined the company a few days before the move.

It was Krill himself. "Okay, Crazy Horse. The Division artillery has the river plain in front of you registered. We've got a TOT for tomorrow at 1100 hours. Unless on a fire mission for somebody else, it will be all the division heavies, plus the smaller ones of Bozoni's regiment. I'm also having Carlsen's regiment, on your right, join in. That'll last a couple of minutes, then we'll do it all over again about five minutes later. A couple of Bozoni's tubes will try for that narrow south ramp, but I don't know how successful they'll be. Be sure you're all well buttoned up in case my gunners forget your address and send a few general delivery."

Horace told the platoon leaders that a TOT was being shot their way next morning. McCoy explained to Fisco that TOT meant "time-on-target," which meant that preparation of the shells and firing of all the artillery was accomplished so that everything arrived on the target at the same time. "If those arty dick heads get it right, it will be a hell of a blast out of nowhere for the Chin-ee boys to wonder about."

By eleven the next morning, the company was awaiting the artillery demonstration. Some of the men were down below, but most remained topside in their bunkers. There was the sudden sound of many incoming rounds. All who knew what that trilling shriek meant hoped that Monastery would be cleared. It was. Abruptly the plain in front of them erupted in almost a single gigantic explosion. Great chunks of earth belched upward, sending clouds of dust and debris sailing into the sky then settling lazily back into the holes gouged in the flat ground. Five minutes later, it happened again.

Captain Crayley was in First Platoon position with his attention focused on the ramp. Of the two firings, nothing landed on the south slope. Horace got, not unexpected, a sour taste in his mouth. It meant that the principal place of attack could be defended only by what he had in place on Monastery.

◆   ◆   ◆

For the first time, the Chinese had something to say. They did so immediately. Less than four minutes after Krill's second barrage, their initial delivery was made. Many more quickly followed. They were from one-hundred-twenty millimeter mortars that sent huge loads of explosives in a high trajectory to plunge nearly straight down on George Company. A cloudburst of mortar bombs landed on them. Then, in precision movement, the shells started marching behind them toward the main American lines. This continued for several minutes until the explosions were within a hundred yards of the American positions. Then, the barrage abruptly stopped.

Krill was on the wire almost as soon as the Chinese shelling stopped. "Are you all right up there?"

"We're okay here."

"Casualties?"

"A few splinters. We were all pretty well hunkered down while our guys were doing the TOT"

"They plowed the field behind you pretty good, I'm told. Looks like they have you sealed in up there."

"Looks like it. We'll see how hospitable we can be when they visit us."

"All right, Captain. It sounds to me like you got your balls wound tight enough. Keep me up to speed." The line clicked off.

The Chinese mortars resumed about thirty minutes after Krill's call, but in a different manner. A hit would land on Monastery; then several minutes later, a shell would land in the flat fields behind the stone pillar in front of George's brother companies of Bozoni's regiment.

From the first round fired in this new pattern, the Chinese never stopped. Day and night, three and four shells an hour would land topside; one or two would hit in the plain back of the company. The company was being told that Monastery was now targeted. They were being told that heavy bombardment could be delivered on them at any time. The random firing was just to let them know that the enemy had them in their thoughts, and when the Chinese decided to come, there would be little chance of rescue from the friendly forces behind George Company. They were now in harm's way.

The continual harassing mortar fire had limited success in its intended effect of screwing nerves tight. Many, though not all, of the company, while cautious, came to almost ignore a hit unless it was directly over their heads. None of the shells hit narrow Main Street, which continued to be a safe communications trench. The walls of the former monks' quarters, which were now heavily fortified bunkers, were high enough for the men to move about in relatively safety, even as shell shards streaked over their heads.

◆　　◆　　◆

On the third day of the occupation of Monastery Ridge, Harry Princeton was entertaining three of the new men with his Hollywood tales. He had managed to recapture from the company clerk a few of the more succulent shots from his star-strewn portfolio by convincing Corporal Trent that if he didn't give them up, Harry would booby trap Trent's boots so that the ensuing blast would blow his balls off. Trent, of course, wasn't taken in by Harry on the balls blow-off scam, but Yale University had taught him to think on a grander political level, several floors above the basement thinking usually generated by the resident philosophers of George Company. He believed—and so told Harry—that Harry had a constitutional right to own, comment upon, and display his hoary icons. So Trent had given back a few of the best crotch shots. The corporal was also looking forward to the first sergeant's outburst when McCoy again confiscated the skin pics and was challenged by Princeton on constitutional grounds. Trent was sure that their discussion would be politically illuminating.

Near the end of one of Harry's show-and-tell performances, a mortar round hit almost directly overhead. The blast shook the theater and the audience. Fisco, the new commo man, who was still struggling to display the veneer of the nerveless old timers, fell to the dirt floor, knees doubled to his chest, "What the fuck, Sergeant, doesn't this ever stop?"

Harry gave him a smarmy look—though he thought it portrayed serene confidence—"Stop, you say? Stop? Hell no, it doesn't stop. When them Chin-ee boys"—he also had adopted Mallen's label—"want to keep you thinking of them, it don't stop. Kid, look at it as part of the fun we're all havin' just by being up here."

◆   ◆   ◆

The evening of the fifth day, the weather started to kick up. Until then, each day had dawned gloriously with the sun streaming onto the river plain, touching, then embracing, the monastery's rock wall. It was truly the land of the morning calm. Later, a light pearly haze drifted up from the soft earth, turning golden as the sun disappeared behind the peaks to the southwest of the stone pillar. Even the nights had been brilliantly clear until the fifth day.

A cold wind started small eddies in the dirt of the plain as the sun was setting. Dusty tendrils circled and rose, brushing against the stone columns. There was a smell, even a feel, of rain, but none came. The wind grew in force and skittered down the Main Street in errant gusts that swirled through the openings of the bunkers to corkscrew against walls and back out into the street.

A cranky tension came upon the company. The sporadic mortar rounds didn't grind their teeth as much as the wind. They settled down for the night in a very twitchy mood.

Just before midnight, the Chinese ground attack came. It started with a rapid increase in mortar fire, but it didn't hit George. The shells fell in the fields behind the tower. Then, abruptly, the firing stopped. During the next hour, nothing happened. For the first time in three days, no mortar rounds landed on Monastery. It was as if the Chinese just wanted to give George Company a wake-up call for the next event.

And then it came. The men on the ridge became aware of an increasingly noisy chatter coming from the plain in front of them. It grew to a sound like a drunken party coming away from the big game. Suddenly, green signal rockets that looked like Roman candles sliced across the front length of the tower. Three horns sounded wavering blasts. It was hard to see in the dark, but it gradually became apparent that the enemy below had gathered itself into a large formation standing in front of, and looking up at, George. Many in the crowd began yelling and several started banging wood noise makers and metal gongs. Small arms fire—rifle and automatic weapons—began cracking up from the plain. But the mob was now almost directly below and most of their shots simply sailed straight up, never hitting the steep wall of stone or the bunkers on top.

Crayley called on his mortars for illumination flares with most of them to go up over the south ramp. He also directed them to keep some light all around the tower. He told McCoy to ask Regiment for artillery illumination. As soon as the flares were parachuting down, Horace talked to First Platoon in position above the ramp. They reported many enemy soldiers seemed to be trying to get organized to come up the ramp, but so far they were having trouble coming together. The Second Platoon leader said he thought he could take care of the stumbling bunch in front of him with rifle fire only. Clare did not respond. The report from the backside was that no enemy soldiers could be seen on the flat fields between Monastery and the main American lines.

From Buffo Mallen's bunker came word that some Chin-ee boys were attempting to scramble up the north trail, but their effort was noisy and clumsy and the lattice work of traps was blowing them apart.

More light arrived from the artillery. It gave the company a good view of the proceedings below. The flares, jerking in the wind, cast darting black-and-white shadows on the attackers. Many had no weapons. They were simply extras on the opera stage milling around and yelling up at the stone monolith.

So far, no one on Monastery had fired a shot. Crayley, on the wire to his platoon leaders, confirmed their joint evaluation of what was happening. "It's just a probe. Most of that mob is probably high on snorts of their magic white powder. We've seen it before. This mob scene was created to test our panic level. They hope to spook us so we'll fire everything we have at them. Somewhere out there in the dark are some cool eyes waiting to spot the positions of our automatic weapons."

The platoon leaders, all having time in Korea, agreed. That is, all except Clare and, Horace noted, Sergeant Ortega, the unit's second in command. Sergeant Osborne, one of the squad leaders, spoke for the platoon, but Horace was too busy to give it much thought. He simply put it down to Ed's continuing petulance at the placement of his platoon farthest from the ramp, which certainly looked like keeping him away from the area of most activity when the real attack came. "Okay," said Horace, "we've shown we're not just off the turnip truck. There's probably not more than a couple of hundred or so dancing around out there. Everybody stay in position. Nobody moves. Hear me again. Everybody stay in your position. I don't want any movement at all. Take care of those in front of you. Let's get rid of them. Rifle fire only, unless it gets more serious. First Platoon, you can open up with one of your lights."—a reference to the .30 caliber machine guns positioned in the platoon—"If you use it, move it to a new firing port when you're finished."

"Second Platoon, tell Boffo"—he was closest to it—"to roll a crate of grenades down the notch trail."

"Everybody stay alert. Maybe this will turn into something real. But I don't think this is the time."

The men of George opened up on the happy throng in front of them. Rifle fire exploded from every port facing the Chinese. A single machine gun hosed down the south ramp. Grenades rained on the scramblers below. In ten minutes, the trumpets sounded. The mob noise abruptly toned down, but movement continued. A few luckless souls, too high to realize the party was over, kept up the racket until swatted by one of their sober leaders.

In less than an hour, it was all over. The Chinese were gone, taking their dead and wounded with them. The river plain was quiet. The only sound was the wind whistling through the rocky passages of the tower.

Crayley gave orders to stand down. The artillery was informed and thanked for their work. The platoon leaders counted noses. Weapons were checked, quick cleaned, and reloaded. George Company mortars fired more illumination, while Wowser took a five-man search party around through the tower to make sure that no lucky climbers had somehow made it to the top.

Within minutes of the close of action, the radio came to life.

"This is Gibraltar Six. Over." Krill's radio sign.

Horace had to stop and think, "Glitter White George Six. Over."

"This is Krill. We'll forget radio discipline for the moment. Hell, they know who I am and you, too, probably. I waited until the noise stopped. But I can't get through on the wire. The land lines must be cut. What went on up there?"

"It was only a probe. They were just foolin' around to see if we were awake—and they were looking for weapons' positions and routes up."

"Casualties?"

Horace hesitated before putting such information in to the airwaves, then, "None, except for one chipped finger nail. We're in fine shape."

"Anything else?"

Horace had been mulling something over since he had scouted through the lower levels of the monastery. "Gibraltar Six," he couldn't bring himself to say "General" on an open radio. "I suggest that the special communicator at your headquarters get on so he can talk to his brother who is with me. He can pass on my message to you."

Krill, who had been informed of the Cruz twins, said, "Wait." Soon, a rapid voice speaking unintelligible words came in loud and clear.

Crazy Horse handed the radio mike to Cochise so he could talk to his brother, Geronimo. Crayley gave the message to Cochise. This started a discussion between the general, Horace, and the twins, which finally concluded with an approval for the idea Horace proposed to Krill.

The radio conversation ended. The George command group was still in the CP when the radio suddenly blared. "Hello you damn bastard Americans. What you do in Korea?" It was a brusque Chinese voice, heavy, angry, puzzled. "What you talk on radio? I think crazy talk. No one understand, even you. Why you do such foolish talk? We listen all time, but we no care what you say. We knock damn you off the tall rock anyway, soon." The transmission clicked off.

Crayley looked around the CP. He nodded at and handed the mike to McCoy who considered for a moment, "Knock me off? You silly slant-eyed fuck. You couldn't knock a fly off your prick." He looked around for compliments. All the commo men gave him a thumbs up. The captain just winked. Corporal Trent looked glum.

Wowser continued, "That's our new radio scrambler system. I feel real sorry for you if you couldn't understand it. It was very interesting." He waited, but got no Chinese reply. "And if you are dumb enough to think you want to tangle with us, we'll slice your dog meat assholes into chop suey." He ended his transmission with an arm swing snap of the microphone and looked around again quite satisfied with his reply. He had done his job of expressing bombastic, cocksure defiance in nearly gibberish terms to the Chinese intruders.

The men stared at the radio, willing it to speak to them again. It was silent for several minutes. They had just about given up when, without even the hiss that usually proceeded a radio call, it sudden spoke to them. But this time it was a different speaker. "Ah, Lieutenant Crayley, I hope that rude person wasn't you. I think American Army officers are not so crude in their speech, especially the commander of G Company, who has been given the important, but impossible, task of holding the stone tower where you now sit. Unfortunately for you, we have been given the task of removing you from your place, and I have always been successful in my efforts for the Peoples Republic Volunteer Forces in Korea."

Horace picked up the mike. "Well, general, and you sure sound like you are at least a general, I've got my job. You've got yours. Unfortunately for you, this company has never failed its missions"—he didn't think it wise to refer to Iron Mountain—"and we wouldn't think of starting now. We're here lookin' down, and you're there looking up.

You've got a hell of a job even getting to us, and we both know it. It looks to me like the odds are all in my favor."

Crayley paused trying to think of an appropriate parting shot. Suddenly Fisco grabbed the mike from his hand, "And besides that, you shit-face gook, Lieutenant Crayley is now Captain Crayley. Didn't your spies tell you that?"

Horace and McCoy looked at Fisco in astonishment. One week in the company, and he's ragging the enemy in a big-time broadcast to which both Krill and Bozoni were also probably tuned in. It was right for Crayley and McCoy to be the company mouthpieces, but for a raw-ass recruit to seize center stage was bad manners, like pissing in the punch bowl. Wowser glared at Fisco, his face telling the new boy that he had just pulled his pud in front of the wrong people.

The smooth voiced Chinaman came on again. "Ah, Captain Crayley, congratulations on your promotion. I have not yet received that news. We may or may not speak again, but be assured that when we place a marker over your grave, assuming we will find you, we will be sure to correctly identify you as 'Captain.'" The radio went dead.

CHAPTER NINETEEN

It was just less than two hours later that Horace got the question that, for a few seconds, shuttered his brain to a full stop. He had been moving through the company, talking calmly to its members, letting the new men see the quiet confidence of their commander, asking them how they had faired during the probe, and assessing their reaction to their first shots fired in anger. He was in First Platoon when its leader, Master Sergeant Noma, casually asked him, "I assume Ortega and the new kid got back okay?"

Horace turned to face him, "What do you mean? Did who get back from where?"

"Ortega and what's his name?"

"What are you talking about?"

Noma took a long, deep breath before he replied, "Jesus! You don't know."

"Know what?"

"A few minutes after that Chinese circus started performing, before they got organized on the ramp, Ortega and—Jeez, I don't know his name—came through here. Benny said that Lieutenant Clare wanted him and his helper to go down the ramp to see if they could circle around and maybe figure a way to hit those people while they were bouncing around down there. He said he would return through here and then tell Clare if it looked good. If so, Clare planned to bring his whole platoon through here and try to wrap up a bunch of the Chinks."

"Why the hell didn't you alert me? You heard me tell everybody to stay in place."

"I know. I reminded Benny of your order, but Clare told him that he had cleared Benny's travel plans with you, because both of you guys had already discussed the likelihood of a probe—'cause it always happens when a new bunch shows up—and you had given the green light to Clare's idea."

"For crissakes, Noma,"—he grabbed the sergeant's shoulders with both hands—"there were probably two hundred of them down there and only two of ours."

"Yes, sir, I know."

Horace released his grip on Noma's shoulders and patted them gently in apology for his angry outburst and assuring the sergeant that it wasn't directed toward him.

Noma continued, "Benny and me discussed that point. I told him it was crazy. He knew it, and he didn't feel good. He told me he had tried to get Clare to let him go alone, let the new kid—what's his name—stay behind. But Clare wanted the rookie to get a feel of it under an experienced hand like Ortega. And, as you would expect, Benny said, 'orders is orders.'"

"My god. They went down the ramp and just disappeared into that rabble."

"Yes, sir. If they ain't back before now, they ain't coming back."

Horace was back in the CP, when Clare arrived in response to an order to see the captain. Crayley told others in the bunker room to find something else to do and to do it some place else.

As the last man pushed through the entrance, Clare started, "I would have gone myself, but I thought that the company shouldn't risk losing half of its officers' strength at just this time. Besides, I had to get the platoon ready in case Ortega found an opening."

"What was the new man's name?"

"Not sure. He's only been with us four, five days. I think maybe it was Bullock."

"What the hell was on your mind in sending two men, one just a kid, down into that bunch? Two against two hundred!"

"Those numbers don't matter. Ortega was experienced. I thought the new boy could learn."

"Learn what? How to get killed?"

Clare waited just a heart beat, then turned, "That's the trouble with you, Horace, you want to run the war without anybody getting hurt."

Crayley took a step back, then quietly, "That's just about what you said in Tokyo. People in combat, or those who think they're in combat, frequently end up dead."

"Yeah, that's right. And you don't like it. The problem with you, Big Chief Washout is that you're way overrated. You've got no balls left for what's needed here."

Horace backed off another step, then moved forward. "Listen to me, you little prick, this is a company in the U.S. Army and, God knows how, you're an officer in it, who obeys orders, cares for his men, and gets the job done."

"Well, what the fuck is the job supposed to be? When the real fight starts, my platoon's not going to be in the fun zone, 'cause you stuck us out on the north end where an octopus couldn't scale the wall. I saw that an opportunity was, maybe, available, that maybe we could sneak down and blow away some of those rice eaters. And I sent an experienced sergeant to check it out. I was using my initiative, like I'm supposed to do.

"You disobeyed my orders that everybody was to stay in place."

"Hell, that's not important. I recognized an opportunity."

"You label it 'opportunity.'" He stepped forward and grabbed Clare's collar with both hands on both sides of his head, pulled Clare to himself—"I call it murder."

Horace dropped his hands from Ed, "I've known you—what is it now—less than a month, and already you've killed three men who, for crissakes, were all on our side."

"What do you mean 'three'?"

"Have you forgotten your drop kick in Tokyo?"

"Oh, that one. That was justifiable. We all agreed."

"No, we didn't all agree. We just bugged out."

They both stopped, breathing heavily. They moved sideways around the room, warily with their eyes on each other. Finally, Clare spoke as if the matter had been cleared up. "Well, I'm gonna need a new platoon sergeant. I'm thinking of jumping Hardesty a couple of grades, and giving him the job. He seems to me to be ready and he's certainly aggressive enough."

Horace cut in quickly, "No. Not Hardesty. Nobody right now, just leave it alone."

Horace continued, this time in a quiet, measured tone, "You just don't get it, do you, Ed?"—he waited. "I'll spell it out for you, Lieutenant Clare. You're finished in this company. More than that, I'm going to finish you in this Army. As soon as I can, I will get charges prepared to court-martial you for disobeying a direct order resulting in the deaths of two of your men."

Ed just looked at him, not stunned, not even surprised. "I could see this coming. I knew you'd lost your nerve after we bailed out in Tokyo. You gutless wonder, you wanted to go to the Provost Marshal that day. If you can get me court-martialed for this, your conscience will swallow the little trucker corporal because I'll be in the bag for something, different, but still in the bag."

Horace started across the room toward him. "Wait," demanded Clare, one hand up in a stop motion. "Hear me out." Crayley stopped in midstride. "I think you should reconsider your great court-martial idea, because if you go forward with it, I will open up Tokyo." Clare waited, looking intently at Horace, "Yeah, that's right. I'll get it out in the open. I think the possibility of that turn of events will take some wind out of your blow-hard threat."

Clare continued, "And my story of the alley will be different than you incorrectly remember. For example, you'll be surprised to learn that the kick to the head of the dumb fuck was delivered by Lieutenant Horace Crayley. And he did it when that poor little corporal was flat on his back, out cold, completely out of the fight."

"What the hell bullshit story is that?"

And Clare went on, "I just watched, horrified at what this murderous officer was doing. After all, I was the junior member of our group. The other two were veteran combat officers. There was simply nothing I could do. It went down so fast."

Horace was struck dumb. He was speechless. He looked at Clare, finally saying,

"You're really crazy, a certifiable nut case. Only you're forgetting there's an antidote to your fantasy—Buddington. Bud was there. His story will be the same as mine."

"Bud won't do that. Why, you ask? Well, it's simple, he's dead."

Horace's gut lurched upward. "What are you talking about?"

"I guess I didn't tell you. I heard about it when I went back to Regiment to check on my Purple Heart. He was on patrol the night before. They tangled with a large group of gooks, and he got thoroughly drilled."

Horace sighed, lost in thought for a moment, then said, "He was a good man."

"Yeah, but no good to you as a backup to your version of the Tokyo alley."

Horace stumbled into some radio equipment, sat down heavily on a bedroll, but immediately jumped up. "It makes no difference. Your story is a lie like most of what you've done since you arrived. Regardless of your threat, I'll take my chances. You're still looking at a court-martial with the longest list of charges that have a chance to deliver you to the hangman.

"Lieutenant Clare, you're relieved of command of Third Platoon. I'm quite satisfied that Kilkenney"—referring to the Platoon Sergeant of First Platoon—"can take over on a temporary basis and do a hell of a lot better than you can. Furthermore, I don't want anybody in the company to know you continue to exist. So you're confined to your bunker starting now."

Crayley continued, thinking aloud, "I'm not going to tell anybody back there," he motioned over his shoulder in the direction of the American lines, "that you're out as a leader. Either Bozoni or Krill might try to send a replacement for you. I don't want that to happen. The odds are way too high that the chosen one would get taken out before he got a third of the way across that open plain behind us. This situation will stay right here on the top of Monastery until we get back."

A sudden idea hit Horace. "Here's something else for you to think about. No matter what happens to me, I'll make sure that a copy of the charges that will be brought against you gets back to your substitute father, the General. He certainly knows you turned out as a bad seed: a real pathological, misanthropic turd. He'll probably want to discuss your latest adventurers with your mother."

Ed's stomach lurched, but he said nothing.

Horace went on, "And, on second thought, I will tell Sergeant McCoy who probably already knows what you did to Ortega and the new kid, whose name you're not sure of, but, in fact, was Bullock. I'll tell him that if I go down, you're not to take over the company. If you were to do that, you'd get them all killed. If it happens with me, he's to tell Krill everything and let him work it out even if, or especially if, it means letting Wowser run the show. I'll give him something in writing to support what I tell him to do."

"If you get taken out, and I succeed to command," Clare paused, "then I'm in command, and we go to glory, all of us, if necessary, on my order. If that dotty old coot gets in the way, I'll kill him and the rest of those decrepit misfits who buddy with him if they try to back him."

They both waited, both almost out of words. Finally Ed said, "I'm reaching a conclusion that you won't court-martial me. You'll think it over and decide it's not worth the risk to you."

"I won't think it over, and I will do it. I'd like to dump you right now, but I can't get you off Monastery. If I tried that, I'd have to explain to Krill or Bozoni, and that would create a hell of a mess at just the wrong time."

"Yes, it would be tough for you to explain from up here your execution of that kid in the alley."

"Goddamn you, I'll not explain anything except what you did if you're dumb enough to raise that incident in your own court-martial."

Clare's stomach was in a turbulent froth. But his mind was sparking on a way to prevent his hated stepfather from seeing a venomous laundry list of court-martial charges that would carry the ultimate address of an Army hangman. That possibility had to be closed off.

As he started out of the command post, he stopped, his back to Crayley. He stood for some seconds, then slowly turned toward Crazy Horse, his face contorted into a mask of malevolent, almost maniacal, hatred. "Well, Horace, I don't think you'll do it. You just don't have the balls. But, just in case you might get a dose of courage when you leave here, you and I should try to work this out together, while we're still on this rock pile, to persuade you to see the errors of your way. Maybe we can pray a little together here in the monastery."

Crayley thought for a moment. "For now, you just go back to your hole and wait it out. I'll do what I have to do as soon as I can. In the meantime, you hope and I'll pray by myself that the action that's coming doesn't get into the north end. You keep your head down and stay in Third Platoon area, if they'll have you after what you've done to Ortega and Bullock."

"Oh, they'll have me. As Ortega and the kid left, I told the rest of them that you approved their stroll down the ramp, and later I told them you refused my request to take the platoon down to try to rescue them."

For the second time, Crayley felt like he had been slammed with a brick. He just looked at Clare. "You slimy bastard."

There was only sadness, with very little discussion, when daylight revealed the bodies of Ortega and Bullock at the bottom of the ramp. Neatly arranged on their backs, arms outstretched, weapons and boots gone, otherwise two wretched crosses in the dirt, starting to attract flies.

CHAPTER TWENTY

When Lieutenant Colonel Burley and Levinson decided to check the motor pool records for the Crazy Horse threesome, the sergeant had said, "How hard can it be?" He was about to find out how hard it could be. The motor pool was huge. It was the major vehicle transport facility for Central Tokyo, housing two hundred fifty-six vehicles of various sizes. He had only one sure date: the date of Luther's death. He decided to work backwards. He asked the motor pool for their records of use or turn-ins after use by multiple-officer occupants for the day of Corporal Potts' death, plus the five preceding days.

Right then the scent that was already several days moldy started to get rancid. In the first place, the records weren't very good. The motor pool administration was reasonably content if, at the end of each day, they had two hundred fifty-six vehicles inside the fence or use tags showing who had them.

Some of the vehicle tags showed multiple occupancy use. But, upon reflection, the pool thought that probably not all transport use had been so carefully recorded. Only the driver's rank, sometimes, was noted. Such detail about other occupants was not entered. On Luther's death day alone, there had been requests, check-outs, or check-in of one hundred eleven multiple-use jeeps of which seventy-six showed officer drivers. In the five preceding days, the total number was three hundred thirty-six. After several days of motor pool clerks combing listlessly through the files, a packet was put together for the CID review.

When the usage information and the four hundred twelve, maybe officer, maybe multiple-use, tags were dropped on Levinson's desk, he looked at the stack of papers as if someone had delivered a large, near-petrified turd on the flat surface and slid it gingerly toward him. And the really bad part, so far as the investigation was concerned, was that the Crazy Horse trio didn't appear on any of the tags in the stack. Their jeep, the record of which was still in the motor pool files, showed a single officer request, Major Dan Clare, for a jeep to be driven by Mr. Hamanaka.

Levinson saw his theory going down the toilet. He looked at the stack without touching it for two days, then decided to discuss the matter with the PM "The Luther Potts case is going nowhere."

"Explain."

So Aaron Levinson told Colonel Burley the really sad story of the four hundred twelve motor pool tags on his desk.

"And so, what's next?"

"I don't know. We don't have the people to try to follow four hundred and twelve leads. Probably a lot of them are back in Korea spread all over the landscape. Even if we found some, it would take two Army careers to check out the stories that they would tell."

"So maybe it was two pals that did him?"

"No, we've got nothing in that direction, especially if we can't check out their story of the three loots."

"So?"

"I'm stumped. Maybe this will end up in the too-hard basket. Let me fumble through it some more today. I'll come back tomorrow."

"Okay."

However, it was that very afternoon that the investigation opened for them.

Colonel Burley liked and admired Major Goetz. He was very pleased to have a combat officer of his reputation somewhat under the colonel's command, if only temporarily, because of Barney Goetz's enforcer role in the officer's clubs. He had asked the major to come to his office. Perhaps after a few minutes of polite conversation they would go to the club for a few convivial drinks. But they never made it.

After Goetz's short recitation of what he had been doing, it was the PM's chance to explain to the major how difficult his days were as Provost Marshal. In this litany of his burdens, the colonel got around to Luther Potts. He told Goetz how hard he, personally, had been working on this case; how he, personally, thought Luther's two pals had turned on him, but that his personal sense of fair play and justice required him to give the fullest attention to their story of the three lieutenants, which he personally thought was just a red herring the real killers were trying to drag across the trail. He then went on in great detail about the mass of records, mostly bad, which the motor pool had provided. He finished up by telling the major, manfully, that he, personally, would check through all of it so as to be sure to get the full story of whatever was available.

At the mention of "three lieutenants," a big one, a middle-sized one, and noisy little one, Goetz was pulled to attention. "The records don't give you any good lead, then?"

"No, they're not very helpful."

"I'm sure there's no connection, but I do know of three loots on R and R from Korea during your time window who may fit the 'big, middle, little' description."

"You do? How?"

"These three came into the club. Two were okay, but the little one was a cocky brat. He just got his first CIB and he was 'lord of the walk,' especially toward an engineer corporal who was making extra money as a waiter that day. I finally had to toss all of them entirely because of attitude of the little noise box. They all came in the next day to meet the little guy's brother, Dan Clare. You know Dan. He's a surgeon at Tokyo General."

"'Tiny Tim' was still mouthing off, and Dan could see he was pushing into trouble with me, so he came up with a place outside of town for them to cool off for a day or two."

Colonel Burley brightened. "Well, by god, that's a lead we'll have to follow. Thanks, Barney."

The next day, Levinson got busy. Sure that his brother had nothing to do with Luther's death, Major Clare was totally cooperative. He identified the Fuji View; no, he hadn't gone with them; didn't know what they did or who they saw, except he knew they had met at least one of the nurses at the hospital because she had mentioned meeting his brother; did know they returned on the same day that Luther went down; no, he didn't know what time they left the hotel or when they arrived in the city; no, he hadn't seen his brother, but knew he was back in Korea because he had received a short note thanking him for setting up the Fuji View outing.

The Fuji View itself was next on the schedule for Sergeant Levinson and Corporal Matsumoto. They took a leisurely ride in an open jeep on a beautiful day. The sergeant hoped that any interviews could be dragged out so that he could get two or three days of R and R for himself. The corporal just hoped that there would be a room full of Pachinko machines, a vertical pinball game activity to which he was addicted and which the hotel did not have.

No guests at the hotel when they got there had been in residence during the visit of the Crazy Horse gang. However, the hotel records were in good shape, and Levinson quickly obtained a list of occupants during the critical time period. But, even as he scanned it, he recognized the track of several artful dodgers. Major Clare had told them that the hotel's principal guest list was members of medical staffs from various facilities in and around Tokyo. But the list seemed to indicate that more than half the guests came from faraway units with strange sounding names. One captain identified himself as a member of the 416th Balloon Observation Group, supposedly stationed in Taiwan.

Matsumoto traveled an even murkier path. By telling the Mama-san the purpose of his visit involved the death of an American soldier, he might as well as told her that he wanted the help of hotel employees to assassinate the emperor. By the time the first interview was set up, it was apparent that Mama-san had given her orders. The hotel business was going very well. She had a nice repeat trade. By and large, the guests were pleasant, intelligent, and well mannered. The name of her hotel was not going to appear in any *Stars and Stripes* article concerning a dead GI in Tokyo.

Each member of the staff could barely remember if they had been to work yesterday, much less during the designated time period. The staff numbered more than sixty, but Matsumoto quizzed only seven. He got nothing and recognized that he could do it fifty, or a hundred, or a hundred and fifty times more with the same result, His last question to Mama-san was if any employee who had been at work on the day of departure was not present for questioning. Only one, a specialty gardener who came in once a week had been there on that day, and he was not due back for five days.

Back in Tokyo, the PM was told that the Fuji View evidence trail was cold, only the specialty gardener, maybe, was an interview prospect.

The three nurses were quickly located. Sure, they had met Dan Clare's brother, plus a tall likeable chap, Buddington by name, and an attractive, tough, but sensitive officer with the odd name of Crazy Horse. They had had dinner and a pleasant evening with them. They had not seen them the next morning, because they had taken a jeep for a picnic on the lakeshore. They had no idea when the three loots left the hotel.

On the identified work day, Mr. Matsumoto was back at Fuji View to interview Mr. Fukao, the specialty gardener. Mr. Toshio Fukao was seventy-seven years old. His specialty was rock-garden design. Upon his arrival for work, Mama-san told him that representatives of the U.S. military would be asking him a very few questions. And she also delivered the company line, which was simply the Japanese equivalent of "dummy up."

By the time Mr. Matsumoto arrived, Mr. Fukao was seething. This wasn't unusual, because Mr. Fukao was usually in a flaming bad mood after a short while tending the rock garden. Before Mama-san had been promoted to oversee the service and ground staff, two years ago, Mr.

Fukao had been an everyday employee. In fact, he had been one for thirty-eight years; his only job being the design and care of the forty-yard long rock garden paralleling the entry drive. Mama-san had three years less service, and Mr. Fukao thought it a great breach of protocol and good manners that he was now subject to her direction. He had nearly suffered an apoplectic fit when she reduced his work time to one day a week. His revised job now required only that he modify the garden design once a week, and the service staff was required to keep the garden clean and the weekly design immaculately maintained.

Of course, it was never maintained according to his clear eye and contemplative thought process, so that by the time he had spent an hour or so waiting for his new vision for the coming week to come into consciousness he was slipping into a red rage. He had already decided he would not be silent as ordered by Mama-san. She had told him nothing, but if it involved the U.S. Army and silence was the command, maybe if he told the truth, and he could never do more or less than that, it would somehow cause trouble for Mama-san.

After the appropriate greetings, Mr. Matsumoto launched his interview. His first questions confused Mr. Fukao.

"Were you here on the designated day?"

"Of course."

"Where did you work that day?"

"Right here, of course, on the rock garden."

"The whole day that you were here?"

"Of course." Mr. Fukao had no idea what these silly questions were about. Of course he would be here at the rock garden. This was his only job. Where else would he be?

"Did you see three U.S. Army officers on that day?"

"Of course. Many more than three. They were all around."

"No, I'm interested in three male officers. They were always together, a tall, medium, and short height threesome. Did you see something like that?"

To Mr. Fukao, who was five feet three inches, all American Army officers looked tall. "I saw many American officers, all sizes."

"Well, did you see any officers driving away in a jeep?"

"I saw many officers driving many jeeps. I don't know where they were going."

"Did you ever see a jeep with only three officers in it driving out of the hotel grounds?

"Yes."

"How many jeeps like that?"

"Just one."

"Just one, the whole day?"

"Yes."

"What time was that? Do you know?"

"Yes, it was 10:50 in the morning."

"How do you know it was 10:50?"

"A truck was to deliver a certain amount of smooth blue stones for the garden no later than 11:00. I had just looked at my watch and put it away when the jeep with three officers drove by."

Matsumoto needed a written statement. They went into one of the small hotel common rooms. The corporal dictated a statement containing the gist of Mr. Fukao answers to his questions. Mr. Fukao wrote in his own hand. After finishing it, he read it carefully and signed it, but did not give it to Matsumoto. He explained that such a letter had to have his personal seal on it, and the seal was at his home. He would stamp the seal on the letter and send it to Tokyo. The corporal gave him an Army envelope so that the letter could travel through the Army postal system.

Matsumoto's interview was finished, but there were problems that he didn't know about. The three officers Mr. Fukao saw were not Crayley, Buddington, and Clare. They were their three nurse companions from the night before, who were motoring for their lakeside frolic. The three infantry officers had left shortly after eight when Mr. Fukao, just arriving for work, had been in the tool shed getting his necessary equipment for the day's activity. When he saw the three nurses leave, the jeep was past him, and he saw only the backs of their heads. Their hair was coiled up on top of their heads and bunched under their standard-issue Army officer hats. So far as Mr. Fukao was concerned, he saw three people seated in a jeep, departing the grounds, who looked just like Army officers—which they were.

Matsumoto told the story of the Fukao interview to the PM and Levinson, including that he had obtained a written, signed statement which was on its way via Army post.

The colonel turned to the two of them, "Well, if the gardener's statement says that, it may put the cap on the three loots' investigation. But, you,"—nodding toward Matsumoto—"said "this old guy is really old, maybe"—pointing toward Levinson—"you ought to go to Korea, talk to those three."

"Okay, but let's wait till we see the Fukao statement."

Back in his own office, the sergeant was not happy. He'd said, "Okay," to the colonel about a trip to Korea, but he didn't mean it. A few months back, he'd gone to Korea to talk to a captain about a then-pending investigation. The PM had initially asked that the captain be returned to Tokyo so he could be questioned. A blistering reply came back from the captain's regimental commander. It told Colonel Burley in seething terms that the captain was busy "fighting his ass off." He would not be pulled from his company to accommodate the Tokyo military police exercises. If they wanted to talk to him, they could damn well send "one of their Twinkies to Korea."

Levinson pulled that detail, and he would never forget it as long as he lived. He was smart enough to wear a plain uniform without insignias, so they didn't know if he was a private or a field marshal. It didn't do any good. The regimental adjutant scalded his butt before he was sent off with a guide to climb two of the tallest, straight-up peaks he had ever seen. If the whole town of Tokyo had been tilted on its side, it would not have been as tall as those mountains.

When he found the company, they were spread along the crest of a high valley swale and they were awaiting a Chinese attack. Before nightfall, the captain he was to interview and who was the company commander handed him a carbine and assigned him to a squad. The Chinese came and came and came. Levinson was petrified. He never moved. He managed to stay out of it by hunkering down in one of the squad bunkers while the fighting swirled about him.

The next morning, he was able to ask the captain only six questions before the requirements of the situation pulled the commander away. Worse, there were a small number of Chinese behind them, between the company and the battalion headquarters. Levinson couldn't leave. He had to stay another night, during which he actually had to fire his carbine in the general direction of North Korea. Also, one of his bunker mates got drilled through the face, toppled off the firing port, and almost rolled over Levinson.

Levinson thought to himself, "I ain't going back to Korea to interview anybody. I'll shoot Luther's two friends, and we'll write it all off as a bad traffic accident."

Three days later, Mr. Fukao's statement arrived. Corporal Matsumoto was away on official business in Fukuoka. The PM was in Osaka on a boondoggle of his own. Levinson took the statement to one of the civilian clerks, Mr. Kawaguchi, for a translation. The critical part of the statement was that Mr. Fukao had seen three Army officers leave the hotel at 10:50 in the morning. The statement was translated as, "I saw the jeep with the three Army officers leave the hotel at 10:50."

Levinson seized on the single word—"the"—that, to him, being a declaration that meant that the gardener had actually identified and seen the three lieutenants that Levinson was interested in—not just any three Army officers in a jeep. That interpretation allowed him to finish his final report.

When the PM returned, Levinson told him, "We have the statement of an eyewitness that our three R and R visitors left the premises at 10:50 in the morning. Luther died about 11:30, give or take a few minutes, depending on when the other two guys wake up. There's no way under the sun that the three loots could have made it back to Tokyo by that time. It's a good two-and-one-half hour drive from the Fuji View. That's the end of it as to the three of them." he paused, "and we got nobody else. It's over. Let's move on."

The PM heard the conclusion then said only, "There's something bothering me, but I can't grab it. Let me think on it."

The PM's indecision was a little unsettling to Levinson. What more was needed? Usually, his investigation recommendations were routinely accepted. He was quite satisfied that the gardener's observation took the three R and R officers out of the picture. To him, Luther's file should go into the dead-letter box. They had no leads. The trail was cold. Time to get out of it and move on. He couldn't understand why the colonel wanted to hang on to it.

Unknown to Levinson, the PM had a different agenda. Lieutenant Colonel Burley didn't like Major Dan Clare very much. In fact, he didn't like him at all. Five months before, there had been a little unpleasantness in Burley's stockade, which resulted in nine prisoners, inside the wire for various minor offenses, being hustled to Tokyo General for repair of their officially minor injuries. But a few of them weren't so minor and one of the prisoners, the recipient of a broken nose, two cracked ribs, and a broken arm, was the nephew of the mayor of a large Midwestern city, who had the usual political friends. The anticipated outcry followed and included an investigation of Burley's guards, the actions of which had resulted in the nine prisoners taking a hospital tour. The investigation committee was not large, comprising only Army doctors and lawyers. Their report was foreordained: many prisoners had gotten out of hand, the guards responded, nine inmates got hurt, injuries not excessive in view of the need to regain control and establish order in the stockade. It noted that all prisoners had recovered and were back to regular assignments, which happened to be sitting out the rest of the sentences in the stockade.

One member of the committee hadn't gone along in the expected manner. Major Dan Clare had an inflammatory view of the guards' control techniques. He had actually tried, unsuccessfully, to file a minority report, which, if filed, would have done Burley's remaining career absolutely no good. In all his years of service, Burley had never forgotten or forgiven such breaches of etiquette. His memory flashed Major Clare's name through the "get even" part of his cortex frequently to remind him that payback was an accepted Army ritual.

When the PM had learned that Dan Clare's brother might legitimately be considered as part of the Luther Potts investigation, he had taken a few minutes of quiet contemplation reflecting that "what goes around, comes around." Though he had not displayed any undue enthusiasm for Levinson's investigation of the events at Fuji View Hotel, his hope that something good would come out of it gave him a warm feeling whenever the cares of his office tended to unduly burden him. That's why, when Levinson finally reported his conclusion that the three loots were not the guys they were looking for, the PM experienced a deflation of his private potential glee. He felt let down, and he wasn't ready to let go of it. So he told Levinson he would think on it, and he started to think.

Levinson waited for what he considered to be the appropriate polite time, while the colonel thought. Then, thinking that the colonel had lapsed into a comma, he started to leave. The PM said, "Wait."—Levinson turned—"Do we know where our suspects are?" Levinson noted the use of the word, "suspects."

The sergeant was puzzled. "They're back in Korea."

"Thanks," with a scowl. "Where in Korea, as between Pusan and the Yalu?—where? Find out their location. You may have to go over there and really nail this down."

Even though it was a warm day, Levinson was shivering as he went out of the PM's office.

CHAPTER TWENTY-ONE

Charlie Pope was the third side of a triangle, who with Harry Princeton and Boffo Mallen gave "old timer" support to Wowser's pronouncements—whenever their words of wisdom might benefit by quiet, and they thought subtle, further dissemination to the troops—by their clucking of tongues and sage wagging of heads. None of the men paid much attention to the three supporting players. They simply did, and quickly, whatever the first sergeant said. However, the three thought themselves pillars of their close community, and McCoy usually found a way to thank them for their efforts on his behalf.

Besides acting or actually being feeble and generally worn out, Charlie's other noteworthy attribute was his ugliness. He was the ultimate scumbag. He had a tired, lined, old face and hit-or-miss strands of hairy beard poking out of it at odd angles from strange places. Charlie's hair, what there was of it, contributed to the illusion of age. On top it was not uniformly laid out. It seemed to sprout in clumps as if small explosions inside his head had blown patches of stringy fiber through the hard surface. These trailing threads straggled down both sides of his face. His skin was concrete grey with flecks of yellow that randomly appeared and disappeared. There was a puffiness around two, small, spit-colored eyes and a mouth that fell off to a sagging oval on the left side.

Charlie's mouth gave him trouble. His remaining teeth hurt a lot. Much of the time, he had a habit of massaging them with his tongue, sometimes helped by a finger and occasionally by a soft, unlit cigar that rolled around in the left side oval. At such times, Charlie was always prepared to wince when one of his comrades likened the cigar in his face to a turd peeking out of a puckered asshole. He had heard that theme many times, and he had even answered to it some years ago at a now-famous roll call when the first sergeant of his company had bellowed at a soldier arriving late to formation, "Ass Face," the top sergeant had inquired, "where the hell have you been?" Getting no immediate response and thinking he had been ignored—a possibility not within contemplation—the sergeant let go again much louder, "Ass Face!"

At the other side of the formation, Charlie, startled to hear what he recognized as his call sign, shouted, "Present for duty. Present for duty. Always present for duty, Sergeant."

Charlie was fond of telling people, any people, "It's a hard life." When Charlie said it, people believed him. Actually, Pope did labor hard in his chosen line of work. But it wasn't soldiering, or at least not garrison soldiering. His particular ramble was being one of the Army's lost souls. Secure in the embrace of Mother Khaki, Charlie skittered through life on a serene sea of contentment—usually adrift in a fog bank. He was one of the walking welfare cases. In an organization in which everybody had somebody to lookout for, Charlie needed a whole platoon of keepers.

Always present, but never around except in the chow and pay lines, he was an uncapturable spot of light flitting through the vision of company officers who infrequently thought they saw him. But if they reached out to grab him, he wasn't there—or, he was on his way to sick call, or the chaplain, or the Red Cross, or to get the company mail.

Charlie became—very early on—a blender. He blended into the group, always on the edge. He got so he could blend into trees, bushes, mounds of earth, and later, into buildings, trucks, even tanks. Commanders of units had been surprised to learn that Charlie Pope was in their outfit. Always present for duty, but never seen and never available for work.

Charlie's special skill that permitted him the good life was that he was a facilitator. He could facilitate, in ways unknown, a menu of things arcane and bizarre that delighted those seeking his services.

Before his Army days, he had been a minor helper of a midlevel mob boss in New Orleans. Watching him and his organization, Pope had learned how many things could get done if law, morals, and ethics were not closely observed. So when in 1937, it had become necessary for Charlie—speedily, really speedily—to find a new line of work in a safe place, he had slipped into the Army recruiting office. At that time, a lot of men better than Charlie sought to join the Army and grab onto three squares a day and a dry bed, so his first attempt to enlist was rejected.

But Charlie's New Orleans boss had stepped in. This budding, but soon to be pruned, nabob supplied Charlie with two tall, sinuous girls just off the boat from Trinidad. Pope introduced these ladies to the enlistment sergeant, and the sergeant, fascinated by their lilting tongues, speech wise and otherwise, signed up Charlie and two other friends of the girls and would have enlisted Adolf Hitler, if they had asked him.

Pope entered a new, but still nonworking, phase of his life. He found it quite congenial. Many of those in positions to ease his burdens found his talents as a facilitator to be useful and most agreeable in a variety of ways. So Charlie prospered, comfortably and slovenly, right up to December 7, 1941.

After that, things had turned a little sour, especially when Charlie actually had to go overseas to a theater of war. But, after Adolf and Eva were barbecued in Berlin, and the victors cut up the pie, Charlie's duty in the occupation of Germany had been lush beyond his wildest dreams. But then came mid-June 1950, and after a period of time, which was enough to get him beyond the horror days of the first year in Korea, Charlie found himself on a boat and then, finally, in George Company with—he hoped—his old friend Wowser McCoy.

During his first survey of Monastery Ridge, McCoy had decided upon the job for Pope that would be the most likely to keep him occupied, out of the way, and least likely to get killed. After discussion with Charlie's platoon sergeant, Wowser told Pope he could rack out in

Boffo's bunker, but his job would be tending the generators. McCoy impressed upon him the critical importance of the power source, particularly for the company's radio communications. Radio batteries were always in short supply, and Captain Crayley—he told Pope—would throw him over the side if the generator failed and the batteries were dead.

The well-lit, but still musty cavern—slightly noisy, but warm—where the electric station resided was just fine with Charlie. He could spend as much, or as little, time as he liked down in the rock hole so long as the generators did their job.

Besides that, it was far enough into the rock that the sounds of any explosive clamor that was sure to take place would be hardly more than a muffled thump down in his hole. Charlie hated loud noises. They hurt his ears. They made his head twitch with a clanging ring. Because of this hurtful sound problem, he had a strong aversion to firing his rifle—a strange malady for an infantryman. Not only did firing his rifle hurt his ears, he did not like to clean his weapon. After the Iron Mountain debacle, the men of Charlie's platoon were convinced he never fired a shot during that aborted effort. All in all, the generator room assignment was a neat fit of a somewhat square peg into a nearly round hole.

CHAPTER TWENTY-TWO

Jen Po-Wei was thirty-six years old. He was a big man, well over six feet and just over two hundred pounds. Because of his size, attained while still in his midteens, the people of his village ridiculed him as an odd fit in their little community. His father put him to the hardest tasks on the family's tiny plot of land. He was loaned for a fee to others who needed heavy—usually grindingly ponderous—labor.

This family and village life made it easier for him, in fact, made him glad to be pressed into the service of the man who would become the nation's Great Leader when Mao's Communist force had passed through his area during his nineteenth year.

He had married, even though quite young for such an event, immediately prior to entering Mao's peasant army. The village chiefs had initially forbidden a marriage, but those elders had learned from a persuasive discussion with the local Communist commander, who having decided that Jen, and a few others, should serve a greater cause, also thought it a good idea for his new men to have loving memories of home.

Jen had been fighting since that year, 1935: first against various warlords, then against Chiang Kai-Shek's soldiers, then the Japanese, then again Chiang's Army, until Chiang's retreat and escape to Taiwan in 1949.

After that, Jen returned to his village for the first time since he left fourteen years earlier. He found he was respected, even admired. He was reunited with his wife who he barely remembered. He got acquainted with his thirteen-year-old son who he was pleased to see was not of the towering stature of his father and thus was better accepted by the villagers than Jen had been. His stay at home had been short because there was much work to be done in the new China, some of it requiring, from time to time, assistance from Mao's trusted veterans.

Peacetime duties, getting on with the new world order, had not lasted as long as Jen hoped they would. In June 1950, rumors circulated in his unit that a war was underway somewhere on the eastern edge of China. It didn't concern him, so he paid no attention to it. But, a short time later in early October, he received marching orders, and he found himself moving toward the Yalu River border between China and North Korea as part of a massive force of "volunteers."

With his unit he had gone into Korea in November. Soon, they were engaged in heavy fighting. He was surprised to find that the enemy soldiers were not only of South Korea, but also America. Initially the Chinese volunteers had great success, but after violent, massive Army sweeps north and south on the peninsula in winter and summer over some of the most tortuous mountains he had ever seen, so shatteringly freezing or suffocatingly hot that he thought he would not survive another season, he found himself sitting on the north side of a dry river plain, studying a rock tower in the middle of the plain, which was inhabited by Americans. He was studying the stone tower because he and a few of his men meant to go up on it. They would do so through a narrow cleft on the stone side facing him.

Jen was a small-group leader. Usually, he had sixty to one hundred men under his command. For his present assignment, he had thirty-five. Most of them were younger by a few years than he, but all were veterans of many years and all hand picked—a highly skilled team for this special project.

His group was in the ground less than a hundred yards in front of the north face of the tower. It had taken two nights to get this close through furtive, quick movements—a dash, a fast crawl—always hoping to avoid the illumination flares put up sporadically by the American artillery.

Two nights earlier while still distant from the tower, his team had watched the first probe, trying to spot the automatic weapons emplaced on the stone spire. His group was nothing like the drunken, or drugged, unfortunates who had danced around in the field. The reaction of the Americans did not hearten Jen. No haphazard panic firing: only one automatic weapon, then only rifles and grenades, which had been enough to reduce the probers to a mass of runaways, although more than half would ever run again.

The American reaction to the probe was important information to Jen. He now knew that his team was going against experienced soldiers. But he was confident that however experienced they were, they would not match his men who he knew had been fighting much longer than the men on the rock. The Americans brought men to Korea. They stayed for maybe, a year and a half but probably less; then they were gone. It was true, however, that many of them had been in a big war a few years before, and this group could be difficult, but generally, their young men could not match his veterans.

Jen's team was ready. They were all in the flat field with him, spread out, taking advantage of every hole, every depression, every bush to stay hidden during the day. They were awaiting favorable weather conditions, which they had been told would arrive by nightfall.

His men were still wearing the two-piece, quilted-cotton uniform that was their winter garb. It was not yet warm enough to discard these outer garments, particularly when they had to lay out in the river plain for two nights. They wore padded-cotton headgear with bulky ear flaps. Their shoes were poorly made of canvas like fabric with thin soles. Jen thought that such shoes were probably an advantage in the rocky trail climb that was to come. They had all entered the plain with a three-day supply of precooked food, mostly rice with some beans, peppers, and garlic.

The team was well armed. They had short-barrel machine rifles—not the latest Russian models, but with a high rate of fire and quite serviceable—automatic pistols, ample magazines or clips of ammo, several grenades per man, and each also carried three small packets of powerful explosive. A coil of rope went around each man's body, and every one of them also carried a thirty-inch length of thin pipe, two inches in diameter and packed with dynamite. These pipes had threaded ends to be screwed together to form a single pipe of any length. He had earlier learned that the Americans called them Bangalore torpedoes. Jen called them long stick bombs.

The pipes were critical to his task. The long stick bombs would be slid under the barbed wire and suspended booby traps heavily strung in the cleft trail. When detonated, they would blow the wire, booby traps, and any mines that lay close to the surface.

Jen's planning, but not his objective, stopped with his team's successful ascent to the top, and he did expect to get to the top. He reached that conclusion when he realized that the Americans could not fire directly into the notch trail. They were depending on the barbed wire and traps they had laid to keep the trail secure.

After reaching the top, his actions would depend on circumstances and targets of opportunity. His leader had suggested two desirable targets, if either or both appeared possible once the team had scaled the tower. The first was the American CP. If this command post could be located and eliminated perhaps the entire position would be won. The determination of a second target had been arrived at by observation. The Chinese had seen through small openings in the rock walls of the bunker rooms that illumination, though not sharply bright, was available at all times. Also, twice they had been startled by a large high-intensity light shining down the south ramp. This beam had been sited by Horace to give the company visibility if movement was observed or sensed. Crazy Horse had tested the lamp twice for short periods each time; partly to assure himself it worked and partly for the enemy. It would give them something to consider if they were thinking of a nighttime silent sneak up the slope.

The illumination in the rock did give the Chinese commander something to consider. He told small-group leader Jen-Po that the

Americans must have a power generator in the stone tower that not only provided light but would also power radio communication. With land wire gone, if the team could find and destroy the generator, the American commander would have only short-lived batteries. A communication failure might be of great benefit when Jen's leader decided to launch his full-scale attack. So the team's second possible objective was to find and disable the generator.

He accepted the two suggested objectives, but Jen knew that his principal purpose was to create as much surprise, fear, and havoc as possible while learning as much as possible about the position. He allowed only short spells of worrying about whether anyone would be able to take back any information to his superiors.

In the initial stages of his planning he had thought he might be able to cause enough terror and panic in the close confines of the bunkers that he and his assault team could capture the stone tower. But, after watching the probe, that possibility did not look promising. Nonetheless, orders were orders, so they would do a lightning strike with, he hoped, maximum damage. Then, they would get out as quickly as they could with as many of his men as were still alive and moving.

CHAPTER TWENTY-THREE

On the sixth and seventh days, the weather continued to worsen. By late afternoon on the seventh, the wind was howling down the flat river course. Towering storm clouds were building up. Under them, low, thin, streaking clouds of mist slammed against the prow nose of the ridge. Main Street became a wind tunnel as air currents channeled down its length. The men of G Company kept well away from the entrances of their bunkers, finding tasks that they could do against the back walls of their stone cells. Finally, as night fell, the storm broke. Lightning streaked around the monastery with photoflash intensity. Magnificent low-register thunder followed with such booming majesty that even in the bunkers the men could feel the vibrations. Fat drops of rain, too heavy to be carried by the wind, drove straight down on the company in a roaring deluge.

At the first lightning stroke, Charlie Pope jumped to one of the firing ports of the bunker he shared with Mallen. He knew the cannon shot of thunder was coming. He wanted to see what he was in for after the first shot. Eye-numbing slashes filled the sky as far as he could see.

"Well, Boffo, I think I must check on the generator. With this storm and all, I certainly must keep full juice on line."

"Sure, Charlie. Tend to your power station. I'll see ya when the weather clears."

Pope was gone in a second. He grabbed his rifle, two blankets, some K-rations and was across Main Street and into the corridor leading to the generator station before the second thunderclap.

Almost directly below Boffo, but far below, was Jen Po-Wei. To him the storm was a blessing and a curse: a blessing because what he intended to do would be helped by it and a curse because the pouring water could turn notch trail into a plunging cataract. As the storm increased, he waited for an expected call. He cradled an American field telephone to his chest. It had been taken long ago in the early days of the war. As they had moved across the plain to get into position, a wire trailed behind them back to his superior who would tell him when to move. The phone vibrated against his chest. He could not hear the raspy bell. He listened. He looked at the lighted dial of the watch his commander had given him and which must be returned. He said only a few words, then put the phone on the ground. He would not use it again.

His team was within forty yards of the tower. The eight men he had designated were close to him. They had already gathered the sections of long stick bombs from most of the other men. Jen gave his orders. The bomb team stood up for the first time in two days and moved toward the cleft trail. They had no concern about being seen in the raging storm.

Jen thought it wouldn't be difficult to get the stick bombs into place. He had a good view of the Americans when they had booby-trapped the steep trail. They had wired and mined only the middle third of it. Leaving the bottom of the trail open gave the Chinese all they needed. Jen's team quickly screwed the pipe lengths together and, moving well into the trail opening and some distance up, they laid the long pipe on the path and slid it upward, screwing sections on to extend its length. The pipe moved easily under the lattice work and barbed wire. It was not heavy enough to detonate pressure mines under the dirt, and, Jen hoped, any trip wire would be at least six inches above the trail.

The eight men returned to Jen in less time than he had allotted for the task. On the hour, a heavy salvo of mortar shells hit in several places on the top of the tower and on the First Platoon bunkers over-looking the south ramp. Jen had kept the electric box. He attached the wire extending back to him from the lowest section of pipe. He gave the box handle a sharp crank. The Bangalore torpedo blew, but Jen could not distinguish the blast in the roar of the rain, thunder, and exploding mortar shells.

Jen and his men were up immediately and trying to sprint up the trail—but stumbling and lurching through the mud in their now sodden, heavy clothing. They made it through the blasted middle portion without losing a man and kept going. As the path became more vertical, they started up the rock sides of the notch. It was this move that nearly broke the back of the team. Water was now pouring down the notch. As they scratched for handholds, searched with toes, and probed with the soles of their shoes for a foothold on the nearly unclimbable slick stone walls matted with slippery bits and pieces of vegetation, water drenched and soaked them and their heavy loads. Jen wondered if the storm by itself would defeat them, but he would not let that happen. Leading by his example and will, he continued to push them upward through the waterfall.

In the CP, Crazy Horse jerked to attention with the arrival of the enemy mortar rounds. "What the hell is that for?" he inquired of the room. Quickly, he was on the wire phone to First Platoon.

"Noma, what do you see on the ramp?"

"Can't see much. One hit on the ramp. A lot on us."

"Well, they won't come until they turn off their tubes. And I doubt they will try to come up here with any size force in this weather."

"I'm with you."

"Okay, when the mortars stop, keep a sharp eye on that avenue into your position. Let me know if they start up in your direction."

Horace turned to Wowser. "Which way will they come?" Wowser just shook his head.

Jen and the first of his men were wedged into the rock at the top of the notch before the mortars ceased firing. He pressed the glowing dial of this commander's watch to his right eye. As the last rounds exploded, he and two men went through a narrow passageway, sliding along the streaming wet wall of a bunker and stepped into Main Street. He took quick glances right and left down the street. Though the illumination was weak, it was enough. He gave himself the slightest moment to appreciate the resources of the Americans. Imagine, lights in this sort of place.

The open entrance of a bunker was three feet from them. Jen looked back down the narrow passage. It was full of his men pushing toward him. It was time to start. He motioned to the first of his two companions, who pulled pins from two grenades and looked at Jen, who nodded. The men tossed the grenades with an easy underhand motion into the bunker.

After Charlie Pope left to attend the generators, Mallen decided to get comfortable, maybe get a little shut eye before taking his sentry turn. He also decided he was hungry. He crouched over a ten-in-one rations box in the corner and started rummaging through the food. He found what he was looking for, a can of weenies and beans and some crackers. Like everybody else, he carried his dime-size can opener on his dog tag chain and was removing it from around his neck when he heard two hissing objects enter the bunker.

Mallen hit the floor and started rolling. "Grenades, Jesus, grenades!" was his instant thought. He was rolling behind the ration box as the explosions came. The lower two thirds of his body was not behind anything. The searing fragments ripped into him.

At the instant of the explosion, Jen and one man were through the entrance, their short barrel burp guns already spraying the room in two directions waist high. No one in the room. Had they launched their raid against empty bunkers? Where were the American devils? Then, in the corner, they saw one figure on the floor. He probably hadn't been hit by the midlevel rip they had delivered.

Mallen could not move his legs and didn't want to move his body as the automatic fire lashed above his head. It stopped. He couldn't help himself. He pushed up on one elbow and saw two bulky figures in the center of the room. He was still hungry. Where had his dinner gone? They saw him. One looked at him, pointed his weapon and fired.

Boffo didn't have time to register on who these people were. He just died.

Jen looked around. It appeared to him that all his men were in the street or crowding at the passageway outlet. He wanted to find the Command Post. Now he was glad that the storm was still roaring on them. In weather like this, it was nearly impossible to maintain command control. But, up here, the narrow street kept his team in close physical proximity. They could not be driven into dispersed clumps by this vicious weather.

Jen thought the CP must be toward the south end, where any commander would know that if a serious Chinese attempt were to be made, it would be up the south ramp. He indicated to his men the direction they would take. They started, moving cautiously but steadily through the raging weather, throwing grenades, and splattering automatic fire through any opening.

The first two bunkers they came upon were killing grounds: seven men in the bunkers, all down after the grenades and heavy fire through the entrances. But, from two bunkers just ahead of them, on opposite sides of the street, came the first response; a Browning automatic rifle from one side fired short bursts. From the other side two rifles, one near ground level, the other higher up, both fired blindly down the street. Two of Jen's men went down. The others pushed back into the bunkers they had just blown out. Jen gave quick orders. Disciplined heavy fire was directed at the Americans. Jen held up to see if they were suppressed. In less than a minute, the Chinese started to move again, more slowly this time.

The assault team was headed in the right direction. Horace's CP was closer to the south end. Despite the deluge still pounding them, George Company could damn quick recognize grenades and automatic weapons inside their own perimeter.

"Where the fuck is that coming from?" yelled Wowser as the sounds of the moving street battle reached them.

Even as he reached for the phone to the platoons, Horace issued his first order, "Kill all the lights." Power lines from the generator were routed through the CP. McCoy was closest to the distribution board. He jerked the switch and all illumination on the street and in the firing bunkers went out. The captain grabbed Trent, "Get to the entrance. What do you see?"

Trent, timid and very unhappy, peeked around the corner just as the lights went out. He went blind. But, just as he was pulling back into the CP, there were two explosive lightning strokes. For an instant everything was revealed, and he could see the length of the street in perfect clarity. Nobody in view.

Horace spoke to his platoon leaders, thinking much faster than he could talk—then remembering he had to speak slowly so he could be understood over the wire—and took a heaving, deep breath. "The Chinese are up. They must have come by the notch trail. So far I think they are staying in the street. They may be moving south, wait," he looked at Trent, who shook his head, couldn't see them—"Everybody stay in bunkers. And that means everybody. Do not move out. I'm going on top of the bunkers. Give me a minute to get up. Keep your fire in the street, and lay it on. And, for crissakes, remember three or four of us will be up on the roof! Out."

The CP had a narrow stairway to an opening to the roof. From there, it was easy to move along the tops of the bunkers down the length of Main Street. Crazy Horse looked around the bunker. Not a group to inspire confidence for what he had in mind. "Harry,"—motioning at Princeton—"you and Trent take those"—pointing at two shot guns. "You,"—jabbing at Fisco, the new man—"ever fire one of these?"—he handed over a Thompson submachine gun. Fisco, wide-eyed, was barely able to nod. "Good, you and I will use a couple of them to fire down the street ahead of us. Harry and Fred will clear out the holes and the corners." Trent winced. To all of them, Horace said, "Take all you can carry."

Princeton and, reluctantly, Trent each grabbed a bag of shotgun shells and three or four grenades. Fisco slung two bandoliers of Thompson magazines around his neck. The captain loaded up and also stuck two phosphorous grenades in his pocket.

Horace turned to McCoy. "You and Cochise stay here. If you can raise anybody on the radio in this storm, tell 'em what's happening. Send it clear. Give any orders to the platoons you think are necessary. See you in church."

Crayley turned to his team. "Let's go," he said, pushing the three toward the stairs. Princeton went up, Fisco pushing him from behind. Trent was frozen. Horace, behind him gave him a gentle prod with his gun barrel. He leaned toward him and in a conversational tone said, "Get your ass in gear, Trent. The party's starting."

Trent was locked into his space. This had not been covered in his classes at Yale. He couldn't do it. His mouth was suddenly full of heavy, sour mush. He had a high-pressure, critical need to piss. He would not go up on that roof. The captain was in his ear again, speaking in a near whisper. "C'mon, Fred. We're needed topside. Be sure to take an umbrella."

Somehow Trent willed his legs to move up the stairs. When he emerged on the roof, the howling storm nearly smashed him. The rain, not drops, but jet spears traveling flatways across the roof with the driving force of huge waves, was so thick he could breathe only by covering his mouth with his hand. Again, he was riveted immobile. He looked numbly at Harry.

"For crissakes, kid, get with it. We got work to do," Harry said as he pushed Trent across the roof toward the street. Crazy Horse's four-man fire team was finally organized and starting out just as, on the street below, Jen was starting to move his men, in short, quick rushes, making sure that each bunker they passed contained only dead or those too wounded to care. Crazy Horse's crew moved faster, trying to close with the invaders.

The Chinese, still a long distance up Main Street, were continuing south toward the CP. They cleared one more bunker, which had only two men in it. As they regrouped and started south again, there was a sudden lull in the storm. The wind stopped. The rain ceased. It became nearly quiet. From behind them to the north, they heard loud talking. They did not understand the language. If they had, they would have known it was a comedy show on the Far East Radio Network.

In a bunker almost on the northern rim of the monastery, five members of the patrol that Ortega had earlier taken to the Poppy Bowl were trying to enjoy a program beaming from the Armed Forces station in Seoul. They had no awareness of what was happening. The raging storm and blaring radio had masked the sounds of the fire fight going on to the south of them.

Kimball, the senior man in the bunker, was trying to hear McCoy on the wire net. He shouted for the radio to be quiet. Hardesty, who had assumed control of the entertainment, reached for the volume knob, turned it the wrong way, and the program blasted even louder just as the storm went eerily quiet. Hardesty quickly reversed the knob, not off, but softer. It was too late. Jen had heard it. He decided that the voices were probably from the American CP. He stopped his men, gave orders, and the group turned and started north.

Horace, now on the roofs, was trying to locate the Chinamen somewhere in the street below. He couldn't find them, until a burst of weapons fire pinpointed their positions. Crazy Horse went after them. But now his fire team was trailing them instead of charging toward a head-on collision. Running along the rooftops, they caught up with the back of the Chinese assault group. Even in the driving rain, but helped by the continual lightning flashes, Crayley could see far enough ahead to realize there were a hell of a lot of Chin-ee boys on Main Street.

Princeton pulled Trent to the edge of a roof motioning with his shotgun at the backs of the enemy who were moving at a fast walk up the street throwing grenades and firing into openings. The nearest of them was only ten yards away. Trent, who was still terrified, could not bring himself to even look at them. He tried to pull out of Harry's grasp. Princeton put his mouth to Trent's ear, "You cowardly fuck, just point and let fly." Trent swallowed the heavy rancid bile in his throat, took a slight lean over the edge of the roof, pointed his gun at the backs of the enemy below him, and, at the same time as Harry, pulled the trigger.

Five of the Chinamen went down. Trent was shocked. "My God. These things really work." He pumped a round in, fired, and saw one head disappear in a splendid pulpy mush; pumped again, fired, two more hits. "Hell, this was all right. It was better than that. It was,"—he fought for the word—"exhilarating." Another round fired—a miss. The Chinamen nearest Harry and Fred had scrambled into the bunkers they had just cleared. That didn't help them. The angle of the walls and the narrowness of the street made it impossible to get a clear shot up at this sudden source of trouble, big trouble. All Trent and Princeton had to do was step to the edge of the roof and shoot, then duck back a few paces, and they were unhittable.

Trent stepped to the edge. Two Chinamen were cautiously peering out a bunker entrance. As they looked upward, their faces were pelted by the driving rain. They pushed out farther, searching the roof line. Fred fired. The two heads exploded. "Hot damn. This is better than sex." He became, strangely, aware that he had what, in another time and place, would have been a very serviceable erection. But he had no trouble realizing that there was nothing he could do with it in the present circumstances. For good measure, he let fly with another round. "This is absolutely marvelous. Where are some more of these Chink bastards?"

The captain and Fisco moved up with the two shotgun shooters. They were keeping up steady automatic fire into the street and into any opening that might shelter the enemy. Men in the bunkers, both ahead and behind Jen, were firing mostly blindly down the street, which was thickening with flying lead.

A bunker just ahead of them had a large opening to the roof. While Trent and Harry were at street edge, three of the Chinese attacking force started through the roof entry. Crayley saw them first, and before they could bring their weapons to bear, he cut them nearly in half. They flopped like cut-string marionettes back down through the opening.

Trent thought if there were three, there were more. He ran across the roof holding two grenades. He managed to pull the pins on both as he continued to hold them in his fists. As he neared the entry, he let the safety handles pop off. With two seconds to spare, he reached the roof opening and dropped the grenades through. There was an almost instantaneous blast within the bunker. Trent bent over the hole, poked the muzzle of his shotgun in and waggled it around firing twice. He looked into the room. There were five or six lumpy forms not moving except for one who seemed to be struggling to get up.

Trent was surging with maniacal rage. He was savoring and feeding it. He aimed again and pulled the trigger. The head of the struggling lump disintegrated into bits of meat and bone vapor that swirled around the room. Adrenaline was pumping him like a balloon. He felt he would soar into the storm. He detached from his body, looked down at himself and what he was doing—"Looking good"—he complemented himself. He remembered Crazy Horse telling the recruits, "We fight to stay alive"—yeah, that's what it's about—but he never expected it would be so satisfying.

Crazy Horse and Fisco were at the edge of the roof, maintaining constant fire down the length of the street. The Chinese were being hit from their front from the bunkers farther north and from the four-man wrecking crew at their back and over their heads.

Jen decided it was time to leave. He knew that he was not going to capture this place by himself, and he was starting to wonder how many of his team would make it off the stone pillar. Two shrill bleats on his whistle; orders were shouted. Three men started firing wildly at the roof line behind them, trying to keep the GIs away from the edge. Four men at the front started moving very rapidly, throwing grenades in front of them, and quickly following up the explosives by spraying into the bunkers as they moved by, leaving more firepower to pour into the blown rooms from others of their comrades hurrying along behind them.

Crayley and Fisco raced forward to catch up with the retreating enemy. Horace saw three of them slip into a corner where the street made a slight jog. He fired into the blocked space hoping ricochets would do the job. He reached even with their hiding place on the opposite side of the street, pulled the pin on a phosphorous grenade, and pitched it into the dark angle. It bounced off the walls and exploded in the confined space. A dazzling burst of light was followed by wild screams. The three men, their quilted uniforms and hair starting to burn and showering sizzling incandescent flecks on their faces and hands, lurched out of their corner. Crazy Horse hit them with a heavy burst, and they toppled into the street, their bodies sputtering in the rain.

Jen kept his team moving, clearing bunkers, trying to hold off the rooftop attack. He no longer heard the loud voices that had turned him around earlier, but he was still searching for the company CP.

In the Ortega squad room, they knew the Chinese were advancing toward them. Kimball tried to get his group ready. Rollins and Fine moved closer to the entrance. Kezar started opening another box of grenades. Hardesty, reaching for his helmet, knocked the radio off its rock ledge. It hit the floor with a loud squawk and blared for an instant until crushed by Kimball's boot.

Jen's head jerked to the sound. The CP had announced itself again. Strangely, it seemed to be in the second to the last bunker from the north end. Two grenades were thrown along the street in front of the entrance; a third followed a couple of seconds later. The first two went off together, clearing the entry. Rollins and Fine shielded by pillars on either side of the entrance, jumped into the entry opening hoping to beat the charge they knew would be coming after the blast. The third grenade blew them lifeless back into the bunker.

Jen and the first man following him rushed in, firing at all corners of the room. Hardesty was hit and fell down still trying to find his helmet. Kezar got off one shot—a miss, then was stitched by a five-shot pattern. Kimball, with the wire net phone still to his ear, felt for an instant a rip across his chest. Jen looked closely. Not much equipment for an American CP, but five enemies down. He fired a short burst at each body, made another quick scan of the bunker, and hurried out the entrance.

At first, Charlie Pope could not hear the sounds of the fight overhead. But, as Jen's team moved north, they came to the tunnel corridor leading to the generator room. Then Charlie could hear very well what was happening. As he thought on the activity above, he decided that his room was too well lit. Even though all lights were off, the control panel of the operating generator was illuminated, and it was enough to cast a shadowy glow throughout the room. But there was nothing he could do about it except shut off the generator, and he knew he couldn't do that. He was very sure that Crazy Horse would be pretty well pissed if they suddenly lost all power.

He moved as far away from the entrance as he could. He went behind the two spare generators sitting near the far wall from the entrance. There were several equipment boxes nearby. He dragged them around the spares and hunched down behind the pile with his eyes on the entrance.

Just as Jen's commandos went by the generator tunnel, Fisco had caught the end of the group with two short bursts. In automatically jerking away from Fisco's shots, two of the Chinamen had dodged into the tunnel. By then, Trent and Princeton's guns were booming at the tunnel entrance. Hoping to find a way around the fire point, the two scurried down the dark passage way. They could see a dim flutter of light coming out of the rock wall ahead of them, and they sensed a gentle rumble of machinery that seemed to come from the light source.

They pushed on and came to Charlie's safe hole. They peered cautiously into the room. It was empty except for machinery. Realizing they had stumbled onto one of their leader's objectives, they saw an opportunity to redeem themselves for failing to stay in the fight going on above them. They moved to the whirring machine. They quickly fixed two packets of explosives to it. Then, back at the entrance, they placed more explosive around the entry.

Charlie watched them get ready to blow the generator and entomb him in the rubble. Their backs were to him. "Enough," he thought. "Enough is already too much." Pope stuffed bits of cotton waste into his ears, uncoiled his body, and stood up in a half crouch. His rifle was held at waist level pointing in the general direction of the two Chinamen. From fifteen feet away, he fired the full eight-round clip as fast as he could pull the trigger. The modest recoil of the rifle resulted in a neat dispersal pattern. All eight shots hit the two demolition experts: five into one of them, three for the other. They went down without ever seeing Charlie.

Pope reflected on the event for a moment. Strange, his ears didn't ring and his head didn't hurt as much as he expected. That was good, but there was a downside. Now it was clear his rifle had been fired, and somebody was sure to make him clean it.

The battle in the street, in the bunkers, and on the roof was raging with lunatic intensity, and it was going on in a thunder storm gone mad. The wind had risen to what seemed like typhoon force. The monastery was the vortex of a swirling jet stream. Main Street was a wind tunnel with its pedestrians being slammed and bounced against the confining bunker walls. Rain was driven down, sideways, and up. It was coming like horizontal grapeshot. Men felt like they were underwater, pulling for the surface, gasping for air. Lightning pulsed all about them, illuminating, with accompanying thunder rolls, the scene like a dance hall spinning globe spotting the inmates of the asylum.

Crayley was on the roof edge. The slanting driving rain pinging off his eyes and permitted him only a misty view of the street below. He was searching for the retreating Chinamen, but could see only the backs of two of them running for the north rim, trailing the remainder of the assault force, somewhere ahead of them.

Two quick lightning strikes cleared his vision. There, down below much closer, was one of them in the entrance of a bunker firing in staccato machine bursts and swinging the barrel so that he hit roof lines on both sides of the street. Horace leveled down on him. The movement caught the eye of the man below who stared at Crayley. Horace swung his weapon down toward the man, but Crayley did not shoot. At the last instant, he recognized the outline of an American helmet. And he recognized more. The shooter below was Ed Clare. For Horace, the speed of the scene abruptly slowed to a jerky, plodding motion illuminated by strobe flashes of lightning. Ed was aiming his carbine at him. He threw himself onto the roof even as he saw Clare's trigger finger close. A burst from the carbine, on full automatic, chipped the edge of the roof at his feet. He took off his own helmet, squirmed onto the roof of the next bunker and cautiously peered over the ledge. Clare, searching the roof line, saw him, snapped off two wild shots and jumped backward into the bunker.

The realization of what was happening was like a stunning body blow, which quickly became a surging rage. His mind raced. Clare knew that Crayley's team owned the roofs, and he had been waiting for him, hoping to take him out, hoping to get command of the company and take it to his version of glory land, attempting to solve all his problems with one shot. But Horace had seen enough, fast enough. Action became real time again. Venomous acid bile was forced back down his throat. He felt a soothing calmness as he acknowledged and accepted the decision that Ed had made for him. A phrase came to him, "Well here we are Ed, working this out together just as you suggested."

Fisco was beside him on the roof. The captain pointed at the bunker, yelling to Fisco above the roar of the storm, "One of them is in there! You pour it through the window. I'll unload through the entrance."

A lone Chinaman, racing to catch up with his disappearing comrades, suddenly appeared directly below them. As he passed the bunker, he paused to fire a short burst from his machine pistol into the room. Horace shouted, "Mine," and moved to take out the runner. Crayley fired at the enemy soldier, who was propelled through the entrance, sprawling on the dirt floor with one foot in the street. Fisco started ripping Thompson machine gun fire through the open window. Satisfied that the Chinaman was down, Horace waited a moment, then laid three long bursts through the bunker entrance. With the Chink obviously taken out, Fisco wondered why the captain kept shooting, but he took the cue, slammed another magazine into this weapon, and put half the new load through the window.

Jen was in serious trouble, and he knew it. One more bunker ahead and then he would be fighting only a rear guard action, while what men he had left would try to get away. The Chinese made it to the north end of Main Street. Here they could get up on top of the bunkers. Five men were ordered up to hold off the Americans from behind rock extensions of the perimeter wall. The first two were met by Crayley and Trent and cut down at the roof edge. The other three managed to scramble behind the rock shields where, according to Jen's orders, they would try to hold off the topside Americans, who were tearing their team apart.

The rest of the Chinamen shrugged off the ropes they carried made quick splices, secured the lines, and tossed them over the rock face. Immediately, they went over the side in a hurried, almost falling, descent. Jen took a quick look at his three men on the roof; they were certainly lost. He knew they understood that a small group leader was too important to join their defense. He went off Monastery in a quick slide to the ground.

Harry and Trent managed to get to a tall stone chimney close enough so that the three Chinese were within shotgun range. They kept up a rattling fire as Crayley and Fisco moved in, then, all four closed on the Chinamen, firing rapidly. One of the Chinese broke, leaping for an escape rope. The other two died on the roof. Trent rushed to the parapet where the escaping man had gone over. He was still on the rope going down rapidly, hand over hand. Trent leaned over with his shotgun in one hand. He watched the man for a few seconds. Then, casually, pulled the trigger. The man dropped to the rocks below. "Good," said Trent.

◆   ◆   ◆

With the last Chinaman in a heap at the bottom of the tower, Crayley gave orders to stay in the bunkers to await the mortar barrage that would surely come. It came, but it didn't last long.

Horace asked the platoon leaders for a careful head count. No response was received from Third Platoon at the north end. McCoy and two men headed that way. It was bad where the last minutes of the attack had taken place. The platoon leader was dead, and the other bunkers of the platoon had more dead and wounded. It was in the next to last bunker that Wowser came upon the men of Ortega's patrol. He had difficulty recognizing Hardesty. He saw the form, he knew the man, but his face was that of a scowling old man with sagging folds sliding down his forehead and his hairline nearly resting on his eyebrows. McCoy looked closer and understood what happened. Hardesty had been hit in the back of the head. The skin and muscle holding his face in place had been severed so that those features slid toward his chin, making a thick layer of folds held up by attachment to his jaw. He looked ancient.

McCoy returned to the CP where the list was being made up. He gave the count, which included Lieutenant Clare. The, he motioned the captain outside. "I thought you might want to see Ed."

"I'll see them all. Was there anything special about him?"

"Well, yes and no," Crayley waited, "somehow Clare and a Chink got in that room together and decided to turn this into their private war. There was a real lead hailstorm in that place; rock walls were ripped in every direction by ricochet hits. It was like the two of them were run over by a threshing machine." He waited for Horace's reaction.

"Strange how the two of them ended up in the same bunker at the same time."

"The thing that's odd to me is how it was able to go on so long when they were only about five feet apart blasting at each other." There was silence as McCoy looked at his score sheet again.

After a long moment, Crayley said, "I want you and Trent to put together an action report that will get Harry and Fisco and Trent—boy that Trent was a surprise, he was great—good citations out of last night's work. And get creative. Include Lieutenant Clare for a big one." He paused, "His father will like that."

◆   ◆   ◆

George Company had won the round, but at a stiff price: twenty-one dead, two more who would go soon, and another eleven who would survive but were out of action. But it was not one sided. The other count was twenty-four dead Chinamen, no wounded. The bodies went over the side of the north parapet, away from the prevailing wind.

Even before the box score was completed, General Krill was on the radio. Crayley had Cochise give the report. There were several questions from the general with answers from Horace translated by the two brothers. Finally, Cochise said to his captain, "The general wants to know if we can hold out."

Crazy Horse thought for a moment. Then took the hand set from Cochise. He fingered the "speak" button a few times to simulate static or other transmission trouble, then, "Gibraltar Six, this is Crazy Horse. We're having some radio problems, but in answer to your last question—Hell yes, damn straight, we can hold here. We can stay here till Christmas. We're still waiting for them to get serious. Out."

By first light, the rain had stopped. Order was returning. In the First Platoon at the ramp end, Private Robinette, a new man who had come up with the last batch of replacements just before the move to the monastery, was still pumping adrenaline even though the First Platoon had not been in the fight. Still, as far as Robinette was concerned, it had been a hell of a battle, and he had been in the thick of it. He was exulting about the magnificence of their victory. He was out in Main Street excitedly striding about when he became aware of a bad smell, a very foul odor. He stopped his arm waving bravado when be became aware of an unpleasant, sodden, sticky wetness around his lower calf where his pants were bloused into his combat boots. He investigated. It came to him suddenly. He was shocked. "Who shit in my pants?" he demanded of the group around him. "Who did it?" He got no answer. He couldn't fathom how such a thing could happen.

His squad leader spoke to him. "Remember McCoy's speech a little while back?"

Robinette thought, "I don't remember real good. It wasn't much."

The squad leader replied, "He told you to keep a tight asshole. Now you know why."

CHAPTER TWENTY-FOUR

The Provost Marshal was in is office doing the cross word puzzle in his daily Far East edition of the *Star and Stripes*. His schedule was open most of the day, except for lunch with Major Goetz. On his way in that morning, he had seen Sergeant Levinson who had been out of the office, up north, for a few days on coordinating matters with the PM in the Sendai area. Seeing Levinson, he recalled he was still thinking on the Luther Potts case, and he told the sergeant to see him after lunch. He entered, "Levinson—1400" on his appointment calendar, thinking as he did that he should get his mind set on what he wanted to do. So he started to think on it.

He still liked his first thought. Send Levinson to Korea to determine if the gardener's observation could be verified by the participants. If so, it was probably over. If not, then it was a real nice piece of detective work that could lead to a short column, probably on about page four of the *Stars and Stripes*, which might be a good entry on Burley's record in the event that General Ridgeway might be looking for a new PM at Far East Headquarters. And, quite incidentally, of course, such result might give vascular surgeon, Dan Clare, heartburn for which he didn't have a cure.

He reviewed the file in his mind. His office had drawn a blank. Basically, he was nowhere. Levinson's report, still on his desktop, said end it. It was just one that had gotten away from them. He thought further, asking himself if any outside voices were being heard. No, that sector was quiet. Luther's trucking company had quieted down to the point of silence. At first, members of the company had been noisily vocal about the progress in the investigation, but as time passed and, unknown to Burley, especially as the enthusiasm of Fanelli and DeBow gave way to cautious hope that Luther's ghost would find a different place to haunt, concern of those two for Luther started to turn even more inward to their own interests. They had successfully planted, in the trucking company, their initial explanation that they had been attacked by five strangers. Although they dearly wanted to tie the three lieutenants to Luther's death, they had determined not to open that can of worms; they had decided that the matter of Luther's knife work on the littlest lieutenant, which nobody knew about, could not be cleverly explained at this late stage. Inasmuch as it looked to them like they were being forgotten, they decided to let sleeping corporals lie.

Colonel Burley recognized that no one, and nothing, was pressuring him on this one. But the idea of sticking it to Dan Clare through his brother continued to resonate. He left to meet Major Goetz for lunch.

On the day before he was to have lunch with Burley, Goetz had received a phone call from Major Dan. "I've just received some bad new. I'm not up to a run this afternoon."

"Anything I can do?"

"I don't think so. I've just heard that my brother, Ed, was killed three nights ago."

"Good God. I'm so sorry to hear that."

"Me, too. He and Crayley were up on some pinnacle that was under attack, and Ed didn't come through it."

"Dan, I'd like to help."

"Thanks, we'll see," he continued, "I wonder who's next."

"What do you mean, 'next'?"

"You remember that tall one, Buddington was his name?"

"Sure."

"Well, one of my senior nurses, Barbara Radley, apparently hit it pretty good with him while they were at Fuji View. They started corresponding. But a few days ago, she got a black border letter from one of his buddies. He got killed shortly after they returned to Korea. That's two out of three."

Goetz waited before answering, "I really would like to help, Dan. Please let me know if I can."

◆   ◆   ◆

After the usual pleasantries, the PM asked Goetz if there was any gossip at the hospital.

"No hospital gossip, but I did get some unpleasant news yesterday. Remember I told you about the R and R lieutenants who Dan Clare sent to Fuji View?" Burley nodded, "Well, two of them are KIA: the big one and Dan's little brother." He filled out the rest of the story for Burley.

On the way back to his office, the PM reached a point of flushing the Luther investigation, but he was scheduled to see Levinson that afternoon. He might as well get the most current view before he trashed the case.

Levinson arrived. The colonel seated at his desk looked up at him, "So—?"

"So I finally was able to contact the PM of their division. I told them their names, and he immediately sparked on Crayley. He doesn't know Ed Clare or Buddington, but he'll find out and get back to me. He tells me that this Crayley—by the way, he's a captain now—is today's Division hero. Seems his company had some tough outpost duty and during a hell of a storm a few nights ago, a lot of Chinese got into their position, and they fought them eye-to-eye in the midst of a driving, lightning-riddled, torrent."

"Anyway, Crayley beat them off, and now they're sitting on some stone spire waiting for the next attempt, which the Division commander thinks will be the big one. The general, by the way, it's Krill—you may recall seeing his name in the *Stars and Stripes* from time to time—thinks that Crayley is the best thing to happen to the Army since the A-bomb."

"I asked if there was any chance the three could come back to Division Headquarters if I was to come to Korea to talk to them."—even as he said Korea again, he started to shake—"He started to laugh so hard he could barely talk." He told me that if I was serious, I, or my boss, could ask Krill directly. He wouldn't do it. He was kind enough to remind me that Krill has a thoroughly justified reputation as a fire-spouting dragon, and if I, or my boss, did ask Krill to pull those guys off line that he would be too busy to attend my, or my boss's, funeral.

The PM said, "Let me think on it. Sit down while I consider where we are." Levinson slouched in a chair. Burley thought to himself: *Levinson doesn't know that Clare and Buddington are dead. The Division PM didn't know their names, and he certainly didn't know they are now on Division records as KIA.*

The PM didn't tell Levinson. He continued to think to himself. *Two of them gone, one left, and maybe he's a hero or about to be one. And then there is the general. Sure as God made green apples, I won't go head-to-head with the Division commander on an issue of investigative procedure—especially against a guy like Krill.*

The PM turned to Levinson, "I've thought on it enough. I've concluded that the gardener's direct observation is the capstone. If you agree with my conclusion,"—he looked at Levinson for a confirmation. Levinson, who thought that the colonel's insightful determination was very like the recommendation he had given him several days before, shook his head up and down vigorously—"then, the investigation is over." He handed Luther's file to him, "Lose it."

On his way out of the office and the building, Levinson dropped the file into the basket for "Pending Investigation—No Action Required." It would go to archival storage. Levinson wondered what had taken Burley so long thinking on it.

CHAPTER TWENTY-FIVE

The day after Jen's assault, Crayley went with McCoy and Harry Princeton down into the engineer explosives room. They again surveyed the inventory. All three of them were of the same mind. The Chinese would come again. The next time with massive force, and they would certainly come up the south slope. The three reached conclusions, and Harry went to work with six men of First Platoon.

They packed shaped charges against the south wall and buttressed them heavily with a mat of sand bags and timbers scrounged from the monastery. Behind the charges were two rows of the napalm drums. They manhandled these into a canted position and built heavy earth berms behind each row. They then packed sandbags and dirt packed around each drum. A white phosphorous, sixty mm mortar shell was suspended in each drum, and they fixed a quarter-pound block of TNT to the bottom.

After two days of work from Harry and his detail, Horace and McCoy came down to inspect the result, Harry was waiting for them. He had a clipboard with many notes and angled lines on several pages. The captain asked few questions. His quick, knowledgeable inspection confirmed that the place was correctly set up as he had ordered. As he turned to Princeton for a final comment, Harry pushed his clipboard at him, "Ya see, Captain, I got all the angles planned right here. We need only three cameras. Lighting is no problem. We can fill in sound later, I could direct it and get a real good shot."

Harry was back in Hollywood. His clipboard pages were the camera angles layout of the best way to present what the room was set up to do. Horace looked at him. "I'm not sure the scene will play just this way," he said, tapping Harry's clipboard.

Crayley looked at McCoy. "When we're ready for this, I want you down here with him—and I mean with him. Keep him away from the igniter crank until you hear from me." Wowser looked only at Harry, but he nodded toward Horace.

Then, they waited. They waited under clear blue skies with errant soft breezes starting to mellow—marvelous days with not a cloud, nor for that matter, not a Chinaman, to be seen. The veterans knew that the job remaining for the Chinese was a day job. They would need good observation and visual control for the effort, but not such a good day that American air power could get off the ground to help the monastery defenders.

So George Company relaxed in the near balmy weather. Although at leisure, they were getting ready for what they all knew was coming. Four days after the attack up the notch trail, the wind picked up; clouds started forming, then billowed down the river valley like convoys of full-sheeted sailing ships. Under the clouds, fog began to slide into the plain to surround the lower levels of the ridge. The company started to twitch as if it were a string instrument in the hands of a clumsy tuner. The men got testy with one another. Easy bantering was replaced by short grunts. Tempers flared over imagined insults, which in the past had been given and received without reply. Horace, Wowser, and other seniors took notice of the spreading tremors, and they were satisfied. The company was getting itself ready for the next round.

◆   ◆   ◆

In the low foothills facing Monastery Ridge, Jen Po-Wei waited in the covered-trench entry to the nearly perfectly camouflaged, mostly underground, command center of the Chinese division, which had responsibility to capture the stone tower. He was nervous being in such a place. He looked again at his weapon, assuring himself for the tenth time it was untouchably clean. A small-group leader had no business with men of such high rank. But he was also curious. He expected he would be asked to account for his leadership failure in the attack up on the steep trail. He had lost nearly all his men. He should not have survived, but he did. And here he was.

Severe criticism and, probably, demotion did not require attention of officers of division rank. Even if it were to be worse—even if he were to be executed for the failure of his attack—such action could be ordered by his immediate superior. But that officer had said very little to Jen; only questioning him about how the Americans had managed to drive him off the tower. Yet here he was and still alive—not even under guard. Very curious.

His name was called. He was led into an underground room, which actually had a small tent erected inside it. In the tent was the general commanding the division as well as Jen's regimental commander. The two officers again questioned him intensely about the actions of the Americans. That was all. The meeting was short.

Jen was not to be demoted; not to be disciplined. In fact, he had been promoted. The general told him that his report of the reaction of the Americans against the attack persuaded the general that a series of small bloodying sorties against the stone tower would take too long with no guarantee of eventual success. The division had its own timetable to meet, and, therefore, a massive, overwhelming force would be used in a swarm assault on the position. The attack, of course, would be up the south slope, and—surprise!—Jen would command the attack.

The general was making available to the effort, to be used as necessary, one of his larger regiments—more than two thousand men. Because of the narrowness of the ramp, the general realized, and regretted, that it would be difficult to get all the manpower in the assault at the same time. But that was Jen's problem.

Finally, the general in answer to an unspoken, but obvious, question from Jen—Why me?—said, "You are given this duty because your reputation of many years is good; your success in reaching the top of the stone tower; you may have eliminated their commander; and, finally, you brought me good information about the Americans—the most valuable information. We now know the tower is not defended by easily frightened fearful children and that our capture of their outpost will be very difficult."

◆   ◆   ◆

At the same time as Jen was making his way back to his unit, Crayley was finishing a radio report to Krill and Bozoni. He passed the hand set to Cochise, "Tell your brother I think they'll come tomorrow, or, at the latest, the next day, and I think it will be the main event. This weather is good for them. The forecast is for more of this high overcast and low fog, which means that spotter and support aircraft won't fly. Also, tell him to pass the word that I don't want artillery unless this turns into a doomsday scenario" Cochise looked at him as he pondered how to translate "doomsday," then decided to use the Apache equivalent of "kicking our ass." Crayley continued, "The big tubes can't hit the ramp. If they try, it's more likely they'll hit us up here." The message went from Cochise to Geronimo. After a pause, Krill spoke, "Message understood. Out."

Crazy Horse moved into the First Platoon CP just after midnight of the fourth day. McCoy went down with Harry at the same time. Cochise trailed along with Wowser. Trent and Fisco stayed at the company CP

Three times during the hours of darkness, Horace ordered illumination flares from the Regiment's artillery because a watcher thought he heard something on the south ramp They exploded overhead and herky-jerked their way down—bobbing, sliding, falling as their parachutes swirled in the wind currents over the monastery. The light split into erratic streaks on the ramp, creating the illusion of movement where there was none.

No booby traps or trip flares planted in the ramp exploded. But Crayley thought that most of those devices had already been blown by mortar and artillery rounds that had landed on the narrow roadway.

As first light began to seep through the overcast, the company found itself suspended on a rock island in a gray soup sea. A heavy fog layer had settled on the plain; its surface was halfway up on the monastery walls. Nothing and no one else to be seen. They were alone in the universe.

Gradually, the sun beat through the overcast, which did not disappear but moved higher. The fog began to break up. Men moved closer to the firing ports. The machine gunners straightened and smoothed the ammo belts in the breech of their weapons.

A strong wind suddenly blew down the valley. The fog around the monastery was, within several seconds, torn into shreds and wisped into the sky.

◆   ◆   ◆

The attack started as the fog began to dissipate. It came to the company with the sound of heavy shells being launched from many Chinese mortars, now in position much closer to the company. But none of the rounds landed on, or very near to, them. They were landing behind monastery—between George Company and the other line companies of the Regiment. And the Chinese were firing smoke. Explosive shells followed shortly, but the smoke continued.

Horace and the others recognized the drill. The Chinamen were sealing them off from their friends who would be unable to see and who would suffer grievous casualties if they tried to cross the river plain to help.

As soon as the enemy mortars started firing, Crayley put a call to all three of his platoons. "Tell the members of the orchestra to assemble at First Platoon."

As the last ground fog disappeared, the south slope came into view. The leader of First Platoon turned to Crayley and said, "My God, Captain, the place is alive with those maggots." The surface of the ramp seemed to be moving. There was no place not occupied by diligent Chinese soldiers, who were plastered against the ground but crawling with awkward bulky movements up toward the monastery. The padded cotton arms and legs, humping up and down as they squirmed toward the top, formed a dirt- and grass-stained seamless carpet. The closest of the attackers was less than seventy yards from the base of the rock wall above which First Platoon was anchored.

Almost at once whistles and bugle blasts commenced a series of command signals. Immediately, the George Company noise makers joined in. Their bugles and trumpets blared. The trombone delivered a blowzy sliding gargle. The air-raid siren was loud enough to awake Chinese fire brigades on the Yalu River. The din of the company's effort overtook the command sounds of the enemy signalers, who redoubled their decibel output and added several loops to their bugle calls. This was answered by a particularly spirited rendition of "When the Saints Come Marching In" by the one company trumpeter who had musical training.

Crazy Horse did not know if the company's concert confused the crawling troops about what their leaders were telling them to do. But what he was clear on was, that hearing their own people blasting and wailing away had a million volt energizing effect on his men. He felt a breaking surf of adrenaline rolling over the company. It was Fisco who said to Trent, "Ah, screw 'em. They ain't so tough. Just three of us and the captain beat their ass the other night."

With the fog gone, Crayley saw how near the leading elements were. His men were pushing and crowding into the rock walls facing the south ramp. The firing steps were full. The barrels of the machine guns were vibrating in the twitchy hands of the gunners. Still looking at the scene before him, Crazy Horse said to First Platoon leader, "Okay, see what you can do."

The Chinese opened up first. A thick volley of automatic fire roared up from the slope and beat against the bunker walls. It increased in volume as every soldier on the ramp joined in. The men on top hardly flinched. They replied with a hailstorm of rapid fire into the attackers. The Chinese were packed on the slope, so George Company hardly had to aim. They just kept drilling downslope into the ramp.

The machine guns—all three of them—surprised Jen, who had seen only one on the night of the first weapon-seeking demonstration, when it opened up in methodical fashion. They sprayed along the leading lines, progressing up the ramp. It was almost like hosing along furrows of a planted field. The beaten zone left by the bullets moved leisurely along the front edge of the attack. But the edge never moved backward. The escalator movement of the assault continually provided men clawing upward. In a very short while, a barricade of bodies started to build up at what had been the line of farthest advance. Those in back still continued their advance until they reached the growing stack. They tried to clamber over it, and then, getting hit, flopped into place, more body bricks in the heightening wall.

A small number of the attackers, by some means almost beyond reality, made it through the murderous fire pouring down on them. These few were pressed against the wall at the base of First Platoon's position. One Chinese soldier tried to attach an explosive package to the base of the wall. The defenders saw this, and a dozen grenades bounced down the rock face. The small hand bombs exploded in rapid sequence. All those Chinese lucky, or unlucky, enough to have made it that far were torn apart by the fragments.

Horace called for a quick report from the other platoons. Nothing. There was no enemy effort anywhere on the tower perimeter, except at the notch trail. There, a small group was again trying to force a way up the steep path. But this time, Second Platoon was calmly observing the climbers, looking down their throats. The timid Chinese attack completely failed when platoon members rolled a cascade of grenades down the trail. Now, the platoon reported to Horace, two men were sitting on three cases of grenades and casually pitching one or two down the rock cleft every minute or so.

At the south ramp, the carnage continued. More bodies were stacked at the blocked line of advance. The Chinese were taking devastating losses. By all odds, the attack should start to break up. But still they came on. Maybe the Chinese commander thought the sight of several hundred riflemen swarming up the slope would so unnerve the Americans that they would collapse in panic.

But fortune did not favor the Chinamen. George Company had a commanding, high-ground position, and they took full advantage of it. Jen's superiors could see the attack was starting to falter. On the lower ramp, there was less forward movement. Horace could see it, also. The enemy riflemen had begun to seek cover in holes, in folds of the earth, and behind the bodies of their comrades. Yet, there was no clustering as was common in a failing assault; no groups crowded around a particularly inviting deep hole or around a leader who would somehow save and reinvigorate the effort. These were just poor souls scabbing into the ground, trying to burrow in.

Crazy Horse thought to himself, *"Is this it? Is this the best they can do?"*

◆   ◆   ◆

Then, the first shell hit. It came with little advance notice: no ranging fire, just a sharp crack from close in, then a slamming crunch into First Platoon. It was perfect, a direct hit on one of the machine guns position with shattering effect. The walls of the monks' sleeping cells had never been built to withstand high-velocity, flat trajectory fire.

Horace and First Platoon leader moved quickly to the blown gun port. The gun was destroyed, and its crew as well as three riflemen in the room were down. Shell fragments and rock shards had swirled through the bunker like the blades of a giant shredder. The entire room, including the ceiling, was painted with blood strokes. The platoon's medic was already there and probing. He looked up as Crayley came in, "Three dead, Captain. Janero is out now, but he'll die in a few minutes. The others will probably make it if we aren't up here too long."

"Okay. Do what you can and get all of them out of here."

A second and third shot arrived. The first, too high, barely ticked off one of the wooden beams lately laid over the thin flat rock roof. The second came too low, nearly at the base of the wall. Neither did any damage.

Horace, back at the platoon CP, was easily able to spot the enemy weapons. There was no difficulty identifying them. "By damn, those are thirty-seven millimeter anti-tank guns. Where the hell did the gooks find those relics?" This weapon was small, easily transportable, simple to operate, and completely useless for its original purpose. Though designated "anti-tank," it was much too small to do more than ping the armor of modern tanks. It had not been employed by the American Army for years. Horace thought that probably these guns had been given to the South Korean Army well before the present war and been captured by the invading Northerners.

Although outmoded by the press of technology, there they were in his binoculars. The Chinese were using them, and it was clear to Horace that they were just fine for knocking out selected gun sites and surrounding rock walls. They were out in the open less than seven-hundred yards away in a narrow small gully, not more than twenty or thirty-feet deep. It was a dry creek bed that in earlier times had carried a stream into the flat river plain.

The little gully was precisely in line with the south ramp. Its opening to the river plain was dead on to the line of the slope. The gun emplacements could be easily seen. Their crews were visible, industriously loading and firing. And, in their protected place, they were safe from any artillery Horace could call in.

Another round slammed in, its slivers whirling like airborne butcher knives from wall to wall in the targeted bunker. More men down; others moved away from firing positions seeking cover against this new threat. Whistles and bugles sounded. The enemy on the south ramp were on the move again. They were coming out of their holes, and the slope was filling with bodies erect and striding upward. First Platoon could see that if the thirty-sevens continued to pound away, they would turn the platoon position into an open-air shooting gallery. More than adequate as in the words of Private Robinette, "They're beating the crap out of us." He made that as his last war observation about a minute before one of the A.T. rounds blew a basketball size hole through his chest.

Crayley grabbed the wire phone to his mortar section, giving direction and range. He could not hear the thunk of the shells as they launched out of the tubes, but he intently watched the enemy gun position. The first rounds were to the left and beyond the thirty-sevens. He gave change of direction and range to the mortarmen. Two more anti-tank shells arrived but low with little damage. The second flight of mortars was closer—more fine tuning directions, more rounds out—and then the American shells came close enough to send the Chinese crews into their holes. Three mortar rounds hit nearly on the guns. Cautious heads poked out of the holes; then, the gun crews were up and resumed firing. Two shells hit two bunkers—more George men down. First Platoon was being cut up pretty good with another machine gun out. On the slope, a good-sized group of Chinese scrambled over the pile of their dead and started to move toward the wall.

Horace watched three more mortar rounds hit close to the guns, but the crews were already back in their holes. "This time I want three willy-peter shells. Hold the high explosive until I say—and send me an observer." The white phosphorous mortar rounds arrived nearly on target. They exploded almost together, close to the center of the triangle of guns. A billowing cloud of shiny white flakes blossomed upward, then fell as soft rain onto the guns and into the crew slit trenches. Within seconds, the crews leaped out of their holes grabbing and clutching or frantically brushing themselves where the deadly tiny chips of fire were burning and burrowing into their bodies. The heads of two of them were ablaze.

"Now, pump out the HE!" The explosive shells hit. The gun crews were still dancing around, jumping and screaming, erect and vulnerable, when the mortar barrage arrived. It worked as intended: the willy peter got them out of their holes, and the HE scraped them off. As far as Crazy Horse could tell, they all went down. *"Well,"* he said to himself, *"that's as close to perfect as we'll ever see."*

He knew he had them stymied. To be effective against the First Platoon walls, the Chinese anti-tank guns had to have direct line of sight—a circumstance in which they were also visible from the monastery. He turned to the observer from mortar section. "See those guns?" The observer nodded. "Okay, those tank guns are out of action now. If anybody tries to start 'em up again or tries to move them, hit them with both white phosphorous and HE Got it?"—another nod. "Good. They're all yours."

First Platoon leader was finding out how badly his section was hurt. The thirty-sevens had scored heavily against his position. Eight monks' cells that had been converted to firing bunkers for his men had faced the ramp. Of these, five had crumpled with many casualties. The remainder of his platoon was disorganized and loopy. Their firing toward the slope was scattered, weak. He gave the captain a quick report.

Horace turned his attention to the ramp once again. There were as many bodies moving as when the attack started—and they were really on the move now. He saw their leading line was past the body barricade pushing to the base of the wall. The fire from below intensified. The attackers had been energized by the damage done by their AT guns. The Chinese had found their second wind. Bullets were cracking into First Platoon. More men were being hit. The last of the platoon's machine guns was out—blown apart or hopelessly jammed.

Crayley called Trent in the CP. "Send two squads and a machine gun from Second Platoon." Then Horace punched the line to the engineer cavern. McCoy responded.

"Are you and Harry still awake?"

"Of course, Number One. What can we do for you?"

"Are you ready?"

"Of course."

"Standby."

Wowser to Harry. "Get off your dead ass. We have to start earning our pay."

Horace took another look. More Chinese were at the bottom of the ramp crowding others to start up the slope. In addition to several already at the wall, he saw many more closing in. He had seen enough. "McCoy, are you still there?"

"Still here, Crazy Horse."

"Do it!"

"Fire in the hole!"

Horace turned to look at the ramp. Down below, McCoy and Princeton ran out of the engineer store room. Wowser carried the field phone, and Harry cradled a black box, both of them trailing wire behind. They went up one level and stopped.

The engineer room had been prepared as the captain ordered. Near the dirt wall farthest from the entrance were three rows of heavy sand bags behind and jammed against four shaped charges—one hundred sixty pounds of TNT—spaced evenly along the outward wall. This dynamite load was nearly one hundred feet below and, because of the angle of the ramp, nearly fifty feet outward of First Platoon but no more than fifteen feet beneath the south slope. Behind the shaped charges in their prepared canted position were the two rows of primed napalm barrels—fifteen in front, ten lined up twelve feet behind the first row.

Harry closed the firing circuit. Even though Crazy Horse knew what was coming, he was not prepared for the massive jolt. The rock tower shuddered with the blast that shot dirt, rock, and Chinamen soaring out, into, and over the troops laboring up the ramp below the explosion. A great gap, a trench twenty-feet wide, was ripped across the full width of the ramp. Many of those below the new trench were felled by the explosive debris propelled into them. Firing from the slope abruptly stopped as bodies and parts of bodies of their former comrades rained down on the attackers. The company was as stunned as the attackers. They quit shooting and just stared. Horace found himself thinking, "*The wind is picking up again*," amazed that he could actually hear it.

Then from downslope, the whistles started. No bugles, just whistles at first. Gradually, Crayley became aware, for the first time, of shouted commands from the few Chinese leaders still on their feet. As Crayley watched, he was astonished. The Chinese were actually resuming the attack. They were getting to their feet, running up the ramp into the trench, the upper side of which was now open into the engineer room.

"Are you two still among the living?"

"Wowser replied, "Yes, sir. That was a real kick. We enjoyed it very much. How does it look from up there?"

"It cleaned off a lot of undesirables from the ramp. But those bastards are regrouping and coming again. They really have steel balls."

"We've got something to temper that aggressive attitude."

"Hold it a minute. I want more of them in that trench you two just dug." Crazy Horse turned his attention to the ramp once again. He watched the leading element jump into the gap and struggle to get out the top side. He saw the hole was crammed with the enemy. "Okay," into his handset, "start the barbecue."

Almost immediately, there was another blast, different from the sharp crack of the shaped charges. This one rumbled, then choked and gulped like something trapped in the earth was disgorging a foul, bubbling lump of matter. The first rack of searing napalm vomited out of the hole: a tumbling, slow-moving, fiery river. This was no thin sheen of napalm, a mile long and an inch thick dropped by air force jets at five hundred miles an hour from two thousand feet. This was a thick, enveloping blanket from hell that rolled down the ramp and swallowed the fleeing, panic-stricken attackers. For those who had been struggling to climb through the new trench there was no escape. The deep ditch became a boiling pond, igniting all the swimmers in it.

Those far down on the ramp could see it coming. They abandoned the slope and raced toward the gully where the anti-tank guns sat. Horace heard the mortar observer call to shorten the range and to "Fire for effect." Mortar shells, mostly antipersonnel but some willy peter, commenced to fall amongst the fleeing soldiers. Later, Horace remembered thinking to himself, *"Good thinking. I'll have to remember this kid's name."* Those in the trench, wounded or dead on the ramp, were engulfed and became charcoal stick figures. There was silence in the company—an unearthly silence. George Company just watched as the rolling flame cleaned the ramp. Chinese bugles started; this time, as urgent, staccato snaps. The soldiers who could still move did not turn back toward the ramp. They increased their rapid movement away from Monastery Ridge. The attack was over.

CHAPTER TWENTY-SIX

There were still Chinese alive on the ramp. On the left edge of the slope there was a line of stubby, bushy pine trees of a type found on the lower hills of Korean mountains. These trees had been planted by the careful work of the monks more than two centuries earlier. The reason for the plantings, if there ever was one, had been lost many years before. Though full-grown and mature, these ancient pines were barely twenty feet tall. Over time, their branches had twisted and turned up, down, and round about, so that they formed a thick hedge no more than twenty-five feet wide the length of the ramp up to the monastery wall.

Jen had been directing the attack from just behind the leading edge in the center of the line. When the advance bogged down in the face of the initial First-Platoon barrage, he called for his trump weapon, the anti-tank guns. Their action had nearly stopped the withering fire from above, and he was getting his lines in order to resume the push when he became aware that the left flank seemed to be melting away into the trees. He saw that some of his men—far too many—had crowded into the tree lane, seeking to be lost in the low branches, and were not in the fight.

The Americans, so far, had not directed much of their firepower into the trees, not because they didn't know there were Chinese in there, but because the glut of targets on the open ramp was a more compelling attraction.

Jen had moved into the trees when the George Company mortars put his thirty-sevens out of action, but only after they had done great damage to the tower defenders. Jen shouted and cursed at his men, trying to get them back into the battle and to join their comrades, who were starting to make some headway against the Americans. To keep up the momentum, he needed all the men he could muster. By pushing and shoving his way through the low branches, he found that here and there were small open areas where he could see for more than a few feet. There were far fewer of his men seeking refuge than he had at first thought.

He was aware that, even without him, movement up the ramp had started again, and he was about to return to a center position when an enormous explosion erupted behind him. He was jolted into the air and dumped on his back and head. The trees swirled in a curious dizzying pattern around him. He heard several piercing sounds that he recognized as whistle commands. His head started to clear, but it took more than a minute to realize what had happened. He wobbled to his feet, skidding crabwise down the pitch of the slope and bouncing off trees like a marble in a pinball machine.

Then, he saw the deep trench, thirty feet down slope, that the blast had created. On the lower side of the gap, he saw his men strewn like rag dolls across the landscape. He also saw some of his junior leaders collecting soldiers, starting them across the new trench, still trying to get to the wall. As the blast gap started to fill with his men scrambling to get through the new barrier, he thought, *"They've played their last tile. We've got them now. We'll blow their wall apart from underneath them and finish them off."*

His thoughts for his final assault plan were shattered when a great geyser of oily flame launched out of the hillside. He saw napalm gobbing into the trench, coursing down the ramp, and smothering everything in incandescent slop. Even as he was trying to wring from his brain a response to the firestorm falling on his men, he heard the sharp bugle calls. The attack, his attack, was finished. He slumped onto the low branches, unable to even fall to the ground.

The two explosions—shaped charges, then napalm—set off wild cheers in George Company. Most of the men raced to the First Platoon's position to view the results. They were clapping one another on the backs and recounting the event. Those who had been at the other end of Monastery, not even close to the ramp attack, were already telling each other of their heroic actions; were already practicing and rewiring their memory of their own participation in the blowout defense of Monastery Ridge.

Charlie Pope, much admired in the company for his sterling defense of the generator room, was awakened from his slumber by the shaped charge send-off, which rattled everything in his power station chamber. Charlie was fully awake when the napalm blasted out. He decided he should go topside to see how the Chinese cooking was progressing. On Main Street, he collided with others hurrying toward the ramp. But Charlie didn't join that rush. Instead, he went to Boffo Mallen's place of previous existence, the bunker above the notch trail. Only two riflemen, new to the company, were following the captain's order to stay in place. They were looking at the river plain in front of them, between the monastery and the Chinese lines. There, on that flat dry bed, was the remainder of Jen's assault force. Those who had managed to get off the ramp in front of the napalm had swung through the deep draw where the thirty-sevens were, gathering the rest of the troops who had been waiting for the final charge on stone tower, and the whole swarm had changed course, streaming around Monastery back to home base.

Charlie took in the scene at once. "Holy fuck. Look at that. It's a goddamned goat rodeo."

"You," he turned to one of the new men, "go tell the captain there's a ton of them running for China in the flat land."

"You." he turned to the other man, "get a machine gun crew over here now, with a shit-load of ammo."

By the time the machine gun team arrived, Charlie was loudly bellowing the complete lyrics of a song about a hero chaplain pressed into duty on Pearl Harbor Day, "Praise the Lord and pass the ammunition."

"Gimme that gun," Pope barked at the team as their weapon was being set up in a firing port. "Ah, yes, you little slanty assholes. This is

for Boffo." Charlie commenced fanning the field below, lazily travers-
ing in an arc of nearly a half circle. In front of him, lumpy cotton figures began a series of forward flips as Charlie's wandering fire caught
them in the back and tumbled them in an acrobatic front roll.

Less than three minutes after the machine gun opened up, the first
artillery shells—requested by Crazy Horse from Division—started
landing. When General Krill received Horace's call, he had ordered all
the Division heavies, plus cannon companies of all the regiments to hit
the river plain. He even got some of the super heavies—two hundred
forty millimeters—from Seventh-Corps artillery to join in. It was a
devastating bombardment. The field was littered with bodies. Charlie
looked up from his machine gun as another belt was being loaded.
"Very satisfying. Very satisfying, indeed," he said.

Wowser, trailed as usual by Cochise, and Harry went to join the
captain and most of the rest of the company on First Platoon's parapet
to watch the broken remnants of the Chinese attack move away from
Monastery. In a short time, it was nearly silent with only an undercur-
rent of occasional gulps from the napalm bubbling in the trench. The
fired petroleum fumes were thick and unpleasant, but, as remarked by
one nasally alert observer, "This crap smells awful, but it's better than
those charcoal chicken sticks out there."

◆   ◆   ◆

"McCoy," Crayley turned to the first sergeant, "we've been in this
place long enough to know what to look for. It's quiet down there, a
few sparks and a little mushy, but I don't see anything moving. Let's
hop over the wall. You take Cochise with you and we'll look for anything to identify their unit. It's unlikely that we'll find much, but if we
do, we can tell Krill who we chopped up. He'll like that. Stay above the
fire pit you and Harry made. No reason to get down slope into that
mess of fried crickets. Nothing to be found there."

"Okay, Captain. I'll see if any of them thought to bring their passports to the show." Wowser, with a helping hand and arm from Horace, labored over the wall followed by Cochise doing a quick leap to the ground.

Trent, cradling his new favorite weapon, one of the company's shotguns, arrived just as McCoy disappeared over the wall. "What's up?" Trent addressed Horace. He felt he could be conversational and, if it suited him, somewhat flip with the captain. This was because he thought they were real battle buddies now after the night attack up the notch trail. Trent's wild-man performance had lead to his acceptance as one of the company's certified bone-cutting killers. He was still the company clerk, but he had also proved himself to be a remarkable handyman in the company's line of work.

"McCoy's gone over to look for identification of those rump roasts down there."

"Hey, Wowser,"—a greater breach of protocol than his query to the captain, but one which Trent was sure would be tolerated, even if only barely—"need some help carving the turkey?"

No answer, just a hand wave off by McCoy who, with Cochise close behind, had started toward the tree line, searching the bodies clustered between the base of the wall and the fire trench.

"Come with me, Cowboy," Horace touched Trent's arm, "you can keep these Asiatic hordes from overrunning me." The captain and the corporal vaulted the wall and moved toward the opposite side of the ramp away from the trees.

◆   ◆   ◆

Jen Po-Wei cleared his head of the shock of the American's explosions. He had pulled himself out of the branches into which he had slumped and was sitting in a tiny clearing. He recognized two of his men, who were staring at him. They had the expectant look of ones waiting for his next orders. But he had none. *"It's over,"* he thought, *"can't these plowboys see that? The attack is finished. I'm finished."*

Jen stood up carefully. He turned slowly around. He saw only three more of his people half hidden outside his open area. He snapped his fingers. The crack sounded to him like a rifle shot, but it was no more than a sharp tick. The three heard and moved toward him. Jen sat back down. Still no thought of action. Maybe he should try to plan a way out for his five followers. Then again, maybe not. The only way was down the ramp, and the Americans were in complete control of that route.

Then, through the bushy limbs, he saw two figures slowing making their way toward the trees. They were looking carefully at the bodies on the ground. He watched them steadily as they continued their search mission. As they got closer, he could see that the leader was a small tub of a man, far above the age of any he had seen on his night attack or of any of those he could see lining the wall above on the stone tower. The one accompanying him seemed to Jen to be a bodyguard. He continued his observation. This soldier was really old for the kind of work the Americans were doing. *"What was he doing in this place?"* Then it was clear to him. This old man had to be a commander, at least the chief of those on the stone tower, and, Jen hoped, maybe a much more senior officer who had been on the stone tower as an observer. He would kill this stumpy old fool—put an end to his studious examination of those good men stretched out on the slope. He continued to wait. The man's path was taking him into the trees. If he continued his course, he would deliver himself to Jen.

Crazy Horse and Trent finished their search at the far side of the ramp. They turned and started toward McCoy and Cochise who were nearing the tree line. When they turned, Jen saw them for the first time—only two and too far away to help the old man.

The Chinese leader waited. He saw that the short commander stopped to look carefully at one of the bodies. He prodded it with a short rifle, half turned it over, and looked again. Then, satisfied, returned his carbine to the cradle of his arm and started forward.

Wowser and Cochise entered the tree lane no more than thirty feet above Jen. But, as they entered, he lost sight of them. No matter, he knew where they were. By hand signals, he told his five men the direction of their fire, and that they were to shoot only when he did. He wanted another look at the two and waited for them to move into his view through the intermittent sight openings allowed by the branches.

One of his men stood up to get a better stance. "Fool," hissed Jen motioning him down. It was too late. Cochise had seen the movement, and he fired first with his carbine on full automatic. He salvoed where he had seen the standing man suddenly appear, but he aimed low because he had also seen the man duck down. Cochise caught the three Chinese with a wide pattern, and they all fell together in a collapsed embrace. Wowser, startled by Cochise's quick action, got himself quickly into the fight. Without ever seeing a target, he sprayed the area in front of him.

Although the two Americans were still hidden from him by the low tree limbs, Jen directed a burst into the spot where had last seen them. His remaining two soldiers were slow in reacting, and one was knocked back in a heap without ever getting his weapon's safety off.

Cochise continued to fire in short bursts, moving through the trees. Finally, Jen recognized where the killing shots were coming from and shifted his weapon toward the spot. His first volley caught Cochise in the stomach, hip, and both knees. He fell heavily and did not move.

Wowser redirected his aim, and as Cochise went down, Jen's last remaining supporter took a single shot just above the bridge of the nose. At nearly the same instant, Jen felt a searing heavy thump in his side that spun him around and dumped him onto the ground. Lying on the soft carpet of the tree park, Jen heard the sharp crack of many bullets coming from downslope behind him over his head. Four more of his men, to that point unseen by him, were thrashing up hill through the branches and undergrowth firing wildly. As they approached Jen, they stopped, though still firing up slope.

Near the top of the tree lane, Wowser was moving toward Cochise, who was several feet in front of him, when a burst from a new spot downslope ripped through the trees. He took two hits at the same time: one in the left shoulder, one in the chest. These slugs batted him on his ass, his fall stopped by his back hitting a tree. He sat there for several seconds, then to himself, *"I think I better get up"* He was able to lever himself upright by pushing against and sliding up the tree trunk. When he was finally erect, he decided to rest and consider the situation for a minute or so. Even though he wanted to understand this latest turn of events, he couldn't get his thought processes started, because he couldn't put his finger on what had brought him to this place.

At the sound of the first firing by Cochise, Horace and Trent started sprinting toward the trees looking for targets. When they had taken no more than ten steps, the firing stopped. They kept running. Firing resumed. Then, a new barrage started up from farther down in the tree lane. From the side, Horace could see four figures running up hill, firing as they ran.

Crazy Horse was in the lead. His carbine burst caught one of the four. The other three turned toward them as if on command and fired. Crayley saw their movement, also saw a shallow shell depression and dived in. Trent, not so quick, was hit in the upper right leg. The shot twisted him around, and he spun into the same hole as Horace.

The captain looked at Trent, decided he would last until help arrived. "Gimme that," Crazy Horse said as he grabbed Trent's shotgun. Then he was up, out of the hole, running full tilt at the three Chinamen. They saw him coming, but they seemed frozen at the sight of Crazy Horse charging at them. They were standing almost in parade formation as he commenced firing his heavy buckshot, pumping as fast as he could. The big pellets dispersed nicely and pounded into the three men who, together, seemed to have taken an interest in flying. They exploded backwards and upwards into the trees.

Horace's charge took him into the trees right into Jen Po-Wei's little clearing. Jen, still sitting on the ground, looked up at him while Crazy Horse furiously pumped a now-empty gun. The Chinaman, no more than five feet away, calmly aimed his rifle and pulled the trigger. The last round in his weapon fired. The slug hit the shotgun stock, broke it into four pieces, and each piece of stock and the slug itself slammed into Crayley's right side. He staggered out of the trees and fell.

Startled by the first firing in the tree lane, men of the First Platoon took only a moment to react. By the time Horace fired the shotgun, five of them were over the wall. They saw him go into the trees, heard a shot, saw him stagger backward and fall. There were no more shots in the trees. Seeing their captain go down, they all headed for him.

Jen was alone. His mind was clear. Somewhere upslope nearby was the squat little American commander. He intended to find him and make sure he never left the trees. Still seated, Jen looked around him for a weapon. His rifle and pistol were empty. He had no more ammunition. Near him lay the rifle of one of his soldiers. It was an old hand-operated bolt model. Its open breech was clogged with dirt, but lying on the ground next to it was a bayonet. Jen tested it. It was, according to his standing instructions, razor sharp. He fixed it on the end of his rifle and heaved himself to his feet.

Wowser was riding a flood of remembrances, tremors, and nausea. He knew he was bad hurt because he had a sort of windy feeling in his chest. By pushing his chin against his neck and squinting downward he could see small pink bubbles forming and breaking on his bloody shirt front. He knew that that kind of chest shot usually didn't make it back to the Battalion Aid Station.

"Well, by damn; what the hell, Cochise? Where is that black-eyed demon? Saved my life. Probably not for long; I'm leaking way too much. Don't give a plugged fuck." A loud yell, "I been at this far too long," and a look round. "How the hell did all these Chin-ee boys get here? Chin-ee boys, that's a good name. I'll have to remember that. *Where's Boffo?*"

His passing parade took an abrupt detour. His muttering stopped; his head cleared. He said to himself, *"Enough of this shit. I better get back to duty. Crazy Horse will need me."* He started to move, almost fell, but managed to slouch lumpily back against his tree post. He would rest a minute. Then take up his duties. Maybe Cochise could help. He spotted him lying on the ground several paces in front of him, but it didn't look like he was ready to join up.

He also saw something else, beyond Cochise, lumbering heavily up the slope. *"What the hell is that?"* The figure stopped by Cochise, half turned him over with an unsteady foot, all the time looking at Wowser. Then, the apparition resumed his unsteady march toward Wowser.

It was an enemy soldier; a damn big enemy soldier carrying a rifle. *"Where in hell did the giant Chink come from?"* McCoy suddenly had a serious need for a weapon. He scanned the ground for his carbine. It was not in sight. His right hand fumbled into a pouch pocket of his fatigues. There it was—his short-barrel thirty-eight caliber revolver, a small hand piece much admired in Korea for its utility in close-in work.

It was too late. The big guy was on him, leveling a bayonet at him. McCoy followed his actions with interest. His technique was poor. The Chinaman lunged forward. His foot hit a branch. Instead of skewering Wowser to the tree, the rifle barrel jerked up and the bayonet punched into McCoy's upper left arm. There was no pain in the arm, which had been nearly torn off by the slug he had received a short time before.

The Chinaman pulled back getting ready for another thrust. Wowser's right hand finally got his revolver clear. Jen stepped back to get more strength into his lungs. Then his body went puppet limp; somebody had cut the strings.

When Jen had jostled Cochise, it had brought the soldier back to awareness. He had been hit four times, but still had upper-body movement. He hadn't moved while the big Chinaman had pushed and poked. He saw Jen's first strike at Wowser. He saw him prepare for the second. His own throwing knife was always on his cartridge belt. As Jen lined up, Cochise's arm flashed once. It was his last move. His blade hit the Chinaman in the center of his back just as he was flexing for the final bayonet push.

Wowser saw Jen's face grimace with the effort he was bringing to the last stroke. Then, that face went slack. The eyes filled with a wondering wideness, and he tottered toward McCoy. He collapsed, comfortably, against Wowser with the tree trunk supporting both of them.

The bayonet dropped down, pointing toward the ground. It moved not with great speed, but with the weight of Jen's slumping body behind it. The point of the blade went into Wowser's left boot and kept going. The stiletto slickness of the knife never stopped. It went into the earth through McCoy's foot. *"By damn, that really hurts."* The rifle remained upright at Wowser's left side.

Jen's head had fallen forward to rest on McCoy's right shoulder, his eyes staring past Wowser into a bole of the tree.

McCoy slid his stubby revolver out of the embrace of the body leaning against him, put the muzzle under Jen's chin, and pulled the trigger. The top of Jen's head and half his face exploded in a frothy red mush into the upper branches.

It took many seconds before McCoy could clear his clanging head. Looking around, he decided, *"That'll do it."* He dropped his revolver and took stock of his situation. He was near the end, *"Well, let's do it proper—I always taught them the right way."* With grunting and a shaking effort, Wowser took off his helmet and carefully placed it on the upraised butt of the Chinese rifle and, sighing, leaned back to regard the signal he had left for the searchers who would be coming. *"Boffo"* looking around, *"Boffo, where are you? Oh, there you are. Hold on, old tub, wait for me."*

◆　　◆　　◆

The captain and Trent were hoisted over the wall with maximum exertion, careful handling, and a minimum of concern. Their handlers had examined them on the ground and decided—without medical knowledge, but with much practical experience—that their wounds, while painful, were nowhere near life threatening.

"Captain," it was Fisco, "General Krill, Krill himself, is on the blower."

Horace was half carried, half trundled down Main Street to the radio. "Crayley here, sir."

"Don't I need the smoke signal twins? I have Geronimo here."

"Not needed, sir. The Commies were part of the pageant. They won't hear anything they don't know."

"Well, what happened? I received reports from all three of my regiments that there was a hell of an explosion, then a flame-belching eruption."

"What happened was they decided today was the day. They came. We had prepared a couple of surprises. They worked. We beat the crap out of them. They ran home."

"Are they getting ready to try again?"

"I seriously doubt it."

"Casualties?"

"Several hundred of them. We will be up to our eyebrows in very bad smells in a very short time."

"What about you?"

"We lost several, but we can manage."

"No. I mean about you. They told me you were down on the south ramp and got pinged."

"I'm portable."

"You lose anybody I should know about?"

"Damn sure, sir. Every man that's down is priceless to me."

"All right, Captain. Your men love you without you proving how caring you are in a radio hook up with me."

"Yes, sir. We lost our first sergeant, and I'm really sorry to say Cochise went with him. Sergeant McCoy was an Army treasure."

"I've heard of him: with Custer at the Little Big Horn, the only survivor. I'll give him a good heavy medal, both of them, plus a couple for you and any more in your company that you say."

"Now, Crazy Horse, tell me straight, two questions: Did we really pound them and can you hold the Ridge for me?"

"We slaughtered them. And we can hold Monastery. We bought and paid for it. It's ours." Crayley paused. "In fact, Killer, I can promise you we can hold it. We can keep it till the next ice age. The Chinks didn't get it, and they never will."

And they never did.

978-0-595-46211-7
0-595-46211-1

Printed in the United States
122285LV00008B/89/P

9 780595 462117